SELECTED STORIES

STEFAN ZWEIG

SELECTED STORIES

Translated from the German by

Anthea Bell

and

Eden and Cedar Paul

PUSHKIN PRESS
LONDON

Original texts © Williams Verlag AG Zurich

Fantastic Night first published in German as
Phantastiche Nacht in 1922
English translation © Anthea Bell

Letter from an Unknown Woman first published in German as
Brief einer Unbekannten in 1922
English translation by Eden & Cedar Paul

The Fowler Snared first published in German as
Sommernovellette in 1906
English translation by Eden & Cedar Paul

The Invisible Collection first published in German as
Die unsichtbare Sammlung in 1925
English translation by Eden & Cedar Paul

Buchmendel first published in German as
Buchmendel in 1929
English translation by Eden & Cedar Paul

Twenty-four Hours in the Life of a Woman first published in German as
Vierundzwanzig Stunden im Leben einer Frau in 1927
English translation © Anthea Bell

This edition first published in 2009 by
Pushkin Press
12 Chester Terrace
London NW1 4ND

British Library Cataloguing in Publication Data:
A catalogue record for this book is available
from the British Library

ISBN: 978 1 906548 22 3

Cover: *Charlotte Spaulding Albright* Edward Steichen c1908
© George Eastman House
Bequest of Edward Steichen by Direction of Joanna T Steichen

Frontispiece: Stefan Zweig
© Roger-Viollet Rex Features

Set in 10.5 on 13.5 Monotype Baskerville
and printed in Great Britain by
CPI Cox & Wyman, Reading, RG1 8EX

www.pushkinpress.com

SELECTED STORIES

FANTASTIC NIGHT

Translated from the German by Anthea Bell

A SEALED PACKET *containing the following pages was found in the desk of Baron Friedrich Michael von R ... after he fell at the battle of Rawaruska in the autumn of 1914, fighting with a regiment of dragoons as a lieutenant in the Austrian reserve. His family, assuming from the title and a fleeting glance at the contents that this was merely a literary work by their relative, gave it to me to assess and entrusted me with its publication. I myself do not by any means regard these papers as fiction; instead, I believe them to be a record of the dead man's own experience, faithful in every detail, and I therefore publish his psychological self-revelation without any alteration or addition, suppressing only his surname.*

This morning I suddenly conceived the notion of writing, for my own benefit, an account of my experiences on that fantastic night, in order to survey the entire incident in its natural order of occurrence. And ever since that abrupt moment of decision I have felt an inexplicable compulsion to set my adventure down in words, although I doubt whether I can describe its strange nature at all adequately. I have not a trace of what people call artistic talent, nor any literary experience, and apart from a few rather light-hearted squibs for the *Theresianum* I have never tried to write anything. I don't even know, for instance, if there is some special technique to be learnt for arranging the sequence of outward events and their simultaneous inner reflection in order, and I wonder whether I am capable of always finding the right word for a certain meaning and the right meaning for a certain word, so as to achieve the equilibrium which I have always subconsciously felt in reading the work of every true storyteller. But I write these lines solely for my own satisfaction, and they are certainly not intended to make something that I can hardly explain even to myself intelligible to others. They are merely an attempt to confront an incident which constantly occupies my mind, keeping it in a state of painfully active fermentation, and to draw a line under it at last: to set it all down, place it before me, and cover it from every angle.

I have not told any of my friends about the incident, first because I felt that I could not make them understand its essential aspects, and then out of a certain sense of shame at having been so shattered and agitated by something that happened quite by chance. For the whole thing is really just a small episode. But even as I write this, I begin to realise how difficult it is for an amateur to choose words of the right significance when he is writing, and what ambiguity, what possibilities of misunderstanding can attach to the simplest of terms. For if I describe the episode as small, of course I mean it only as relatively small, by comparison with those mighty dramatic events that sweep whole nations and human destinies along with them, and then again I mean it as small in terms of time, since the whole sequence of events occupied no more than a bare six hours. To me, however, that experience—which in the general sense was minor, insignificant, unimportant—meant so extraordinarily much that even today, four months after that fantastic night, I still burn with the memory of it, and must exert all my intellectual powers to keep it to myself. Daily, hourly, I go over all the details again, for in a way it has become the pivot on which my whole existence turns; everything I do and say is unconsciously determined by it, my thoughts are solely concerned with going over and over its sudden intrusion into my life, and thereby confirming that it really did happen to me. And now I suddenly know, too, what I certainly had not yet guessed ten minutes ago when I picked up my pen: that I am recording my experience only in order to have it securely and, so to speak, objectively fixed before me, to enjoy it again in my emotions while at the same time understanding it intellectually. It was quite wrong, quite

14

untrue when I said just now that I wanted to draw a line under it by writing it down; on the contrary, I want to make what I lived through all too quickly even more alive, to have it warm and breathing beside me, so that I can clasp it to me again and again. Oh, I am not afraid of forgetting so much as a second of that sultry afternoon, that fantastic night, I need no markers or milestones to help me trace the path I took in those hours step by step in memory: like a sleepwalker I find myself back under its spell at any time, in the middle of the day or the middle of the night, seeing every detail with that clarity of vision that only the heart and not the feeble memory knows. I could draw the outline of every single leaf in that green spring landscape on this paper, even now in autumn I feel the mild air, the soft and pollen-laden wafts of chestnut blossom. So if I am about to describe those hours again, it is done not for fear of forgetting them but for the joy of bringing them to life again. And if I now describe the changes that took place that night, all exactly as they occurred, then I must control myself for the sake of an orderly account, for whenever I begin to think of the details of my experience ecstasy wells up from my emotions, a kind of intoxication overcomes me, and I have to hold back the images of memory to keep them from tumbling over one another in wild confusion, colourful and frenzied. With passionate ardour, I still relive what I experienced on that day, the 7th of June, 1913, when I took a cab at noon …

But once more I feel I must pause, for yet again, and with some alarm, I become aware of the double-edged ambiguity of a single word. Only now that, for the first time, I am to tell a story in its full context do I understand the difficulty of expressing the ever-changing aspect of all that lives in concentrated form. I have just written "I", and said that I took a cab at noon on the 7th of June, 1913. But the word itself is not really straightforward, for I am by no means still the "I" of that time, that 7th of June, although only four months have passed since that day, although I live in the apartment of that former "I" and write at his desk, with his pen, and with his own hand. I am quite distinct from the man I was then, because of this experience of mine, I see him now from the outside, looking coolly at a stranger, and I can describe him like a playmate, a comrade, a friend whom I know well and whose essential nature I also know, but I am not that man any longer. I could speak of him, blame or condemn him, without any sense that he was once a part of me.

The man I was then differed very little, either outwardly or inwardly, from most of his social class, which we usually describe here in Vienna, without any particular pride but as something to be taken entirely for granted, as 'fashionable society'. I was entering my thirty-sixth year, my parents had died prematurely just before I came of age, leaving me a fortune which proved large enough to make it entirely superfluous for me to think thereafter of earning a living or pursuing a career. I was thus unexpectedly spared a decision which weighed on my mind a great deal at the time. For I had just finished my university studies and was facing the choice of a future profession. Thanks to our family connections and my own early inclination for a contemplative existence proceeding at a tranquil pace, I would probably have opted for the civil service, when this parental fortune came to me as sole heir, suddenly assuring me of an independence sufficient to satisfy extensive and even luxurious wishes without working. Ambition had never troubled me, so I decided to begin by watching life at my leisure for a few years, waiting until I finally felt tempted to find some circle of influence for myself. However, I never got beyond this watching and waiting, for as there was nothing in particular that I wanted, I could have anything within the narrow scope of my wishes: the mellow

16

and sensuous city of Vienna, which excels like no other in bringing leisurely strolls, idle observation and the cultivation of elegance to a peak of positively artistic perfection, a purpose in life of itself, enabled me to forget entirely my intention of taking up some real activity. I had all the satisfactions an elegant, noble, well-to-do, good-looking young man without ambition could desire: the harmless excitement of gambling, hunting, the regular refreshment of travels and excursions, and soon I began cultivating this peaceful way of life more and more elaborately, with expertise and artistic inclination. I collected rare glasses, not so much from a true passion for them as for the pleasure of acquiring solid knowledge in the context of an undemanding hobby, I hung my apartment with a particular kind of Italian Baroque engravings and landscapes in the style of Canaletto—acquiring them from second-hand shops or bidding for them at auction provided the excitement of the chase without any dangers—I followed many other pursuits out of a liking for them and always with good taste, and I was seldom absent from performances of good music or the studios of our painters. I did not lack for success with women, and here too, with the secret collector's urge which in a way indicates a lack of real involvement, I chalked up many memorable and precious hours of varied experience. In this field I gradually moved from being a mere sensualist to the status of a knowledgeable connoisseur. All things considered, I had enjoyed many experiences which occupied my days pleasantly and allowed me to feel that my life was a full one, and increasingly I began to relish the easygoing, pleasant atmosphere of a youthful existence that was lively but never agitated. I formed almost no new wishes, for quite small things could blossom into pleasures in the calm climate of my days. A well-chosen tie could make me almost merry; a good book, an excursion in a motor car or an hour with a woman left me fully satisfied. It particularly pleased me to ensure that this way of life, like a faultlessly correct suit of English tailoring, did not make me conspicuous in any way. I believe I was considered pleasant company, I was popular and welcome in society, and most who knew me called me a happy man.

I cannot now say whether the man of that time, whom I am trying to conjure up here, thought himself as happy as those others did, for now that this experience of mine has made me expect a much fuller and more fulfilled significance in every emotion, I find it almost impossible to assess his happiness in retrospect. But I can say with certainty that I felt myself by no means unhappy at the time, for my wishes almost never went unsatisfied and nothing I required of life was withheld. But the very fact that I had become accustomed to getting all I asked from destiny, and demanded no more, led gradually to a certain absence of excitement, a lifelessness in life itself. Those yearnings that then stirred unconsciously in me at many moments of half-realisation were not really wishes, but only the wish for wishes, a craving for desires that would be stronger, wilder, more ambitious, less easily satisfied, a wish to live more and perhaps to suffer more as well. I had removed all obstacles from my life by a method that was only too reasonable, and my vitality was sapped by that absence of obstacles. I noticed that I wanted fewer things and did not want them so much, that a kind of paralysis had come over my feelings, so that—perhaps this is the best way to express it—so that I was suffering from emotional impotence, an inability to take passionate possession of life. I recognised this defect from small signs at first. I noticed that I was absent more and more often from the theatre and society on certain occasions of great note, that I ordered books which had been praised to me and then left them lying on my desk for weeks with their pages still uncut, that although I automatically continued to pursue my hobbies, buying glasses and antiques, I did not trouble to classify them once they were mine, nor did I feel any particular pleasure in unexpectedly acquiring a rare piece which it had taken me a long time to find.

However, I became really aware of this lessening of my emotional vigour, slight but indicative of change, on a certain occasion which I still remember clearly. I had stayed in Vienna for the summer—again, as a result of that curious lethargy which left me feeling no lively attraction to anything new— when I suddenly received a letter written in a spa resort. It was from a woman with whom I had had an intimate relationship for three years, and I even truly thought I loved her. She wrote fourteen agitated pages to tell me that in her weeks at the spa she had met a man who meant a great deal to her, indeed everything, she was going to marry him in the autumn, and the relationship between us must now come to an end. She said that she thought of our time together without regret, indeed with happiness, the memory of me would accompany her into her marriage as the dearest of her past life, and she hoped I would forgive her for her sudden decision. After this factual information, her agitated missive surpassed itself in truly moving entreaties, begging me not to be angry with her, not to feel too much pain at her sudden termination of our relationship; I mustn't try to get her back by force, or do anything foolish to myself. Her lines ran on, becoming more and more passionate: I must and would find comfort with someone better, I must write to her at once, for she was very anxious about my reception of her message. And as a postscript she had hastily scribbled, in pencil: "*Don't do anything stupid, understand me, forgive me!*" I read this letter, surprised at first by her news, and then, when I had skimmed all through it, I read it a second time, now with a certain shame which, on making itself felt, soon became a sense of inner alarm. For none of the strong yet natural feelings which my lover supposed were to be taken for granted had even suggested themselves to me. I had not suffered on hearing her news, I had not been angry with her, and I had certainly not for a second contemplated any violence against either her or myself, and this coldness of my emotions was too strange not to alarm me. A woman was leaving me, a woman who had been my companion for years, whose warm and supple body had offered itself to me, whose breath had mingled with mine in long nights together, and nothing stirred in me, nothing protested, nothing sought to get her back, I had none of those feelings that this woman's pure instinct assumed were natural in any human being. At that moment I was fully aware for the first time how far advanced the process of paralysis already was in me—it was as if I were moving through flowing, bright water without being halted or taking root anywhere, and I knew very well that this chill was something dead and corpse-like, not yet surrounded by the foul breath of decomposition but already numbed beyond recovery, a grimly cold lack of emotion. It was the moment that precedes real, physical death and outwardly visible decay.

After that episode I began carefully observing myself and this curious paralysis of my feelings, as a sick man observes his sickness. When, shortly afterwards, a friend of mine died and I followed his coffin to the grave, I listened to myself to see if I did not feel grief, if some emotion did not move in me at the knowledge that this man, who had been close to me since our childhood, was now lost to me for ever. But nothing stirred, I felt as if I were made of glass, with the world outside shining straight through me and never lingering within, and hard as I attempted on this and many similar occasions to feel something, however much I tried, through reasonable argument, to make myself feel emotion, no response came from my rigid state of mind. People parted from me, women came and went, and I felt much like a man sitting in a room with rain beating on the window panes; there was a kind of sheet of glass between me and my immediate surroundings, and my will was not strong enough to break it.

Although I felt this clearly, the realisation caused me no real uneasiness, for as I have said, I took even what affected myself with indifference. I no longer had feeling enough to suffer. It was enough for me that this internal flaw was hardly perceptible from the outside, in the same way as a man's physical impotence becomes obvious only at the moment of intimacy, and in company I often put on a certain elaborate show, employing artificially passionate admiration and spontaneous exaggeration to hide the extent to which I knew I was dead and unfeeling inside. Outwardly I continued my old comfortable, unconstrained way of life without any change of direction; weeks, months passed easily by and slowly, gathering darkly into years. One morning when I looked in the glass I saw a streak of grey at my temple, and felt that my youth was slowly departing. But what others call youth had long ago ended in me, so taking leave of it did not hurt very much, since I did not love even my own youth enough for that. My refractory emotions preserved their silence even to me.

This inner rigidity made my days more and more similar, despite all the varied occupations and events that filled them, they ranged themselves side by side without emphasis, they grew and faded like the leaves of a tree. And the single day I am about to describe for my own benefit began in a perfectly ordinary way too, without anything odd to mark it, without any internal premonition. On that day, the 7th of June, 1913, I had got up later than usual because of a subconscious Sunday feeling, something that lingered from my childhood and schooldays. I had taken my bath, read the paper, dipped into some books, and then, lured out by the warm summer day that compassionately made its way into my room, I went for a walk. I crossed the Graben in my usual way, greeted friends and acquaintances and conducted brief conversations with some of them, and then I lunched with friends. I had avoided any engagement for the afternoon, since I particularly liked to have a few uninterrupted hours on Sunday which I could use just as my mood, my pleasure or some spontaneous decision dictated. As I left my friends and crossed the Ringstrasse, I felt the beauty of the sunny city doing me good, and enjoyed its early summer finery. All the people seemed cheerful, as if they were in love with the Sunday atmosphere of the lively street, and many details struck me, in particular the way the broad, bushy trees rose from the middle of the asphalt wearing their new green foliage. Although I went this way almost daily, I suddenly became aware of the Sunday crowd as if it were a miracle, and involuntarily I felt a longing for a great deal of greenery, brightness and colour. I thought with a certain interest of the Prater, where in late spring and early summer the great trees stand to right and left of the main avenue down which the carriages drive, motionless like huge green footmen as they hold up their white candles of blossom to the many well-groomed and elegant passers by. Used as I was to indulging the most fleeting whim at once, I hailed the first cab I saw, and when the cabby asked where I was going I told him the Prater. "Ah, to the races, Baron, am I right?" he replied obsequiously, as if that was to be taken for granted. Only then did I remember that there was a fashionable race meeting today, a preview of the local Derby, where Viennese high society foregathered. How strange, I thought as I got into the cab, only a few years ago how could I possibly have forgotten or failed to attend such a day? When I thought of my forgetfulness I once again felt all the rigidity of the indifference to which I had fallen victim, just as a sick man feels his injury when he moves.

The main avenue was quite empty when we arrived, and the racing must have begun long ago, for I did not see what was usually a handsome procession of carriages; there were only a few cabs racing along, hooves clattering, as if catching up with some invisible omission. The driver turned on his box and asked whether he should make the horses trot faster, but I told him to let them walk slowly, I didn't mind arriving late. I had seen too many races, and had seen the racegoers too often as well, to mind about arriving on time, and as the vehicle rocked gently along it matched my idle mood better to feel the blue air, with a soft rushing sound in it like the sea when you are on board ship, and at my leisure to view the handsome, broad and bushy chestnut trees which sometimes gave up a few flower petals as playthings to the warm, coaxing wind, which then raised them gently and sent them whirling through the air before letting them fall like white flakes on the avenue. It was pleasant to be rocked like that, to sense the presence of spring with eyes closed, to feel carried away and elated without any effort at all. I was quite sorry when the cab reached the Freudenau and stopped at the entrance. I would have liked to turn round and let the soft, early summer day continue to cradle me. But it was already too late, the cab was drawing up outside the racecourse. A muffled roar came to meet me. It re-echoed with a dull, hollow sound on the far side of the tiers of seats, and although I could not see the excited crowd making that concentrated noise I couldn't help thinking of Ostend, where if you walk up the small side streets from the low-lying town to the beach promenade you feel the keen, salty wind blowing over you, and hear a hollow boom before you ever set eyes on the broad, grey, foaming expanse of the sea with its roaring waves. There must be a race going on at the moment, but between me and the turf on which the horses were probably galloping stood a colourful, noisy, dense mass swaying back and forth as if shaken by some inner turmoil: the crowd of spectators and gamblers. I couldn't see the track, but I followed every stage of the race as their heightened excitement reflected it. The jockeys must have started some time ago, the bunched formation at the beginning of the race had thinned out, and a couple of horses were disputing the lead, for already shouts and excited cries were coming from the people who mysteriously, as it seemed, were watching the progress of a race which was invisible to me. The turn of their heads indicated the bend which the horses and jockeys must just have reached on the long oval of turf, for the whole chaotic crowd was now moving its gaze as if craning a single neck to see something out of my line of vision, and its single taut throat roared and gurgled with thousands of hoarse, individual sounds, like a great breaker foaming as it rises higher and higher. And the wave rose and swelled, it already filled the whole space right up to the blue indifferent sky. I looked at a few of the faces. They were distorted as if by some inner spasm, their eyes were fixed and sparkling, they were biting their lips, chins avidly thrust forwards, nostrils flaring like a horse's. Sober as I was, I found their frenzied intemperance both a comic and a dreadful sight. Beside me a man was standing on a chair. He was elegantly dressed, and had what was probably a good-looking face in the usual way, but now he was raving, possessed by an invisible demon, waving his cane in the air as if lashing something forwards; his whole body—in a manner unspeakably ridiculous to a spectator—passionately mimed the movement of rapid riding. He kept bobbing his heels up and down on the chair, as if standing in the stirrups, his right hand constantly whipped the air like a riding crop, his left hand convulsively clutched a slip of white card. And there were more and more of those white slips fluttering around, like sparkling wine spraying above the grey and stormy tide that swelled so noisily. A few horses must be very close to each other on the bend now, for suddenly the shouting divided into three or four individual names roared out like battle cries again and again by separate groups, and the shouts seemed like an outlet for their delirious state of possession.

I stood amidst this roaring frenzy cold as a rock in the raging sea, and I remember to this day exactly what I felt at that moment. First I thought how ridiculous those grotesque gestures were, I felt ironic contempt for the vulgarity of the outburst, but there was something else too, something that I was unwilling to admit to myself—a kind of quiet envy of such excitement, such heated passion, envy of the life in this display of fervour. What, I thought, would have to happen to excite me so much, rouse me to such fever pitch that my body would burn so ardently, my voice would issue from my mouth against my own will? I could not imagine any sum of money that would so spur me on to possess it, any woman who could excite me so much, there was nothing, nothing that could kindle such fire within me in my emotional apathy! If I faced a pistol suddenly aimed at me, my heart would not thud as wildly in the second before I froze as did the hearts of these people around me, a thousand, ten thousand of them, just for a handful of money. But now one horse must be very near the finishing line, for a certain name rang out above the tumult like a string stretched taut, uttered by a thousand voices and rising higher and higher, only to end all at once on an abrupt, shrill note. The music began to play, the crowd suddenly dispersed. One of the races was over, the contest was decided, their tension was resolved into swirling movement as the excited vibrations died down. The throng, just a moment ago a fervent concentration of passion, broke up into many individuals walking, laughing, talking; calm faces emerged from behind the Maenad mask of frenzy; social groups formed again out of the chaos of the game that for seconds on end had forged these thousands of racegoers into a single ardent whole, those groups came together, they parted, I saw people I knew who hailed me, and strangers who scrutinised and observed each other with cool courtesy. The women assessed one another's new outfits, the men cast avid glances, that fashionable curiosity which is the real occupation of the indifferent began to show, the racegoers looked around, counted others, checked up on their presence and their degree of elegance. Scarcely brought down to earth again from their delirium, none of them knew whether the real object of their meeting in company here was the races themselves or this interlude of walking about the racecourse.

I walked through this relaxed, milling crowd, offering and returning greetings, and breathing in with pleasure—for this was the world in which I lived—the aura of perfume and elegance that wafted around the kaleidoscopic confusion. With even more pleasure I felt the soft breeze that sometimes blew out of the summery warmth of the woods from the direction of the Prater meadows, sometimes rippling like a wave among the racegoers and fingering the women's white muslins as if in amorous play. A couple of acquaintances hailed me; the pretty actress Diane nodded invitingly to me from a box, but I joined no one. I was not interested in talking to any of these fashionable folk today; I found it tedious to see myself reflected in them. All I wanted was to experience the spectacle, the crackling, sensuous excitement that pervaded the heightened emotion of the hour (for the excitement of others is the most delightful of spectacles to a man who himself is in a state of indifference). A couple of pretty women passed by, I boldly but without any inward desire scrutinised the breasts under the thin gauze they wore, moving at every step they took, and smiled to myself to see their half-awkward, half-gratified embarrassment when they felt that I was assessing them sensuously and undressing them with my eyes. In fact none of the women aroused me, it simply gave me a certain satisfaction to pretend to them that they did; it pleased me to play with their idea that I wanted to touch them physically and felt a magnetic attraction of the eye, for like all who are cold at heart I found more intense erotic enjoyment in arousing warmth and restlessness in others than in waxing ardent myself. It was only the downy warmth lent to sensuality by the presence of women that I loved to feel, not any genuine arousal, only

26

stimulation and not real excitement. So I walked through the promenading crowd as usual, caught glances, tossed them back as lightly as a shuttlecock, took my pleasure without reaching out a hand, fondled women without physical contact, warmed only slightly by the mildly amorous game.

But soon I found this tedious too. The same people kept passing; I knew their faces and gestures by heart now. There was a chair nearby, and I took it. A new turbulence began in the groups around me, passers-by moved and pushed more restively in the confusion; obviously another race was about to start. I was not interested in that, but sat at my ease and as if submerged beneath the smoke from my cigarette, which rose in white rings against the sky, turning brighter and brighter and disintegrating like a little cloud in the springtime blue. And at that very second the extraordinary, unique experience that still rules my life today began. I can fix the moment exactly, because it so happens that I had just looked at my watch: the hands were crossing, and I watched with idle curiosity as they overlapped for a second. It was sixteen minutes past three on the afternoon of the 7th of June, 1913. With cigarette in hand, then, I was looking at the white dial of the watch, entirely absorbed in this childish and ridiculous contemplation, when I heard a woman laugh out loud just behind my back with the ringing, excited laughter that I love in women, springing warm and startled out of the hot thickets of the senses. I instinctively leant my head back to see the woman whose sensuality, boldly proclaimed aloud, was forcing its way into my carefree reverie like a sparkling white stone dropped into a dull and muddy pond—and then I controlled myself. A curious fancy for an intellectual game, a fancy of the kind I often felt for a small and harmless psychological experiment, held me back. I didn't want to see the laughing woman just yet; it intrigued me to let my imagination work on her first in a kind of anticipation of pleasure, to conjure up her appearance, giving that laughter

27

a face, a mouth, a throat, a neck, a breast, making a whole living, breathing woman of her.

At this moment she was obviously standing directly behind me. Her laughter had turned to conversation again. I listened intently. She spoke with a slight Hungarian accent, very fast and expressively, her vowels soaring as if in song. It amused me to speculate on the figure that went with her voice, elaborating my imaginary picture as richly as I could. I gave her dark hair, dark eyes, a wide and sensuously curving mouth with strong, very white teeth, a little nose that was very narrow but had flared, quivering nostrils. I put a beauty spot on her left cheek and a riding crop in her hand; as she laughed she slapped it lightly against her thigh. She talked on and on. And each of her words added some new detail to my rapidly formed image of her: a slender, girlish breast, a dark-green dress with a diamond brooch pinned to it at a slant, a pale hat with a white feather. The picture became clearer and clearer, and I already felt as if this stranger standing invisible behind my back was also on a lit photographic plate in the pupil of my eye. But I didn't want to turn round yet, I preferred to enhance my imaginary game further. A touch of lust mingled with my audacious reverie, and I closed both eyes, certain that when I opened them again and turned to her my imagined picture would coincide exactly with her real appearance.

At that moment she stepped forwards. Instinctively I opened my eyes—and felt disappointment. I had guessed quite wrong. Everything was different from my imaginary idea, and indeed was distressingly at odds with it. She wore not a green but a white dress, she was not slim but voluptuous and broad-hipped, the beauty spot I had dreamt up was nowhere to be seen on her plump cheek, her hair under her helmet-shaped hat was pale red, not black. None of my details fitted her real appearance; however, this woman was beautiful, challenging-ly beautiful, although with my psychological vanity injured, foolishly overweening as it was, I would not acknowledge her beauty. I looked up at her almost with hostility, but even in my resistance to it I felt the strong sensuous attraction emanating from this woman, the enticing, demanding, animal desirability in her firm yet softly plump opulence. Now she laughed aloud again, showing her strong white teeth, and I had to admit that this warm, sensuous laughter was in harmony with her voluptuous appearance; everything about her was vehement and challenging, the curve of her breasts, the way she thrust her chin out as she laughed, her keen glance, her curved nose, the hand pressing her parasol firmly to the ground. Here was the feminine element incarnate, a primeval power, deliberate, pervasive enticement, a beacon of lust made flesh. Beside her stood an elegant, rather colourless officer talking earnestly to her. She listened to him, smiled, laughed, contradicted him, but all this was only by the way, for at the same time her nostrils were quivering as her glance wandered here and there as if to light on everyone; she attracted attention, smiles, glances from every passing man, and from the whole male part of the crowd standing around her too. Her eyes moved all the time, sometimes searching the tiers of seats and suddenly, with joyful recognition, responding to someone's wave, turning now to right, now to left as she listened to the officer, smiling idly. But they had not yet rested on me, for I was outside her field of vision, hidden from her by her companion. I felt some annoyance and stood up—she did not see me. I came closer— now she looked up at the tiers of seats again. I stepped firmly up to her, raised my hat to her companion, and offered her my chair. She looked at me in surprise, a smiling light flickered in her eyes, and she curved her lips into a cajoling smile. But then she simply thanked me briefly and took the chair without sitting down. She merely leant her voluptuous arm, which was bare to the elbow, lightly on the back of the chair, employing this slight bending movement to show off her figure more visibly.

My vexation over my psychological failure was long forgotten; now I was intrigued by the game I was playing with this woman. I retreated slightly, moving to the side of the stand, where I could look at her freely but unobtrusively, leaning on my cane and trying to meet her eyes. She noticed, turned slightly towards my observation post, but in such a way that the movement seemed to be made quite by chance, did not avoid my glance and now and then answered it, but non-committally. Her eyes kept moving, touching on everything, never resting anywhere—was it I alone whose gaze she met with a dark smile, or did she give that smile to everyone? There was no telling, and that very uncertainty piqued me. At the moments when her own gaze fell on me like a flashing light it seemed full of promise, although she responded indiscriminately and with the same steely gleam of her pupils to every other glance that came her way, out of sheer flirtatious pleasure in the game, but without letting her apparent interest in her companion's conversation lapse for an instant. There was something dazzlingly audacious about that passionate display, which was either virtuoso dalliance or an outburst of overflowing sensuality. Involuntarily, I came a step closer: her cold audacity had transferred itself to me. I no longer gazed into her eyes but looked her up and down like a connoisseur, undressed her in my mind and felt her naked. She followed my glance without appearing insulted in any way, smiled at the loquacious officer with the corners of her mouth, but I noticed that her knowing smile was acknowledging my intentions. And now, when I looked at her small, delicate foot just peeping out from under the hem of her white dress, she checked it and smoothed her skirt down with a casual air. Next moment, as if by chance, she raised the same foot and placed it on the first rung of the chair I had offered her, so that through the open-work fabric of her dress I could see her stockings up to the knee. At the same time, the smile she gave her companion seemed to take on a touch of irony or malice. She was obviously playing with me as impersonally as I with her, and I was obliged, with some animosity, to admire the subtle technique of her bold conduct, for while she was offering me the sensuousness of her body in pretended secrecy, she appeared to be flattered by and immersing herself in her companion's whispered remarks at the same time, giving and taking in the game she was playing with both of us. In fact I felt vexed, for in other women I disliked this kind of cold, viciously calculating sensuality, feeling that it was incestuously related to the absence of feeling of which I was conscious in myself. Yet I was aroused, perhaps more in dislike than in desire. I boldly came closer and made a brutal assault on her with my eyes. My gestures clearly said, "I want you, you beautiful animal", and I must involuntarily have moved my lips, for she smiled with faint contempt, turning her head away from me, and draped her skirt over the foot she had just revealed. Next moment, however, those flashing black eyes were wandering here and there again. It was quite obvious that she was as cold as I myself and was a match for me, that we were both playing coolly with a strange arousal that itself was only a pretence of ardour, though it was a pretty sight and amusing to play with on a dull day.

Suddenly the intent look left her face, her sparkling eyes clouded over, and a small line of annoyance appeared around her still smiling mouth. I followed the direction of her gaze; a small, stout gentleman, his garments rumpled, was steering a rapid course towards her, his face and brow, which he was nervously drying with his handkerchief, damp with agitation. His hat, which he had perched askew on his head in his hurry, revealed a large bald patch on one side (I could not help thinking that when he took the hat off there were sure to be large beads of sweat gathering on it, and I found him repulsive). His ringed hand held a whole bundle of betting slips. He was puffing and blowing excitedly, and paying no attention to his wife addressed the officer at once in loud Hungarian. I immediately recognised him as an aficionado of the turf, some horse-dealer of the better kind for whom the sport was the only form of ecstasy he knew, a surrogate for sublimity. His wife must obviously have admonished him in some way (she was evidently irked, and disturbed in her elemental confidence by his presence), for he straightened his hat, apparently at her behest, then laughed jovially and clapped her on the shoulder with good-natured affection. She angrily raised her eyebrows, repelled by this marital familiarity, which embarrassed her in the officer's presence and perhaps even more in mine. He seemed to be apologising, said a few more words in Hungarian to the officer, who replied with an agreeable smile, and then took her arm, tenderly and a little deferentially. I felt that she was ashamed of his intimacy in front of us, and with mingled feelings of derision and disgust I relished her humiliation. But she was soon in control of herself again, and as she pressed softly against his arm she gave me an ironic sideways glance, as if to say, "There, you see, he has me and you don't." I felt both anger and distaste. I really wanted to turn my back on her and walk away, showing her that I was no longer interested in the wife of such a vulgar, fat fellow. But the attraction was too strong. I stayed.

At that moment the shrill starting signal was heard, and all of a sudden it was as if the whole chattering, dull, sluggish crowd had been shaken into life. Once again, and from all directions, it surged forwards to the barrier in wild turmoil. It cost me some effort not to be carried along with it, for I wanted to stay near her in all this confusion; there might be an opportunity for a meaningful glance, for a touch, a chance for me to take some spontaneous liberty, though just what I didn't yet know, so I doggedly made my way towards her through the hurrying people. At that very moment the stout husband was forging his own path through the crowd, obviously to get a good place in the stand, and so it was that the pair of us, each impelled by a different passion, collided with each other so violently that his hat flew to the ground, and the betting slips loosely tucked into the hatband were scattered wide, drifting like red, blue, yellow and white butterflies. He stared at me for a moment. I was about to offer an automatic apology, but some kind of perverse ill will sealed my lips, and instead I looked coolly at him with a slight but bold, offensive touch of provocation. As red-hot anger rose in him but then timidly gave way, his glance flickered uncertainly for a moment and then cravenly sank before mine. With unforgettable, almost touching anxiety he looked me in the eye for just a second, then turned away, suddenly seemed to remember his betting slips, and bent to pick them and his hat up from the ground. His wife, who had let go of his arm, flashed me a glance of unconcealed fury, her face flushed with agitation, and I saw with a kind of erotic pleasure that she would have liked to strike me. But I stood there very cool and nonchalant, watched the fat husband, smiling and offering no help as he bent, puffing and panting, and crawled around at my feet picking up his betting slips. When he bent over his collar stood away from him like the ruffled feathers of a chicken, a broad roll of fat was visible at the nape of his red neck and he gasped asthmatically at every movement he made. Seeing him panting like that, I involuntarily entertained an improper and distasteful idea: I imagined him alone with his wife engaged in conjugal relations, and this thought put me in such high spirits that I smiled in her face at the sight of the anger she could barely rein in. There she stood, impatient and pale again now, scarcely able to control herself—at last I had wrested a real, genuine feeling from her: hatred, unbridled rage! I would have liked to prolong this distressing scene to infinity; I watched with cold relish as he struggled to gather his betting slips together one by one. Some kind of devil of amusement was in my throat, chuckling continuously and trying to burst into laughter; I would have liked to laugh heartily at that soft, scrabbling mass of flesh, or to tickle him up a little with my cane. I really couldn't remember ever before being so possessed by an evil demon as I was in that delightful moment of triumph at his bold wife's humiliation. Now the unfortunate man finally seemed to have picked up all his slips except one, a blue betting slip which had fallen a little further away and was lying on the ground just in front of me. He turned, puffing and panting, looked round with his short-sighted eyes—his pince-nez had slipped to the end of his damp, sweating nose—and my sense of mischief used that second to prolong his ridiculous search. Obeying the boyish high spirits that had seized on me without my own volition, I quickly moved my foot forwards and placed the sole of my shoe on the slip, so that for all his efforts he couldn't find it as long as it pleased me to let him go on looking. And he did go on looking for it, on and on, now and then counting the coloured slips of card again and again, panting as he did so; it was obvious that he knew one of them—mine!—was still missing, and he was about to start searching again in the middle of the noisy crowd when his wife, deliberately avoiding my scornful gaze and with a grim expression on her face, could no longer restrain her angry impatience. "Lajos!" she suddenly and imperiously called, and he started like a horse hearing the sound of the trumpet, cast one last searching glance at the ground—I felt as if the slip hidden under the sole of my shoe were tickling me, and could hardly conceal an urge to laugh—and then turned obediently to his wife, who led him away from me with a certain ostentatious haste and into the tumultuous crowd, where excitement was rising higher and higher.

I stayed behind, feeling no wish to follow the two of them. The episode was over as far as I was concerned, the sense of erotic tension had resolved into mirth, doing me good. I was no longer aroused, nothing was left but a sense of sound satisfaction after following my sudden mischievous impulse, a jaunty, almost boisterous complacency at the thought of the trick I had played. Ahead of me the crowd was thronging close together, waves of excitement were beginning to rise, surging up to the barrier in a single black, murky mass, but I did not watch, it bored me now. I thought of walking over to the Krieau or going home. But as soon as I instinctively raised my foot to step forwards I noticed the blue betting slip lying forgotten on the ground. I picked it up and held it idly between my fingers, not sure what to do with the thing. I vaguely thought of returning it to 'Lajos', which might serve as an excellent excuse to be introduced to his wife, but I realised that she no longer interested me, that the fleeting ardour this adventure had made me feel had long since cooled into my old apathy. I wanted no more of Lajos's wife than that single combative, challenging exchange of glances—I found the fat man too unappetising to wish to share anything physical with him. I had experienced a tingling of the nerves, but now felt only mild curiosity and a pleasant sense of relaxation.

There was the chair, abandoned and alone. I made myself comfortable on it and lit a cigarette. Ahead of me the breakers of excitement were rising again, but I did not even listen; repetition held no charms for me. I watched the pale smoke rising and thought of the Merano golf course promenade where I had sat two months ago, looking down at the spray of the waterfall. It was just like this: at Merano too you heard a strongly swelling roar that was neither hot nor cold, meaningless sound rising in the silent blue landscape. But now impassioned enthusiasm for the race had reached its climax again; once more parasols, hats, handkerchiefs and loud cries were flying like sea-spray above the black breakers of the throng, once again the voices were swirling together, once again a shout—but of a different kind—issued from the crowd's gigantic mouth. I heard a name called out a thousand, ten thousand times, exultantly, piercing, ecstatically, frantically. "*Cressy! Cressy! Cressy!*" And once again the sound was suddenly cut short, as if it were a taut string breaking (ah, how repetition makes even passion monotonous!). The music began to play, the crowd dispersed. Boards were raised aloft showing the numbers of the winning horses. I looked at them, without conscious intent. The first number was a distinct *SEVEN.* Automatically, I glanced at the blue slip I was still holding and had forgotten. It said *SEVEN* too. I couldn't help laughing. The slip had won; friend Lajos had placed a lucky bet. So my mischief had actually tricked the fat husband out of money: all of a sudden my exuberant mood had returned, and I felt interested to know how much my jealous intervention had cost him. I looked at the piece of blue card more closely for the first time: it was a twenty-crown bet, and Lajos had put it on the horse to win. That could amount to a considerable sum. Without thinking more about it, merely obeying my itch of curiosity, I let myself be carried along with the hurrying crowd to the tote windows. I was pushed into some kind of queue, put down the betting slip, and next moment two busy, bony hands—I couldn't see the face that went with them behind the window—were counting out nine twenty-crown notes on the marble slab in front of me.

At that moment, when the money, real money in blue banknotes was paid out to me, the laughter died in my throat. I immediately felt an unpleasant sensation. Involuntarily, I withdrew my hands so as not to touch the money which was not mine. I would have liked to leave the blue notes lying on the marble slab, but people were pushing forwards behind me, impatient to cash their winnings. So there was nothing I could do but, feeling very awkward, take the notes with reluctant fingers: the banknotes burned like blue fire, and I unconsciously held my spread fingers well away from me, as if the hand that had taken them was not my own any more than the money was. I immediately saw all the difficulty of the situation. Without my own volition, the joke had turned to something that a decent man, a gentleman, an officer in the reserve ought not to have done, and I hesitated to call it by its true name even to myself. For this was not money that had been withheld; it had been obtained by cunning. It was stolen money.

Voices hummed and buzzed around me, people came thronging up on their way to and from the tote windows. I still stood there motionless, my spread hand held away from me. What was I to do? I thought first of the most natural solution: to find the real winner, apologise, and give him back the money. But that wouldn't do, least of all in front of that officer. After all, I was a lieutenant in the reserve, and such a confession would have cost me my commission at once, for even if I had found the betting slip by chance, cashing it in was a dishonest act. I also thought of obeying the instinct of my twitching fingers, crumpling up the notes and throwing them away, although that would also be too easily visible in the middle of such a crowd of people, and would look suspicious. However, I didn't want to keep the money that was not mine on me for a moment, let alone put it in my wallet and give it to someone later: the sense of cleanliness instilled into me from childhood, like the habit of wearing clean underclothes, was revolted by any contact, however fleeting, with those banknotes. I must get rid of the money, I thought feverishly, I must get rid of it somewhere, anywhere! I instinctively looked around me, at a loss, wondering if I could see a hiding place anywhere, a chance of concealing it unobserved; I noticed that people were beginning to flock to the tote windows again, but this time with banknotes in their hands. The idea was my salvation. I would throw the money back to the malicious chance that had given it to me, back into the all-consuming maw that was now greedily swallowing up new bets in notes and silver—yes, that was the thing to do, that was the way to free myself of it.

I impetuously hurried, indeed ran as I pushed my way in among the crowd. But by the time I realised that I didn't know the name of any horse on which to bet there were only two men in front of me, and the first was already at the tote window. I listened avidly to the conversation around me. "Are you backing Ravachol?" one man asked. "Yes, of course, Ravachol," his companion replied. "Don't you think Teddy has a chance?" "Teddy? Not a hope. He failed miserably in his maiden race. All show, no substance."

I drank in these words. So Teddy was a bad horse. Teddy was sure to lose. I immediately decided to bet on him. I pushed the money over, put it on Teddy, the horse I had only just heard of, to win, and a hand gave me the betting slips. All of a sudden I now had nine pieces of card in my fingers instead of just the one, this time red and white. I still felt awkward, but at least the slips didn't burn in so fiery, so humiliating a way as the crumpled banknotes.

I felt light at heart again, almost carefree: the money was gone now, the unpleasant part of the adventure was over, it had begun as a joke and now it was all a joke again. I leant back at ease in my chair, lit a cigarette and blew the smoke into the air at my leisure. But I did not stay there long; I rose, walked around, sat down again. How odd: my sense of pleasant reverie was gone. Some kind of nervousness was tingling in my limbs. At first I thought it was discomfort at the idea that I might meet Lajos and his wife in the crowd of people walking by, but how could they guess that these new betting slips were really theirs? Nor did the restlessness of the crowd disturb me; on the contrary, I watched closely to see when they would begin pressing forwards again, indeed I caught myself getting to my feet again and again to look for the flag that would be hoisted at the beginning of the race. So that was it—impatience, a leaping inward fever of expectation as I wished the race would begin soon and the tiresome affair be over for good.

A boy ran past with a racing paper. I stopped him, bought the programme of today's meeting, and began searching the text and the tips, written in a strange and incomprehensible jargon, until I finally found Teddy, the names of his jockey and the owner of the racing stables, and the information that his colours were red and white. But why was I so interested? Annoyed, I crumpled up the newspaper and tossed it away, stood up, sat down again. I suddenly felt hot, I had to pass my handkerchief over my damp brow, my collar felt tight. And still the race did not begin.

At last the bell rang, people came surging up, and at that moment I felt, to my horror, that the ringing of that bell, like an alarm clock, had woken me from some kind of sleep. I jumped up from the chair so abruptly that it fell over, and eagerly hurried—no, ran forwards into the crowd, betting slips held firmly between my fingers, as if consumed by a frantic fear of arriving too late, of missing something very important. I reached the barrier at the front of the stand by forcibly pushing people aside, and ruthlessly seized a chair on which a lady was about to sit down. Her glance of astonishment showed me just how wild and discourteous my conduct was—she was a lady I knew well, Countess R, and I saw her brows raised in anger—but out of shame and defiance I coldly ignored her and climbed up on the chair to get a good view of the field.

Somewhere in the distance, at the start, several horses were standing close together on the turf, kept in line with difficulty by small jockeys who looked like brightly clad versions of Punchinello. I immediately looked for my horse's colours among them, but my eyes were unpractised, and everything was swimming before them in such a hot, strange blur that I couldn't make out the red-and-white figure among all the other splashes of colour. At that moment the bell rang for the second time, and the horses shot off down the green racetrack like six coloured arrows flying from a bow. It would surely have been a fine sight to watch calmly, purely from an aesthetic point of view, as the slender animals stretched their legs in the gallop, hardly touching the ground as they skimmed the turf, but I felt none of that, I was making desperate attempts to pick out my horse, my jockey, and cursing myself for not bringing a pair of field glasses with me. Lean forwards and crane my neck as I might, I saw nothing but four or five insects tangled together in a blurred, flying knot; however, at last I saw its shape begin to change as the small group reached the bend and strung out into a wedge shape, leaders came to the front while some of the other horses were already falling away at the back. It was a close race: three or four horses galloping full speed stuck together like coloured strips of paper, now one and now another getting its nose ahead. I instinctively stretched and tensed my whole body as if my imitative, springy and impassioned movement could increase their speed and carry them along.

The excitement was rising around me. Some of the more knowledgeable racegoers must have recognised the colours as the horses came round the bend, for names were now flying up like bright rockets from the murky tumult below. A man with his hands raised in a frenzy was standing beside me, and as one horse got its head forwards he stamped his feet and yelled in an ear-splitting tone of triumph, "Ravachol! Ravachol!" I saw that the jockey riding this horse did indeed wear blue, and I felt furious that my horse wasn't winning. I found the piercing cries of "Ravachol! Ravachol!" from the idiot beside me more and more intolerable, I felt cold fury, I would have liked to slam my fist into the wide, black hole of his shouting mouth. I quivered with rage, I was in a fever, and felt I might do something senseless at any moment. But here came another horse, sticking close behind the first. Perhaps it was Teddy, perhaps, perhaps—and that hope spurred my enthusiasm again. I really did think it was a red arm now rising above the saddle and bringing something down on the horse's crupper—it could be red, it must be, it must, it must! But why wasn't the fool of a jockey urging him on? The whip again! Go on, again! Now, now he was quite close to the first horse. Hardly anything between them now. Why should Ravachol win? Ravachol! No, not Ravachol! Not Ravachol! Teddy! Teddy! Come on, Teddy! Teddy!

Suddenly and violently, I caught myself up. What on earth was all this? Who was shouting like that? Who was yelling "Teddy! Teddy!" I was shouting the name! And in the midst of my impassioned outburst I felt afraid of myself. I wanted to stop, control myself, in the middle of my fever I felt a sudden shame. But I couldn't tear my eyes away, for the two horses were sticking very close to each other, and it must really be Teddy hanging on to Ravachol, the wretched horse Ravachol that I fervently hated, for others were now shouting louder around me, many voices in a piercing descant: "Teddy, Teddy!" The yells plunged me back into the frenzy from which I had emerged for one sober second. He should, he must win, and now, now a head did push forwards past the flying horse ridden by the other jockey, just by the span of a hand, and then another, and now—now you could see the neck—and then the shrill bell rang, and there was a great cry of jubilation, despair and fury. For a second the name I longed to hear filled the whole vault of the blue sky above. Then it died away, and somewhere music started playing.

Hot, drenched in sweat, my heart thudding, I got off the chair. I had to sit down for a moment, so confused had my excited enthusiasm left me. Ecstasy such as I had never known before flooded through me, a mindless joy at seeing chance bow to my challenge with such slavish obedience; I tried in vain to pretend to myself it was against my will that the horse had won, I had really wanted to lose the money. But I didn't believe it myself, and I already felt a terrible ache in my limbs urging me, as if

41

magically, to be off somewhere, and I knew where: I wanted to see my triumph, feel it, hold it, money, a great deal of money, I wanted to feel the crisp blue notes in my fingers and sense that tingling of my nerves. A strange and pernicious lust had come over me, and no sense of shame now stood in its way. As soon as I stood up I was hurrying, running to the tote window, I pushed brusquely in among the people waiting in the queue, using my elbows, I impatiently pushed others aside just to see the money, the money itself. "Oaf!" muttered someone whom I had jostled behind me; I heard him, but I had no intention of picking a quarrel. I was shaking with a strange, pathological impatience. At last my turn came, my hands greedily seized a blue bundle of banknotes. I counted them, both trembling and delighted. I had won six hundred and forty crowns.

I clutched them avidly. My first thought was to go on betting, to win more, much more. What had I done with my racing paper? Oh yes, I'd thrown it away in all the excitement. I looked round to see where I could buy another. Then, to my inexpressible dismay, I saw that the people around me were suddenly dispersing, making for the exit, the tote windows were closing, the fluttering flag came down. The meeting was over. That had been the last race. I stood there frozen for a moment. Then anger flared in me as if I had suffered some injustice. I couldn't reconcile myself to the fact that it was all over, not now that all my nerves were tense and quivering, the blood was coursing through my veins, hot as I hadn't felt it for years. But it was no use feeding hope artificially with the deceptive idea that I might have been mistaken, that was just wishful thinking, for the motley crowd was flowing away faster and faster, and the well-trodden turf already showed green among the few people still left. I gradually felt it ridiculous to be lingering here in a state of tension, so I took my hat—I had obviously left my cane at the tote turnstile in my excitement—and went towards the exit. A servant with cap obsequiously raised hurried to meet me, I told him the number of my cab, he shouted it across the open space through his cupped hands, and soon the horses came trotting smartly up. I told the cabby to drive slowly down the main avenue. For now that the excitement was beginning to fade, leaving a pleasurable sensation behind, I felt an almost prurient desire to go over the whole scene again in my thoughts.

At that moment another carriage drove past; I instinctively looked at it, only to look away again very deliberately. It was the woman and her stout husband. They had not noticed me, but I felt a horrible choking sensation, as if I had been caught in the guilty act. I could almost have told the cabby to urge the horses on, just to get away from them quickly.

The cab moved smoothly along on its rubber tyres among all the other carriages, swaying along with their brightly clad cargoes of women like boats full of flowers passing the green banks of the chestnut-lined avenue. The air was mild and sweet, the first cool evening breeze was already wafting faint perfume through the dust. But my pleasant mood of reverie refused to return; the meeting with the man I had swindled had struck me a painful blow. In my overheated and impassioned state it suddenly went through me like a draught of cold air blowing through a crack. I now thought through the whole scene again soberly, and could not understand myself: for no good reason I, a gentleman, a member of fashionable society, an officer in the reserve, highly esteemed in general, had taken money which I did not need, had put it in my wallet, had even done so with a greedy and lustful pleasure that rendered any excuse invalid. An hour ago I had been a man of upright and blameless character; now I had stolen. I was a thief. And as if to frighten myself I spoke my condemnation half-aloud under my breath as the cab gently trotted on, the words unconsciously falling into the rhythm of the horses' hooves: "Thief! Thief! Thief! Thief!"

But strange to say—oh, how am I to describe what happened now? It is so inexplicable, so very odd, and yet I know that I am not deceiving myself in retrospect. I am aware of every second's feelings in those moments, every oscillation of my mind, with a supernatural clarity, more clearly than almost any other experience in my thirty-six years, yet I hardly dare reveal that absurd chain of events, those baffling mood swings, and I really don't know whether any writer or psychologist could describe them logically at all. I can only set them down in order, faithfully reflecting the way they unexpectedly flared up within me. Well, so I was saying to myself, "Thief, thief, thief." Then came a very strange moment, as it were an empty one, a moment when nothing happened, when I was only—oh, how difficult it is to express this!—when I was only listening, listening to my inner voice. I had summoned myself before the court, I had accused myself, and now it was for the plaintiff to answer the judge. So I listened—and nothing happened. The whiplash of that word 'thief', which I had expected to terrify me and then fill me with inexpressible shame and remorse, had no effect. I waited patiently for several minutes, I then bent, as it were, yet closer to myself—for I could feel something moving beneath that defiant silence—and listened with feverish expectation for the echo that did not come, for the cry of disgust, horror, and despair that must follow my self-accusation. And still nothing happened. There was no answer. I said the word "Thief" to myself again, I said it out loud, "Thief", to rouse my numbed conscience at last, hard of hearing as it was. Again there was no answer. And suddenly—in a bright lightning flash of awareness, as if a match had suddenly been struck and held above the twilit depths—I realised that I only wanted to feel shame, I was not really ashamed, that down in those depths I was in some mysterious way proud of my foolish action, even pleased with it.

How was that possible? I resisted this unexpected revelation, for now I really did feel afraid of myself, but it broke over me with too strong and impetuous a force. No, it was not shame seething in my blood with such warmth, not indignation or self-disgust—it was joy, intoxicated joy blazing up in me, sparkling with bright, darting, exuberant flames, for I felt that in those moments I had been truly alive for the first time in many years, that my feelings had only been numb and were not yet dead, that somewhere under the arid surface of my indifference the hot springs of passion still mysteriously flowed, and now, touched by the magic wand of chance, had leapt high, reaching my heart. In me too, in me too, part as I was of the living, breathing universe, there still glowed the mysterious volcanic core of all earthly things, a volcano that sometimes erupts in whirling spasms of desire. I too lived, I was alive, I was a human being with hot, pernicious lusts. The storm of passion had flung wide a door, depths had opened up in me, and I was staring down at the unknown in myself with vertiginous joy. It frightened and at the same time delighted me. And slowly—as the carriage wheeled my dreaming body easily along through the world of bourgeois society—I climbed down, step by step, into the depths of my own humanity, inexpressibly alone in my silent progress, with nothing above me but the bright torch of my suddenly rekindled awareness. And as a thousand people surged around me, laughing and talking, I sought for my lost self in myself, I felt for past years in the magical process of contemplation. Things entirely lost suddenly emerged from the dusty, blank mirrors of my life. I remembered once, as a schoolboy, stealing a penknife from a classmate and then watching, with just the same demonic glee, as he looked for it everywhere, asking everyone if they had seen it, going to great pains to find it; I suddenly understood the mysteriously stormy nature of many sexual encounters, I realised that my passions had been only atrophied, only crushed by social delusions, by the lordly ideal of the perfect gentleman—but that in me too, although deep, deep down in clogged pipes and wellsprings, the hot streams of life flowed as they flowed in everyone else. I had always lived without daring to live to the full, I had restrained myself and hidden from myself, but now a concentrated force had broken out, I was overwhelmed by rich and inexpressibly powerful life. And now I knew that I still valued it; I knew it with the blissful emotion of a woman who feels her child move within her for the first time. I felt—how else can I put it?—real, true, genuine life burgeon within me, I felt—and I am almost ashamed to write this—I felt myself, desiccated as I was, suddenly flowering again, I felt red blood coursing restlessly through my veins, feelings gently unfolded in the warmth, and I matured into an unknown fruit which might be sweet or bitter. The miracle of Tannhäuser had come to me in the bright light of a racecourse, among the buzz of thousands of people enjoying their leisure; I had begun to feel again, the dry staff was putting out green leaves and buds.

A gentleman waved to me from a passing carriage and called my name—obviously I had failed to notice his first greeting. I gave an abrupt start, angry to be disturbed in the sweet flow of the stream pouring forth within me, in the deepest dream I had ever known. But a glance at the man hailing me brought me out of myself; it was my friend Alfons, a dear schoolmate of mine and now a public prosecutor. Suddenly a thought ran through me: now, for the first time, this man who greets you like a brother has power over you; you will be his quarry as soon as he is aware of your crime. If he knew about you and what you have done, he would be bound to snatch you out of this carriage, take you away from your whole comfortable bourgeois life, and thrust you down for three to five years into a dismal world behind barred windows, amidst the dregs of human life, other thieves driven to their dirty cells only by the lash of destitution. But it was only for a moment that cold fear grasped the wrist of my trembling hand, only for a moment did it halt my heartbeat—then this idea too turned to warmth of feeling, to a fantastic, audacious pride that now scrutinised everyone else around me with confidence, almost with contempt. How your sweet, friendly smiles, I thought, how the smiles with which you all greet me as one of yourselves would freeze on your lips if you guessed what I really am! You would wipe away my own greeting with a scornful, angry hand, as if it were a splash of excrement. But before you reject me I have already rejected you; this afternoon I broke out of your chilly, skeletal world, where I was a cogwheel performing its silent function in the great machine that coldly drives its pistons, circling vainly around itself—I have fallen to depths that I do not know, but I was more alive in that one hour than in all the frozen years I spent among you. I am not one of you any more, no, I am outside you somewhere, on some height or in some depth, but never to tread the flat plain of your bourgeois comfort again. For the first time I have felt all mankind's desire for good and evil, but you will never know where I have been, you will never recognise me: what do any of you know about my secret?

How could I express what I felt in that moment as I, an elegantly clad gentleman, drove past the rows of carriages greeting acquaintances and returning greetings, my face impassive? For while my larva, the outward man of the past, still saw and recognised faces, so delirious a music was playing inside me that I had to control myself to keep from shouting something of that raging tumult aloud. I was so full of emotion that its inner swell hurt me physically, like a man choking I had to press my hand hard to the place on my chest beneath which my heart was painfully seething. But pain, desire, alarm, horror or regret—I felt none of these separately and apart from the others, they were all merged and I felt only that I was alive, that I was breathing and feeling. And this simplest, most primeval of feelings, one I had not known for years, intoxicated me. I have never felt myself as ecstatically alive for even a second of my thirty-six years as I did in the airy lightness of that hour.

With a slight jolt, the cab stopped: the driver had reined in his horses, turned on the box and asked if he should drive me home. I came back to myself, feeling dizzy, looked at the avenue, and was dismayed to see how long I had been dreaming, how far my delirium had spread out over the hours. It was growing dark, a soft wind stirred the tops of the trees, the chestnut blossom was beginning to waft its evening perfume through the cool air. And behind the treetops a veiled glimpse of the moon already shone silver. It was enough, it must be enough. But I would not go home yet, not back to my usual world! I paid the cabby. As I took out my wallet and counted the banknotes, holding them in my fingers, something like a slight electric shock ran from my wrist to my fingertips. So there must be something of my old self left in me, the man who was ashamed. The dying conscience of a gentleman was still twitching, but my hand dipped cheerfully into the stolen money again, and in my joy I was generous with a tip. The driver thanked me so fervently that I had to smile, thinking: if only you knew! The horses began to move, the cab rolled away. I watched it go as you might look back from shipboard at a shore where you have been happy.

For a moment I stood dreamy and undecided in the midst of the murmuring, laughing crowd, with music drifting above it. It was about seven o'clock, and I instinctively turned towards the Sachergarten, where I usually ate with companions after going to the Prater. The cabby had probably set me down here on purpose. But no sooner did I touch the handle of the door in the fence of that superior garden restaurant than I felt a scruple: no, I still did not want to go back to my own world yet,

48

I didn't want to let the wonderful fermentation so mysteriously filling me disperse in the flow of casual conversation, I didn't want to detach myself from the sparkling magic of the adventure in which I had been involved for hours.

The confused music echoed faintly somewhere, and I instinctively went that way, for everything tempted me today. I felt it delightful to give myself up entirely to chance, and there was something extraordinarily intriguing in being aimlessly adrift in this gently moving crowd of people. My blood was seething in this thick, swirling, hot and human mass: I was suddenly on the alert, all my senses stimulated and intensified by that acrid, smoky aroma of human breath, dust, sweat and tobacco. All that even yesterday used to repel me because it seemed vulgar, common, plebeian, all that the elegant gentleman in me had haughtily avoided for a lifetime now magically attracted my new responses as if, for the first time, I felt some relationship in myself with what was animal, instinctive, common. Here among the dregs of the city, mixing with soldiers, servant girls, ruffians, I felt at ease in a way I could not understand at all; I almost greedily drank in the acridity of the air, I found the pushing and shoving of the crowd gathered around me pleasant, and with delighted curiosity I waited to see where this hour would take me, devoid as I was of any will of my own. The cymbals crashed and the brass band blared closer now, the mechanical orchestrions thumped out staccato polkas and boisterous waltzes with insistent monotony, and now and then I heard dull thuds from the sideshows, ripples of laughter, drunken shouting. Now I saw the carousels of my childhood going round and round among the trees, with lights crazily flashing. I stood in the middle of the square, letting all the tumult break over me, filling my eyes and ears: these cascades of sound, the infernal confusion of it all did me good, for there was something in this hurly-burly that stilled my own inner torrent of feeling. I watched the servant girls, skirts flying,

49

getting themselves pushed up in the air on the swings with loud cries of glee that might have issued from their sexual orifices, I saw butchers' boys laughing as they brought heavy hammers down on the try-your-strength machine, barkers with hoarse voices and ape-like gestures cried their wares above the noise of the orchestrions, and all this whirling activity mingled with the thousand sounds and constant movement of the crowd, which was inebriated, as if it had imbibed cheap spirits, on the music of the brass band, the flickering of the light, and their own warm pleasure in company. Now that I myself had been awakened, I suddenly felt other people's lives, I felt the heated arousal of the city as, hot and pent-up, it poured out with its millions in the few leisure hours of a Sunday, as its own fullness spurred it on to sultry, animal, yet somehow healthy and instinctive enjoyment. And gradually, feeling people rub against me, feeling the constant touch of their hot bodies passionately pressing close, I sensed their warm arousal passing into me too: my nerves, stimulated by the sharp aroma, tensed and reached out of me, my senses played deliriously with the roar of the crowd and felt that vague stupor that inevitably mingles with all strong sensual gratification. For the first time in years, perhaps for the first time in my life, I felt the crowd, I felt human beings as a force from which lust passed into my own once separate being; some dam had been burst, and what was in my veins passed out into this world, flowed rhythmically back, and I felt a new desire, to break down that last barrier between me and them, a passionate longing to copulate with this hot, strange press of humanity. With male lust I longed to plunge into the gushing vulva of that hot, giant body; with female lust I was open to every touch, every cry, every allurement, every embrace—and now I knew that love was in me, and a need for love such as I had not felt since my twilight boyhood days. Oh, to plunge in, into the living entity, to be linked somehow to the convulsive, laughing, breathing passion of others, to stream on, to pour my fluids into their veins; to become a small and nameless part of the hurly-burly, something infused into the dirt of the world, a creature quivering with lust, sparkling in the slough with those myriads of beings—oh, to plunge into that fullness, down into the circling ripples, shot like an arrow from the bow of my own tension into the unknown, into some heaven of collective experience.

I know now that I was drunk at the time. Everything was roaring in my blood at once, the ringing bells on the carousel, the high lusty laughter of the women as the men swung them up in the air, the chaotic music, the whirling skirts. Every single sound fell sharply into me and then flickered up again, red and quivering, past my temples, I felt every touch, every glance with fantastically stimulated nerves (it was rather like sea-sickness), yet it came all together in a delirious whole. I cannot possibly explain my complex state in words, it can perhaps best be done by means of a comparison if I say I was brimming over with sound, noise, feeling, overheated like a machine operating with all its wheels racing to escape the monstrous pressure that must surely burst the boiler of my chest any moment. My fingertips twitched, my temples thudded, my heated blood pressed in my throat, surged in my temples— from a state of half-hearted apathy lasting many years I had suddenly plunged into a fever that consumed me. I felt that I must open up, come out of myself with a word, with a glance, unburden myself, flow out of myself, give my inner self away, bring myself down to the common level, be resolved—save myself somehow from the hard barrier of silence dividing me from the warm, flowing, living element. I had not spoken for hours, had pressed no one's hand, felt no one's glance rest on me, questioning and sympathetic, and now, under the pressure of events, this excitement was building up against the dam of silence. Never, never had I so strongly felt a need for communication, for another human being than now, when I was in the middle of a surging throng of thousands and tens of thousands, warmth and words washing around me, yet cut off from the circulating blood of that abundance. I was like a man dying of thirst out at sea. And at the same time, this torment increasing with every glance, I saw strangers meeting at every moment to right and left, touching lightly, coming together and parting in play like little balls of quicksilver. Envy came over me when I saw young men addressing strange girls as they passed by, taking their arms after the first word, seeing people find each other and join forces: a word exchanged beside the carousel, a glance as they brushed past each other was enough, and strangeness melted away in conversation, which might be broken off again after a few minutes, but still it was a link, a union, communication, and all my nerves burned for it now. But practised as I was in social intercourse, a popular purveyor of small talk and confident in all the social forms, I was now afraid, ashamed to address one of these broad-hipped servant girls for fear that she might laugh at me. Indeed, I cast my eyes down when someone looked at me by chance, yet inside I was dying of desire for a word. What I wanted from these people was not clear even to myself, but I could no longer endure to be alone and consumed by my fever. However, they all looked past me, every glance moved away from me, no one wanted to be with me. Once a lad of about twelve in ragged clothes did come near me, his eyes bright in the reflected lights as he stared longingly at the wooden horses going up and down. His narrow mouth was open as if with thirst; he obviously had no money left for a ride, and was simply enjoying the screams and laughter of others. I made my way up to him and asked—though why did my voice tremble and break, ending on a high note?—I asked: "Wouldn't you like a ride?" He looked up, took fright—why? why?—turned bright red and ran away without a word. Not even a barefoot child would let me give him pleasure; I felt there must be something terribly strange about me that meant I could never mingle with anyone, but was separate from the dense mass, floating like a drop of oil on moving water.

However, I did not give in; I could no longer be alone. My feet were burning in my dusty patent leather shoes, my throat was sore from the turbulent air. I looked round me: small islands of green stood to right and left among the flowing human crowds, taverns with red tablecloths and bare wooden benches where ordinary citizens sat with their glasses of beer and Sunday cigarettes. The sight was enticing: strangers could sit together here and fall into conversation, there was a little peace here among the wild frenzy. I went into one such tavern, looked round the tables until I found one where a family was sitting: a stout, sturdy artisan with his wife, two cheerful daughters and a little boy. They were nodding their heads together, joking with each other, and their happy, carefree glances did me good. I greeted them civilly, moved to a chair and asked if I might sit down. Their laughter stopped at once, for a moment they were silent as if each was waiting for another to give consent, and then the woman, in tones almost of dismay, said, "Oh yes, certainly, do." I sat down and then felt that in doing so I had spoilt their carefree mood, for an uncomfortable silence immediately fell around the table. Without daring to take my eyes off the red check tablecloth where salt and pepper had been untidily spilt, I felt that they were all watching me uneasily, and at once—but too late!—it struck me that I was too elegant for this servants' tavern in my race-going suit, my top hat from Paris and the pearl pin in my dove-grey tie, that my elegance, the aura of luxury about me at once enveloped me in an invisible layer of hostility and confusion. The silence of these five people made me sink my head lower and lower to look at the table, grimly, desperately counting the red squares on the cloth again and again, kept where I was by the shame of suddenly standing up again, yet too cowardly to raise my tormented glance. It was a relief when the waiter finally came and put the heavy beer glass down in front of me. Then I could at last move a hand and glance timidly over the rim of the glass as I drank: sure enough, all five were watching me, not as if they disliked me but in silent embarrassment. They recognised an intruder into the musty atmosphere of their world, with the naive instinct of their class they felt that I wanted something here, was looking for something that did not belong in my own environment, that I was brought here not by love or liking, not by the simple pleasure of a waltz, a beer, a wish to sit quietly in a tavern on a Sunday, but by some kind of desire which they did not understand and which they distrusted, just as the boy by the carousel had distrusted my offer, just as the thousands of others out there in the throng avoided my elegance and sophistication with unconscious hostility. Yet I felt that if I could find something careless, easy, heartfelt, truly human to say the father or mother would respond to me, the daughters would smile back, flattered, I could go to a shooting range with the boy and play childish games with him. Within five, ten minutes I would be released from myself, immersed in the carefree atmosphere of simple conversation, of readily granted, even gratified familiarity—but I could not think of that simple remark, that first step in the conversation. A false, foolish, but overpowering shame stuck in my throat, and I sat with my eyes downcast like a criminal at the table with these simple folk, immersed in the torment of feeling that my grim presence had spoilt the last hour of their Sunday. And as I doggedly sat there, I did penance for all the years of haughty indifference when I had passed thousands and thousands of such tables and millions and millions of my fellow men without a glance, thinking only of ingratiating myself or succeeding in the narrow circles of elegant society, and I felt that the direct way to reach these people and talk to them easily, now that I was cast out and wanted contact in my hour of need, was barred to me on the inside.

So I sat, once a free man, now painfully inward-looking, still counting the red squares on the tablecloth until at last the waiter came by. I called him over, paid, left my almost untouched glass of beer and said a civil good evening. They thanked me in tones of friendly surprise; I knew, without turning round, that as soon as my back was turned they would resume their lively cheerfulness, and the warm circle of their conversation would close in as soon as I, the foreign body, had been thrust out of it.

Once again, but now more greedily, fervently and desperately, I threw myself back into the human whirlpool. The crowd had thinned out under the black trees that merged with the sky, there was not so dense and restless a torrent of people in the circle of light around the carousel, only shadowy forms scurrying around on the outskirts of the square. And the deep roar of the crowd, a noise like breathing in desire, was separating into many little sounds, always ringing out when the music somewhere grew strong and frenzied, as if to snatch back the people who were leaving. Faces of another kind emerged now: the children with their balloons and paper confetti had gone home, and so had families on a leisurely Sunday outing. Now there were loud-mouthed drunks about; shabby characters with a sauntering yet purposeful gait came out of side alleys. During the hour when I had sat transfixed at the strangers' table, this curious world had descended to a lower plane. But in itself this phosphorescent atmosphere of audacity and danger somehow pleased me more than the earlier Sunday respectability. The instinct that had been aroused in me scented a similarly intent desire; I felt myself somehow reflected in the sauntering of these dubious figures, these social outcasts who were also roaming here with restless expectation in search of an adventure, of sudden excitement, and I envied even these ragged fellows the way they roamed so freely and openly, for I was standing beside the wooden post of a carousel and breathing with difficulty, impatient to thrust the pressure of silence and the pain of my isolation away from me and yet incapable of a movement, of a cry, of a word. I just stood there staring at the square that was illuminated by the flickering reflection of the circling lights, looking out from my island of light into the darkness, glancing with foolish hope at any human being who, attracted by the bright light, turned my way for a moment. But all eyes moved coldly away from me. No one wanted me, no one would release me.

I know it would be mad to try to describe or actually explain to anyone how I, a cultured and elegant man, a figure in high society, rich, independent, acquainted with the most distinguished figures of a city with a population of millions, spent a whole hour that night standing by the post of a tunelessly squeaking, constantly rocking carousel in the Prater, hearing the same thumping polka, the same slowly dragging waltz circle past me with the same silly horses' heads of painted wood, twenty, forty, a hundred times, never moving from the spot out of dogged defiance, a magical feeling that I could force fate to do my will. I know I was acting senselessly, but there was a tension of feeling in that senseless persistence, a steely spasm of all the muscles such as people usually feel, perhaps, only at the moment of a fatal fall and just before death. My whole life, a life that had passed so emptily, had suddenly come flooding back and was building up in me like pent-up water behind a dam. And tormented as I was by my pointless delusion, my intention of staying, holding out there until some word or glance from a human being released me, yet I relished it too. In standing at the stake like that I did penance not so much for the theft as for the dull, lethargic vacuity of my earlier life, and I had sworn to myself not to leave until I received a sign that fate had let me go free.

And the more that hour progressed, the more night came on. Lights went out in one after another of the sideshows, and then there was always a kind of rising tide of darkness, swallowing up the light patch of that particular booth on the grass. The bright island where I stood was more and more isolated, and I looked at the time, trembling. Another quarter of an hour and then the dappled wooden horses would stand still, the red and green lights on their foolish foreheads would be switched off, the bloated orchestrion would stop thumping out its music. Then I would be wholly in the dark, all alone here in the faintly rustling night, entirely outcast, entirely desolate. I looked with increasing uneasiness at the now dimly lit square, where a couple on their way home now hurried past or a few drunken fellows staggered about only very occasionally: but over in the shadows hidden life quivered, restless and enticing. Sometimes there was a quiet whistle or a snap of the fingers when a couple of men passed by. And if the men, lured by the sound, moved into the darkness you would hear women's voices whispering in the shadows, and sometimes the wind blew scraps of shrill laughter my way. Gradually that hidden life emerged more boldly from the dark outskirts, coming closer to the circle of light in the illuminated square, only to plunge back into the shadows again as soon as the spiked helmet of a passing policeman shone in the reflected street light. But no sooner had he continued on his beat than the ghostly shadows returned, and now I could see their outlines clearly, so close did they venture to the light. They were the last dregs of that nocturnal world, the mud left behind now that the flowing torrent of humanity had subsided: a couple of whores, the poorest and most despised who have no bedstead of their own, sleep on a mattress by day and by night walk the streets restlessly, giving their worn, abused, thin bodies to any man here in the dark for a small silver coin, with the police after them, driven by hunger or by some ruffian, always roaming the darkness, hunters and hunted alike. They gradually emerged like hungry dogs, sniffing about near the lit square for something male, for a forgotten denizen of the night whose lust they could slake for a crown or so to buy a Glühwein in a café and keep the flickering candle-end of life going; it would soon enough be extinguished in a hospice or a prison. These girls were the refuse, the last liquid muck left after the sensuous tide of the Sunday crowd had ebbed away—it was with boundless horror that I now saw those hungry figures flitting out of the dark. But my horror was also mingled with a magical desire, for even in this dirtiest of mirrors I recognised something forgotten and now dimly felt again: here was the swamp-like world of the depths through which I had passed many years ago, and it now rose in my mind again with a phosphorescent glow. How strange was what this fantastic night offered me, suddenly revealing matters closed to me before, so that the darkest of my past, the most secret of my urges now lay open to me! Dim feelings revived from my forgotten boyhood years, when my timid glance was curiously attracted to such figures, yet felt afraid of them, a memory of the first time I followed one of them up a damp and creaking staircase to her bed—and suddenly, as if lightning had riven the night sky, I sharply saw every detail of that forgotten hour, the bad print of an oil painting over the bed, the good-luck charm she wore round her neck, I felt every fibre of that moment, the uncertain heat of it, the disgust, my first boyish pride. All that surged through my body at once. I was suddenly flooded with immeasurable clarity of vision, and—how can I say it, this infinite thing?—I suddenly understood all that bound me to these people with such burning pity, for the very reason that they were the last dregs of life, and my instinct, once aroused by my crime, felt for this hungry sauntering, so like my own on this fantastic night, felt for that criminal availability to any touch, any strange, chance-come desire. I was magnetically drawn to them, the wallet full of stolen money suddenly burned hot on my breast as at last I sensed beings over there, human beings, soft, breathing, speaking, wanting something from others, perhaps from me, only waiting as I was to offer myself up, burning in my fervent desire for human contact. And suddenly I understood what drives men to such creatures, I saw that it is seldom just the heat in the blood, a growing itch, but is usually simply the fear of loneliness, of the terrible strangeness that otherwise rises between us, as my inflamed emotions felt for the first time today. I remembered when I had last dimly felt something like this: it was in England, in Manchester, one of those steely cities that roar under a lightless sky with a noise like an underground railway, and yet at the same time are frozen with a loneliness that seeps through the pores and into the blood. I had been staying there with relatives for three weeks, but spent all my evenings wandering around bars and clubs, visiting the glittering music hall again and again just to feel some human warmth. And then, one evening, I had found such a woman, whose gutter English I could scarcely understand, but suddenly I was in a room, drinking in laughter from a strange mouth, there was a warm body there, something of this earth, close and soft. Suddenly the cold, black city melted away, the dark and raucous lonely space: a being you did not know, who just stood there waiting for all comers, could release you, thaw the frost; you could breathe freely again, feel life, all light and bright in the middle of the steely dungeon. How wonderful for those who are lonely, shut up in themselves, to know or guess that there is something to support them in their fear, something to cling to, though it may be dirty from much handling, stiff with age, eaten away by corrosion. And this, this of all things I had forgotten in that hour of ultimate loneliness from which, staggering, I rose that night. I had forgotten that somewhere, in one final corner, there are always these creatures waiting to accept any devotion, let any desolation rest in their breath, cool any heat for a small coin, which is never enough for the great gift they give with their eternal readiness, the gift of their human presence.

Beside me the orchestrion of the carousel started droning away again. This was the last ride, the last fanfare of the circling light going round in the darkness before Sunday passed into the workaday week. But no one was riding now, the horses went round empty in their crazy circle, the tired woman at the cash desk was raking together the day's takings and counting them, the errand boy was ready with a hook to bring the shutters rattling down over the booth after this last ride. Only I stood there alone, still leaning against the post, and looked out at the empty square where nothing but those figures moved, fluttering like bats, seeking something just as I was seeking, waiting as I was waiting, yet with an impassably strange space between us. Now, however, one of them must have noticed me, for she slowly made her way forwards, and I looked closely at her from under my lowered eyelids: a small, crippled, rickety creature without a hat, wearing a tasteless and showy cheap dress with worn dancing shoes peeping out from under it, the whole outfit probably bought bit by bit from a street stall or junk shop at third-hand, crumpled by the rain or some indecent adventure in the grass. She came over with an ingratiating look and stopped beside me, casting out a sharp glance like a fishing line and showing her bad teeth in an inviting smile. My breath stopped short. I could not move, could not look at her, and yet I could not tear myself away: as if I were under hypnosis, I felt that a human being was walking around me hopefully, that someone was wooing me, that with a word, with a gesture I could finally rid myself of my terrible loneliness, my painful sense of being an outcast. But I could not move, I was wooden as the post against which I was leaning, and in a kind of lascivious powerlessness I felt only—as the melody of the carousel wearily wound down—this close presence, the will to attract me, and I closed my eyes for a moment, to feel to the full this magnetic attraction of something human coming out of the darkness of the world and flowing over me.

The carousel stopped, the waltz tune was cut short with a last groaning sound. I opened my eyes just in time to see the figure beside me turn away. Obviously she felt it tedious to wait beside a man standing here like a block of wood. I was horrified. I suddenly felt very cold. Why had I let her go, the only human being who had approached me this fantastic night, who was receptive to me? Behind me the lights were going out; the shutters rolled down with a rattle and a clatter. It was over.

And suddenly—oh, how can I describe to myself that warm sense like spindrift suddenly spraying up?—suddenly—and it was as abrupt, as hot, as red as if a vein had burst in my breast—suddenly something broke out of me, a proud, haughty man fully armoured with cool social dignity, something like a silent prayer, a spasm, a cry: it was my childish yet overpowering wish for this dirty, rickety little whore to turn her head again so that I could speak to her. For I was not too proud to follow her—my pride was all crushed, trodden underfoot, swept away by very new feelings—no, I was too weak, too much at a loss. So I stood there, trembling and in turmoil, alone at the martyr's stake of darkness, waiting as I had never waited since my boyhood years, as I had waited only once before, standing by a window in the evening as a strange woman slowly began undressing, and I kept lingering and hesitating as she unwittingly stripped herself naked—I stood crying out to God with a voice I did not recognise as my own for a miracle, for this crippled thing, this last scum of humanity, to try me once more, to turn her eyes to me again.

And yes—she did turn. Once more, quite automatically, she looked back. But so strong must my convulsive start have been, so strong the leaping of intense feeling into my eyes, that she stopped and observed me. She half-turned again, looked at me through the darkness, smiled and nodded her head invitingly over to the shadowy side of the square. And at last I felt the terrible spell of rigidity in me give way. I could move again. I nodded my consent.

The invisible pact was made. Now she went ahead over the dimly lit square, turning from time to time to see if I was following. And I did follow: the leaden feeling had left my legs, I could move my feet again. I was magnetically impelled forwards, I did not consciously walk but flowed along behind her, so to speak, drawn by a mysterious power. In the dark of the alley between the booths of sideshows she slowed her pace. Now I was beside her.

She looked at me for a few seconds, scrutinising me distrustfully; something made her uncertain. Obviously my curiously timid lingering there, the contrast between the place and my elegance, seemed to her somehow suspicious. She looked round several times, hesitated. Then, pointing down the street that was black as a mine shaft: "Let's go there. It's dark behind the circus."

I could not answer. The dreadful vulgarity of this encounter numbed me. I would have liked to tear myself away somehow, bought myself off with a coin, an excuse, but my will had no more power over me. I felt as if I were on a toboggan run flinging myself round a bend, racing at high speed down a steep incline of snow, when the fear of death somehow mingles pleasantly with the intoxication of speed, and instead of braking you give yourself up to the sense of falling without your own volition, with delirious yet conscious weakness. I could not go back now, and perhaps I didn't want to. She pressed herself intimately against me, and I instinctively took her arm. It was a very thin arm, the arm not of a woman but of an underdeveloped, scrofulous child, and no sooner did I feel it through her lightweight coat than I was overcome, in the midst of my intense access of feeling, by gentle, overwhelming pity for this wretched, downtrodden scrap of life washed up against me by the night. And instinctively my fingers caressed the weak, feeble joints of her hand more respectfully and purely than I had ever touched a woman before.

We crossed a dimly lit road and entered a little grove where huge treetops held the sombre, evil-smelling darkness in their embrace. At that moment, and although you could hardly make out an outline any more, I noticed that she turned very carefully on my arm, and did the same thing again a few steps later. And strangely enough, while I was, as it were, numbed and rigid as I slipped into this indecent adventure, my senses were perfectly bright and alert. With clear vision that nothing escaped, that took conscious note of every movement, I realised that something was following quietly behind us on the borders of the path we had crossed, and I thought I heard a dragging step. And suddenly—as when a crackling, white flash of lightning leaps across a landscape—I guessed, I knew it all: I was to be lured into a trap, this whore's pimps were lurking behind us, and in the dark she was taking me to the appointed place where I was to be their victim. I saw it all, with the supernatural clarity that one is said to have only in the concentrated seconds between life and death, and I considered every possibility. There was still time to get away, the main road must be close, for I could hear the electric tram rattling along its rails, a shout or a whistle could summon aid. All the possibilities of flight and rescue leapt up in my mind, in sharply outlined images.

But how strange—this alarming realisation did not cool me but only further inflamed me. Today, awake in the clear light of an autumn day, I cannot explain the absurdity of my actions to myself: I knew, I knew at once with every fibre of my being that I was going into danger unnecessarily, but the anticipation of danger ran through my nerves like a fine madness. I knew there was something terrible and perhaps deadly ahead,

I trembled with disgust at the idea of being forced into a criminal, mean and dirty incident somewhere here, but even death itself aroused a dark curiosity in me in my present state of life-induced intoxication, an intoxication I had never known or guessed at before, but now it was streaming over me, numbing me. Something—was it that I was ashamed to show fear, or was it weakness?—something drove me on. I felt intrigued to climb down to this last sewer of life, to squander my whole past, gamble it away. A reckless lust of the spirit mingled with the low vulgarity of this adventure. And although all my nerves scented danger, and I understood it clearly with my senses and my reason, I still went on into the grove arm-in-arm with this dirty little Prater tart who physically repelled rather than attracted me, and who I knew was bringing me this way just for her accomplices. Yet I could not go back. The gravitational pull of criminality, having taken hold of me that afternoon during my adventure on the racecourse, was dragging me further and further down. And now I felt only the daze, the eddying frenzy of my fall into new depths, perhaps into the last depths of all, into death.

After a few steps I stopped. Once again her glance flew uncertainly around. Then she looked expectantly at me.

"Well—what are you going to give me?"

Oh yes. I'd forgotten that. But the question did not sober me, far from it. I was so glad to give her something, to make her a present, to be able to waste my substance. I hastily reached into my pocket and tipped all the silver in it and a few crumpled banknotes into her outstretched hand. And now something so wonderful happened that even today my blood warms when I think of it: either this poor creature was surprised by the size of the sum—she must have been used to getting only small change for her indecent services—or there was something new and unusual to her in the way I gave it readily, quickly, almost with delight, for she stepped back, and through the dense and evil-smelling darkness I felt her gaze seeking me in great astonishment. And at last I felt what I had not found all evening: someone was interested in me, was seeking me, for the first time I was alive to someone else in the world. The fact that it should be this outcast, this creature who carried her poor abused body round in the darkness, offering it for sale, and who had thrust herself on me without even looking at the buyer, who now turned her eyes to mine, the fact that she was wondering about the human being in me only heightened my strange sense of intoxication, clear-sighted and dizzy as I was at one and the same time, both fully conscious and dissolving into a magical apathy. And already the stranger was pressing closer to me, but not in the businesslike way of a woman doing a duty that had been paid for. Instead, I thought I felt unconscious gratitude in it, a feminine desire for closeness. I gently took her thin, rickety, childish arm, felt her small, twisted body, and suddenly, looking beyond all that, I saw her whole life: the borrowed, smeared bedstead in a suburban yard where she slept from morning to noon among a crowd of other people's children; her pimp throttling her; belching drunks falling on her in the dark; the special hospital ward; the lecture hall where her abused body was put on show, sick and naked, as a teaching aid to cheerful young medical students; and the end somewhere in a poorhouse to which she would be carted off in a batch of women and left to die like an animal. Infinite pity for her, for all of them came over me, a warmth that was tenderness without sensuality. Again and again I patted her small, thin arm. And then I bent down and kissed the astounded girl.

At that moment there was a rustle behind me. A twig cracked. I jumped back. And a coarse, vulgar male voice was laughing. "There we are. I thought so."

Even before I saw them I knew who they were. Not for one second, dazed and confused as I was, had I forgotten that I was surrounded, and indeed this was what my mysteriously lively curiosity had been waiting for. A figure now emerged from the bushes, and a second behind it: a couple of rough fellows boldly taking up their positions. The coarse laugh came again. "Turning a trick here, eh? A fine gentleman, of course! Well, we'll see to him now." I stood perfectly still, the blood beating in my temples. I felt no fear. I was simply waiting for what came next. Now I was in the very depths at last, in the final abyss of ignominy. Now the blow must come, the shattering end towards which I had half-intentionally been moving.

The girl had moved quickly away from me, but not to join them. She was in a way standing between us; it seemed that she did not entirely like the ambush prepared for me. The men, for their part, were vexed because I did not move. They looked at each other, obviously expecting some protest from me, a plea, some display of fear. "Oh, so he's not talking!" said one of them at last, threateningly. The other approached me and said in commanding tones, "You'll have to come down to the police station with us."

I still did not answer. One of the men put his hand on my shoulder and gave me a slight push. "Move," he said.

I began to move. I did not defend myself, for I did not want to: the extraordinary, degraded, dangerous nature of the situation left me dazed. But my brain remained perfectly clear: I knew that these fellows must fear the police more than I did, that I could buy myself off for a few crowns—but I wanted to relish the depths of horror to the full, I was enjoying the dreadful humiliation of the situation, in a kind of waking swoon. Without haste, entirely automatically, I went the way they had pushed me.

But the very fact that I moved towards the light so obediently and without a word seemed to confuse the men. They whispered softly, and then began to talk to each other again in deliberately raised voices. "Let him go," said one (a pockmarked little fellow), but the other replied, with apparent decision: "No, that won't do. If poor starving devils like us do such things they put us behind bars. But a fine gentleman like this—he really deserves punishment." I heard every word, and in their voices I detected their clumsily expressed request for me to begin negotiating with them; the criminal in me understood the criminal in them, understood that they wanted to torment me with fears, while I was tormenting them with my docility. It was a silent battle between us, and—oh, how rich in experience this night was!—and in the midst of deadly danger, here in this insalubrious grove on the Prater, in the company of a couple of ruffians and a whore, I felt the frenzied enchantment of gambling for the second time in twelve hours, but this time for the highest of stakes, for my whole comfortable existence, even my life. And with all the force of my quivering nerves, tensed as they were to breaking point, I abandoned myself to this great game, to the sparkling magic of chance.

"Hey, there goes the cop," said a voice behind me. "Our fine gentleman won't like this, he'll be behind bars a week or more." It was meant to sound like a grim threat, but I heard the man's hesitant uncertainty. I went placidly towards the dim light, where I did indeed see light glint on a police officer's spiked helmet. Twenty more paces and I would have reached him. Behind me, the men had fallen silent. I realised they were slowing down. Next moment, I knew, they must retreat like cowards into the dark, into their own world, embittered by the failure of their trick, perhaps to vent their anger on the poor woman. The game was over: again, for the second time today, I had won, I had cheated other strangers of their malicious designs. Pale lantern light was already flickering ahead, and when I turned I looked for the first time into the two ruffians' faces: bitterness and a craven shame looked out of their uncertain eyes. They still stood there, but downcast and disappointed, ready to slink back into the dark. For their power was gone: it was *me* they feared now.

At that moment I was suddenly overcome—and it was like fermentation within me, bursting the staves in the barrel of my breast to pour out hot feeling into my blood—I was suddenly overcome by an infinite, fraternal sympathy for these two men. What had they wanted from me, these poor hungry, ragged fellows, what had they wanted from me, a satiated parasite, but a few miserable crowns? They could have strangled me there in the dark, they could have robbed me, killed me, but they had not; they had only tried to frighten me in a clumsy, amateurish way for the sake of the loose silver in my pocket. How could I, who had become a thief on a whim, out of a sense of audacity, who had turned criminal for the pleasure of my nerves, how could I dare to torment these poor devils further? And my infinite sympathy was mingled with infinite shame at having toyed with their fear and impatience for my own amusement. I pulled myself together: now that I was safe and the light of the nearby street protected me, I must go along with them and banish the disappointment from those bitter, hungry eyes.

With a sudden movement I stepped up to one of them. "Why would you want to report me to the police?" I said, taking care to inject a touch of stress and fear into my voice. "What good will it do you? Perhaps I'll be locked up, perhaps not. But it won't do you any good. Why do you want to make my life a misery?"

They both stared at me in embarrassment. They must have expected anything: cries, threats to make them cringe like growling dogs, not this subservience. At last one of them said, not threateningly at all, but as it were apologetically: "Justice have got to be done! We're only doing our duty, right?"

This comment was obviously prepared for such cases, yet it rang false. Neither of the pair dared look at me. They were waiting. And I knew what they were waiting for. They were waiting for me to beg for mercy and offer them money.

I still remember everything about those seconds. I recollect every nerve that stirred in me, every thought that shot through my mind. And I know what I maliciously wanted at first: I wanted to make them wait, torment them a little longer, relish the pleasure of keeping them on tenterhooks. But soon I forced myself to beg, because I knew it was time for me to relieve these two of their anxiety. I began putting on a show of being terrified, I begged for mercy, asked them to keep all this quiet and not make me wretched. I saw these poor amateur blackmailers begin to feel awkward, and the silence between us was milder now.

And then at last, at last I said what they had been longing to hear all this time. "I'll … I'll give you … I'll give you a hundred crowns."

All three started and looked at each other. They had not expected so much, not now that all was really lost for them. At last one of them, the pockmarked man with the shifty eyes, pulled himself together. He started to speak twice, but couldn't get it out. Then he said—and I felt that he was ashamed as he spoke—"Two hundred crowns."

"Oh, shut it!" the girl suddenly intervened. "You be glad he gives you anything. He ain't done nothing, he didn't hardly touch me. This is too much."

She was shouting at them in genuinely embittered tones. And my heart sang. Someone was sorry for me, someone was speaking up for me, kindness was born of something low and mean, blackmail gave rise to some dim desire for justice. How good it felt, how it responded to the swelling tide of my feelings! No, I must not play with these people or torment them in their fear and shame any longer—enough, enough!

"Very well, two hundred crowns."

All three fell silent. I took out my wallet. Slowly, very openly I held it in my hand. With one move they could have snatched it from me and fled into the dark. But they looked shyly away. There was some kind of secret pact between them and me, not a conflict and a gamble any more but a condition of trust and justice, a human relationship. I took the two notes from the bundle of stolen money and handed them to one of the men.

"Thank you," he said automatically, and turned away. He himself obviously felt how ridiculous it was to thank me for money obtained by blackmail. He was ashamed, and his shame—for I could feel everything that night, I could read the meaning of every gesture—his shame distressed me. I did not want a human being to feel ashamed in front of me, one of his own kind, a thief like him, weak, cowardly, lacking in willpower. I felt pain for his humiliation, and wanted to lift it from him. So I refused his thanks.

"No, it is for me to thank you," I said, surprised at the amount of true feeling in my voice. "If you had reported me to the police I'd have been done for. I'd have had to shoot myself, and you'd have gained nothing by that. It's better this way. I will go right over there, and perhaps you will go the other way. Goodnight."

They stood silent for a moment longer. Then one man said: "Goodnight," and then the other, and last the whore, who had stayed in the dark all this time. The words sounded warm and heartfelt, like true good wishes. I sensed in their voices that somewhere deep in their dark natures they liked me, they would never forget this strange moment. It might perhaps return to their minds again in the penitentiary or the hospice; something of me lived on in them, I had given them something. And the pleasure of giving it filled me as no emotion had ever done before.

I walked alone through the night to the exit from the Prater. All inhibition had left me, I had been like a man missing, presumed dead, but now I felt my nature flowing out into the whole infinite world in a plenitude I had never known before. I sensed everything as if it lived for me alone, and as if in its own turn it linked me with that flow. The black trees stood around me, rustling, and I loved them. Stars shone down from above, and I breathed in their white salutation. I heard singing voices somewhere, and I felt they were singing for me. Now that I had torn away the carapace from my breast everything was suddenly mine, and the joy of lavish abandonment swept me on. Oh, how easy it is, I thought, to give pleasure and rejoice in that pleasure yourself: you have only to open yourself up and the living current will flow from one human being to another, falling from the heights to the depths, rising up again like spindrift from the depths into infinity.

At the exit of the Prater, beside a cab rank, I saw a street trader, tired and bowed over her paltry wares. She had baked goods for sale, covered with dust, and a few fruits; she had probably been sitting there since morning bending over the few coins she had earned, and weariness bent her back. Why not make her happy too, I thought, now that I am happy? I chose a small pastry and put a banknote down in front of her. She began busily looking for change, but I was already walking on and saw only her start of delight, saw the bent back suddenly straighten, while her open mouth, frozen in amazement, sent a thousand good wishes after me. Holding the pastry, I went up to a horse standing wearily in the shafts. It turned and gave me a friendly snort, and its dark eyes showed gratitude when I stroked its pink nostrils and gave it the sweet morsel. And as soon as I had done that I wanted more: to give more pleasure, to feel how a few silver coins, a few notes printed on coloured paper can conquer fear, kill want, kindle merriment. Why were there no beggars here?

Why no children who would have liked to have the bunches of balloons on strings which a surly, white-haired cripple was taking home, disappointed by the poor business he had done all this long, hot day. I went up to him. "I'll take the balloons." "Ten hellers each," he said suspiciously, for what would this elegant gentleman of leisure want with his coloured balloons at midnight? "I'll take them all," I said, giving him a ten-crown note. He swayed on his feet, looked at me as if something had dazzled him, and then, trembling, gave me the string that held the whole bunch together. I felt the taut string tug at my finger; the balloons wanted to be gone, to be free, to fly through the air. Go then, fly where you like, be free! I let go of the strings, and up they suddenly rose like so many coloured moons. Laughing people came up from all sides, lovers emerged from the shadows, drivers cracked their whips and called to each other, pointing out the freed balloons drifting over the trees towards the houses and rooftops. The onlookers all glanced cheerfully at each other, enjoying my happy folly.

Why did I never know before how easy and how good it is to give pleasure? All of a sudden the banknotes were burning a hole in my wallet again, twitching in my fingers like the strings of the balloons just now. They wanted to fly away from me into the unknown too. And I took them, those I had stolen from Lajos and my own—for I felt no difference between them now and no guilt—and kept them ready to be given to any who wanted one. I approached a street-sweeper morosely sweeping the deserted Praterstrasse. He thought I wanted to ask him the way, and looked up with a surly expression; I smiled and held out a twenty-crown note. He started, uncomprehending, then finally took it and waited to see what I wanted in return. But I just smiled at him again, said: "Buy something you like," and went on. I kept looking around to see if anyone wanted something from me, and when no one came up I just handed the money out myself: I gave a note to a whore who accosted me, two notes to a lamplighter, I threw one into the open hatch of a basement bakery, and so I went on, leaving behind me a wake of amazement, thanks and pleasure, I walked on and on. Finally I crumpled notes up and scattered them around the empty street and on the steps of a church, liking the idea of the old ladies who would come to morning service, find all those banknotes and thank God, or of a poor student, a girl or a workman on their way out coming upon the money in amazement and delight, just as I had discovered myself in amazement and delight that night.

I couldn't say now where and how I scattered all those banknotes, and finally my silver too. There was some kind of delirium in me, an outpouring like lovemaking, and when the last pieces of paper had fluttered away I felt light, as if I could fly, and I knew a freedom I had never known before. The street, the sky, the buildings, all seemed to flow together and towards me, giving me an entirely new sense of possession and of belonging: never, even in the most warmly experienced moments of my life, had I felt so strongly that all these things were really present, that they were alive, that I was alive, and that their lives and mine were one and the same, that life is a great and mighty phenomenon and can never be hailed with too much delight. It is something that only love grasps, only devotion comprehends.

There was one last dark moment, and that came when, having walked happily home, I put the key in my door and the corridor leading to my rooms opened up black before me. I was suddenly overcome by fear that I would be returning to my old life if I entered the apartment of the man I had been until this moment, if I lay down in his bed and found myself once more connected with everything from which this night had so wonderfully released me. No, I must not be what I had been before, remote from the real world, I must not be the correct, unfeeling gentleman of yesterday and all the days before. I would rather plunge into any depths of crime and horror, but I must have the reality of life! I was tired, inexpressibly tired, yet I feared that sleep might close over me, and then its black silt would sweep away all the hot, glowing, living emotions that this night had aroused in me, and I might find that the whole experience had been as fleeting and without foundation as a fantastic dream.

But I woke cheerfully to a new morning next day, and none of that gratefully flowing emotion had run away into the sand. Four months have passed since then, and my old paralysis of feeling has not returned. I still bloom warmly as I face the day. The magical intoxication of my experience when the ground of my old world suddenly gave way under my feet, plunging me into the unknown, when I felt the delirium of speed mingled with the profundity of all life as I fell into my own abyss—yes, that flowing heat is gone, but since that hour I have been conscious of my own warm blood with every breath I take, and I daily feel new lust for life. I know I am a different man now, with different senses; different things arouse me, and I am more aware than before. I dare not say, of course, that I have become a better man; I know only that I am a happier man because I have found some kind of meaning in an existence that had been so cold, a meaning for which I can find no term but life itself. Since then I hold back from nothing, for I feel the norms and formalities of the society in which I live are meaningless, and I am not ashamed in front of others or myself. Words like honour, crime, vice, have suddenly acquired a cold, metallic note, I cannot speak them without horror. I live by letting myself draw on the power I so magically felt for the first time on that night. I do not ask where it will carry me: perhaps to some new abyss, into what others call vice, or perhaps to somewhere sublime. I don't know and I don't want to know. *For only he who lives his life as a mystery is truly alive.*

But never—and I am sure of this—have I loved life more fervently, and now I know that all who are indifferent to any of the shapes and forms it takes, commit a crime (the only crime there is!). Since I began to understand myself, I have understood much of many other things: someone's avid glance into a shop window can distress me, the playfulness of a dog can delight me. I suddenly care for everything; I am indifferent to nothing now. In the paper (which I used to consult only in search of entertainment and auction sales) I read of a hundred things that excite me every day; books that once bored me suddenly reveal their meaning to me. And the strangest thing of all is that I can suddenly talk to people outside the bounds of polite conversation. My manservant, who has been with me for seven years, interests me and I often talk to him; the caretaker whom I used to pass by, thinking no more of him than if he were a moving pillar, recently told me about his little daughter's death, and it affected me more than the tragedies of Shakespeare. And this change—although I continue to lead my life in circles of polite tedium so as not to give myself away—this change seems to be gradually becoming evident. I find that many people are suddenly on terms of warm good friendship with me; for the third time this week a strange dog ran up to me in the street. And friends tell me with a certain pleasure, as if speaking to one who has recovered from an illness, that I am quite rejuvenated.

Rejuvenated? I alone know that I am only just beginning to live. Well, it is a common delusion to think the past was nothing but error and preparation for the present, and I can well see that it is presumptuous of me to think that taking a cold pen in a warm, living hand and recording my feelings on dry paper means that I am really alive. But if it is a delusion, then it is the first ever to delight me, the first to warm my blood and open my senses to me. And if I write about the miracle of my awakening here, then I do it for myself alone, for I know the truth of this more profoundly than any words can say. I have spoken to no friend about it; my friends never knew how dead to the world I was, and they will never know how I live and flourish now. And should death strike me in the middle of this life of mine, and these lines should fall into another's hands, that idea does not alarm or distress me. For he who has never known the magic of such an hour will not understand, as I myself could not have understood half-a-year ago, that a few fleeting, apparently disconnected incidents on a single evening could so magically rekindle a life already extinguished. I feel no shame before such a man, for he will not understand me. But he who knows how those incidents are linked will not judge or feel pride. And I feel no shame before him, for he *will* understand me. Once a man has found himself there is nothing in this world that he can lose. And once he has understood the humanity in himself, he will understand all human beings.

LETTER FROM
AN UNKNOWN WOMAN

Translated from the German by Eden and Cedar Paul

'R' THE FAMOUS NOVELIST, *had been away on a brief holiday in the mountains. Reaching Vienna early in the morning, he bought a newspaper at the station, and when he glanced at the date was reminded that it was his birthday. "Forty-one!"—the thought came like a flash. He was neither glad nor sorry at the realisation. He hailed a taxi, and skimmed the newspaper as he drove home. His man reported that there had been a few callers during the master's absence, besides some telephone messages. A bundle of letters was awaiting him. Looking indifferently at these, he opened one or two because he was interested in the senders, but laid aside for the time a bulky packet addressed in a strange handwriting. At ease in an armchair, he drank his morning tea, finished the newspaper and read a few circulars. Then, having lit a cigar, he turned to the remaining letter.*

It was a manuscript rather than an ordinary letter, comprising several dozen hastily penned sheets in a feminine handwriting. Involuntarily he examined the envelope once more, in case he might have overlooked a covering letter. But there was nothing of the kind, no signature, and no sender's address on either envelope or contents. "Strange," he thought, as he began to read the manuscript. The first words were a superscription: "To you, who have never known me." *He was perplexed. Was this addressed to him, or to some imaginary being? His curiosity suddenly awakened, he read as follows:*

"My boy died yesterday. For three days and three nights I have been wrestling with Death for this frail little life. During forty consecutive hours, while the fever of influenza was shaking his poor burning body, I sat beside his bed. I put cold compresses on his forehead; day and night, night and day. I held his restless little hands. The third evening, my strength gave out. My eyes closed without my being aware of it, and for three or four hours I must have slept on the hard stool. Meanwhile, Death took him. There he lies, my darling boy, in his narrow cot, just as he died. Only his eyes have been closed, his wise, dark eyes; and his hands have been crossed over his breast. Four candles are burning, one at each corner of the bed. I cannot bear to look, I cannot bear to move; for when the candles flicker, shadows chase one another over his face and his closed lips. It looks as if his features stirred, and I could almost fancy that he is not dead after all, that he will wake and with his clear voice will say something childishly loving. But I know that he is dead; and I will not look again, to hope once more, and once more to be disappointed. I know, I know, my boy died yesterday. Now I have only you left in the world; only you, who do not know me; you, who are enjoying yourself all unheeding, sporting with men and things. Only you, who have never known me, and whom I have never ceased to love.

I have lit a fifth candle, and am sitting at the table writing to you. I cannot stay alone with my dead child without pouring my heart out to someone; and to whom should I do that in this dreadful hour if not to you, who have been and still are all in all to me? Perhaps I shall not be able to make myself plain to you. Perhaps you will not be able to understand me. My head feels so heavy; my temples are throbbing; my limbs are aching. I think I must be feverish. Influenza is raging in this quarter, and probably I have caught the infection. I should not be sorry if I could join my child in that way, instead of making short work of myself. Sometimes it seems dark before my eyes, and perhaps I shall not be able to finish this letter; but I shall try with all my strength, this one and only time, to speak to you, my beloved, to you who have never known me. To you only do I want to speak, that I may tell you everything for the first time. I should like you to know the whole of my life, of that life which has always been yours, and of which you have known nothing. But you shall only know my secret after I am dead, when there will be no one whom you will have to answer; you shall only know it if that which is now shaking my

82

limbs with cold and with heat should really prove, for me, the end. If I have to go on living, I shall tear up this letter and shall keep the silence I have always kept. If you ever hold it in your hands, you may know that a dead woman is telling you her life-story; the story of a life which was yours from its first to its last fully conscious hour. You need have no fear of my words. A dead woman wants nothing; neither love, nor compassion, nor consolation. I have only one thing to ask of you, that you believe to the full what the pain in me forces me to disclose to you. Believe my words, for I ask nothing more of you; a mother will not speak falsely beside the deathbed of her only child.

I am going to tell you my whole life, the life which did not really begin until the day I first saw you. What I can recall before that day is gloomy and confused, a memory as of a cellar filled with dusty, dull and cobwebbed things and people—a place with which my heart has no concern. When you came into my life, I was thirteen, and I lived in the house where you live today, in the very house in which you are reading this letter, the last breath of my life. I lived on the same floor, for the door of our flat was just opposite the door of yours. You will certainly have forgotten us. You will long ago have forgotten the accountant's widow in her threadbare mourning, and the thin, half-grown girl. We were always so quiet; characteristic examples of shabby gentility. It is unlikely that you ever heard our name, for we had no plate on our front door, and no one ever came to see us. Besides, it is so long ago, fifteen or sixteen years. Impossible that you should remember. But I, how passionately I remember every detail. As if it had just happened, I recall the day, the hour, when I first heard of you, first saw you. How could it be otherwise, seeing that it was then the world began for me? Have patience awhile, and let me tell you everything from first to last. Do not grow weary of listening to me for a brief space, since I have not been weary of loving you my whole life long.

Before you came, the people who lived in your flat were horrid folk, always quarrelling. Though they were wretchedly poor themselves, they hated us for our poverty because we held aloof from them. The man was given to drink, and used to beat his wife. We were often wakened in the night by the clatter of falling chairs and breaking plates. Once, when he had beaten her till the blood came, she ran out on the landing with her hair streaming, followed by her drunken husband abusing her, until all the people came out onto the staircase and threatened to send for the police. My mother would have nothing to do with them. She forbade me to play with the children, who took every opportunity of venting their spleen on me for this refusal. When they met me in the street, they would call me names, and once they threw a snowball at me which was so hard that it cut my forehead. Everyone in the house detested them, and we all breathed more freely when something happened and they had to leave—I think the man had been arrested for theft. For a few days there was a '*To Let*' notice at the main door. Then it was taken down, and the caretaker told us that the flat had been rented by an author, who was a bachelor, and was sure to be quiet. That was the first time I heard your name.

A few days later, the flat was thoroughly cleaned, and the painters and decorators came. Of course they made a lot of noise, but my mother was glad, for she said that would be the end of the disorder next door. I did not see you during the move. The decorations and furnishings were supervised by your servant, the little grey-haired man with such a serious demeanour, who had obviously been used to service in good families. He managed everything in a most businesslike way, and impressed us all very much. A high-class domestic of this kind was something quite new in our suburban flats. Besides, he was extremely civil, but was never hail-fellow-well-met with the ordinary servants. From the outset he treated my mother respectfully, as a lady; and he was always courteous even to little me. When he had occasion to mention your name, he did so in a way which showed that his feeling towards you was that of a family retainer. I used to love good old John for this, though I envied him at the same time because it was his privilege to see you constantly and to serve you.

Do you know why I am telling you these trifles? I want you to understand how it was that from the very beginning your personality came to exercise so much power over me when I was still a shy and timid child. Before I had actually seen you, there was a halo round your head. You were enveloped in an atmosphere of wealth, marvel and mystery. People whose lives are narrow are avid of novelty, and in this little suburban house we were all impatiently awaiting your arrival. In my own case, curiosity rose to fever point when I came home from school one afternoon and found the furniture van in front of the house. Most of the heavy things had gone up, and the furniture removers were dealing with the smaller articles. I stood at the door to watch and admire, for everything belonging to you was so different from what I had been used to. There were Indian idols, Italian sculptures and great, brightly-coloured pictures. Last of all came books, such lovely books, many more than I should have thought possible. They were piled by the door. The manservant stood there carefully dusting them one by one. I greedily watched the pile as it grew. Your servant did not send me away, but he did not encourage me either, so I was afraid to touch any of them though I should have so liked to stroke the smooth leather bindings. I did glance timidly at some of the titles; many of them were in French and in English, and in languages of which I did not know a single word. I should have liked to stand there watching for hours, but my mother called me and I had to go in.

I thought about you the whole evening, although I had not seen you yet. I had only about a dozen cheap books, bound in worn cardboard. I loved them more than anything else in the world, and was continually reading and rereading them. Now I was wondering what the man could be like who had such a lot of books, who had read so much, who knew so many languages, who was rich and at the same time so learned. The idea of so many books aroused a kind of unearthly veneration. I tried to picture you in my mind. You must be an old man with spectacles and a long, white beard, like our geography master, but much kinder, nicer-looking and gentler. I don't know why I was sure that you must be handsome, for I fancied you to be an elderly man. That very night, I dreamt of you for the first time.

Next day you moved in, but though I was on the watch I could not get a glimpse of your face, and my failure inflamed my curiosity. At length I saw you, on the third day. How astounded I was to find that you were quite different from the ancient godfather conjured up by my childish imagination. A bespectacled, good-natured old fellow was what I had anticipated, and you came, looking just as you still look, for you are one on whom the years leave little mark. You were wearing a beautiful suit of light-brown tweeds, and you ran upstairs two steps at a time with the boyish ease that always characterises your movements. You were hat in hand, so that, with indescribable amazement, I could see your bright and lively face and your youthful hair. Your handsome, slim and spruce figure was a positive shock to me. How strange it was that in this first moment I should have plainly realised that which I and all others are continually surprised at in you. I realised that you are two people rolled into one: that you are an ardent, light-hearted youth devoted to sport and adventure; and at the same time, in your art, a deeply read and highly cultured man, grave, and with a keen sense of responsibility.

Unconsciously I perceived what everyone who knew you came to perceive, that you led two lives. One of these was known to all, it was the life open to the whole world; the other was turned away from the world, and was fully known only to yourself. I, a girl of thirteen, coming under the spell of your attraction, grasped this secret of your existence, this profound cleavage of your two lives, at the first glance.

Can you understand, now, what a miracle, what an alluring enigma, you must have seemed to me, the child? Here was a man of whom everyone spoke with respect because he wrote books, and because he was famous in the great world. Of a sudden he had revealed himself to me as a boyish, cheerful young man of five-and-twenty! I need hardly tell you that henceforward, in my restricted world, you were the only thing that interested me, that my life revolved round yours with the fidelity proper to a girl of thirteen. I watched you, watched your habits, watched the people who came to see you—and all this increased instead of diminishing my interest in your personality, for the two-sidedness of your nature was reflected in the diversity of your visitors. Some of them were young men, comrades of yours, carelessly dressed students with whom you laughed and larked. Some of them were ladies who came in motor cars. Once the conductor of the opera—the great man whom before this I had seen only from a distance, baton in hand—called on you. Some of them were girls, young girls still attending the commercial school, who shyly glided in at the door. A great many of your visitors were women. I thought nothing of this, not even when, one morning, as I was on my way to school, I saw a closely veiled lady coming away from your flat. I was only just thirteen, and in my immaturity I did not in the least realise that the eager curiosity with which I scanned all your doings was already love.

But I know the very day and hour when I consciously gave my whole heart to you. I had been for a walk with a schoolfellow, and we were standing at the door chattering. A motor car drove up. You jumped out, in the impatient, springy fashion which has never ceased to charm me, and were about to go in. An impulse made me open the door for you, and this brought me into your path, so that we almost collided. You looked at me with a cordial, gracious, all-embracing glance, which was almost a caress. You smiled at me tenderly—yes, tenderly is the word—and said gently, nay, confidentially: 'Thank you so much.'

That was all. But from this moment, from the time when you looked at me so gently, so tenderly, I was yours. Later, before long indeed, I was to learn that this was a way you had of looking at all women with whom you came in contact. It was a caressive and alluring glance, at once enfolding and disclothing, the glance of the born seducer. Involuntarily you looked in this way at every shopgirl who served you, at every maidservant who opened the door to you. It was not that you consciously longed to possess all these women, but your impulse towards the sex unconsciously made your eyes melting and warm whenever they rested on a woman. At thirteen, I had no thought of this, and I felt as if I had been bathed in fire. I believed that the tenderness was for me, for me only, and in this one instant the woman was awakened in the half-grown girl, the woman who was to be yours for all future time.

'Who was that?' asked my friend. At first, I could not answer. I found it impossible to utter your name. It had suddenly become sacred to me, had become my secret. 'Oh, it's just someone who lives in the house,' I said awkwardly. 'Then why did you blush so fiery red when he looked at you?' enquired my schoolfellow with the malice of an inquisitive child. I felt that she was making fun of me, and was reaching out towards my secret and this coloured my cheeks more than ever. I was deliberately rude to her: 'You silly idiot,' I said angrily—I should have liked to throttle her. She laughed mockingly, until the tears came into my eyes from impotent rage. I left her at the door and ran upstairs.

I have loved you ever since. I know full well that you are used to hearing women say that they love you. But I am sure that no one else has ever loved you so slavishly, with such dog-like fidelity, with such devotion, as I did and do. Nothing can equal the unnoticed love of a child. It is hopeless and subservient; it is patient and passionate; it is something which the covetous love of a grown woman, the love that is unconsciously exacting, can never be. None but lonely children can cherish such a passion. The others will squander their feelings in companionship, will dissipate them in confidential talks. They have heard and read much of love, and they know that it comes to all. They play with it like a toy; they flaunt it as a boy flaunts his first cigarette. But I had no confidant; I had been neither taught nor warned; I was inexperienced and unsuspecting. I rushed to meet my fate. Everything that stirred in me, all that happened to me, seemed to be centred upon you, upon my imaginings of you. My father had died long before. My mother could think of nothing but her troubles, of the difficulties of making ends meet on her narrow pension, so that she had little in common with a growing girl. My schoolfellows, half-enlightened and half-corrupted, were uncongenial to me because of their frivolous outlook upon that which to me was a supreme passion. The upshot was that everything which surged up in me, all which in other girls of my age is usually scattered, was focused upon you. You became for me—what simile can do justice to my feelings? You became for me the whole of my life. Nothing existed for me except in so far as it related to you. Nothing had meaning for me unless it bore upon you in some way. You had changed everything for me. Hitherto I had been indifferent at school, and undistinguished. Now, of a sudden, I was the first. I read book upon book, far into the night, for I knew that you were a book-lover. To my mother's astonishment, I began, almost stubbornly, to practise the piano, for I fancied that you were fond of music. I stitched and mended my clothes, to make them neat for your eyes. It was a torment to me that there was a square patch in my old school apron (cut down from one of my mother's overalls). I was afraid you might notice it and would despise me, so I used to cover the patch with my satchel when I was on the staircase. I was terrified lest you should catch sight of it. What a fool I was! You hardly ever looked at me again.

Yet my days were spent in waiting for you and watching you. There was a judas in our front door, and through this a glimpse of your door could be had. Don't laugh at me, dear. Even now, I am not ashamed of the hours I spent at this spy-hole. The hall was icy cold, and I was afraid of exciting my mother's suspicions. But there I would watch through the long afternoons, during those months and years, book in hand, tense as a violin string, and vibrating at the touch of your nearness. I was ever near you, and ever tense, but you were no more aware of it than you were aware of the tension of the mainspring of the watch in your pocket, faithfully recording the hours for you, accompanying your footsteps with its unheard ticking and vouchsafed only a hasty glance for one second among millions. I knew all about you, your habits, the neckties you wore; I knew each one of your suits. Soon I was familiar with your regular visitors, and had my likes and dislikes among them. From my thirteenth to my sixteenth year, my every hour was yours. What follies did I not commit? I kissed the door handle you had touched; I picked up a cigarette end you had thrown away, and it was sacred to me because your lips had pressed it. A hundred times, in the evening, on one pretext or another, I ran out into the street in order to see in which room your light was burning, that I might be more fully conscious of your invisible presence. During the weeks you were away (my heart always seemed to stop beating when I saw John carry your portmanteau downstairs), life was devoid of meaning. Out of sorts, bored to death, and in an ill humour, I wandered about not knowing what to do, and had to take precautions lest my tear-dimmed eyes betray my despair to my mother.

I know that what I am writing here is a record of grotesque absurdities, of a girl's extravagant fantasies. I ought to be ashamed of them, but I am not ashamed, for never was my love purer and more passionate than at this time. I could spend hours, days, in telling you how I lived with you though you hardly knew me by sight. Of course you hardly knew me, for if I met you on the stairs and could not avoid the encounter, I would hasten by with lowered head, afraid of your burning glance, hasten like one who is jumping into the water to avoid being singed. For hours, days, I could tell you of those years you have long since forgotten, could unroll all the calendar of your life, but I will not weary you with details. Only one more thing I should like to tell you from this time, the most splendid experience of my childhood. You must not laugh at it, for, trifle though you may deem it, to me it was of infinite significance.

It must have been a Sunday. You were away, and your man was dragging back the heavy rugs, which he had been beating, through the open door of the flat. They were rather too much for his strength, and I summoned up courage to ask whether he would let me help him. He was surprised, but did not refuse. Can I ever make you understand the awe, the pious veneration, with which I set foot in your dwelling, with which I saw your world—the writing table at which you were accustomed to sit (there were some flowers on it in a blue crystal vase), the pictures, the books? I had no more than a stolen glance, though the good John would no doubt have let me see more had I ventured to ask him. But it was enough for me to absorb the atmosphere, and to provide fresh nourishment for my endless dreams of you in waking and sleeping.

This swift minute was the happiest of my childhood. I wanted to tell you of it, so that you who do not know me might at length begin to understand how my life hung upon yours. I wanted to tell you of that minute, and also of the dreadful hour which so soon followed. As I have explained, my thoughts of you had made me oblivious to all else. I paid no attention to my mother's doings, or to those of any of our visitors. I failed to notice that an elderly gentleman, an Innsbruck merchant, a distant family connection of my mother, came often and stayed for a long time. I was glad that he took Mother to the theatre sometimes, for this left me alone, undisturbed in my thoughts of you, undisturbed in the watching which was my chief, my only pleasure. But one day my mother summoned me with a certain formality, saying that she had something serious to talk to me about. I turned pale and felt my heart throb. Did she suspect anything? Had I betrayed myself in some way? My first thought was of you, of my secret, of that which linked me with life. But my mother was herself embarrassed. It had never been her way to kiss me. Now she kissed me affectionately more than once, drew me to her on the sofa, and began hesitatingly and rather shamefacedly to tell me that her relative, who was a widower, had made her a proposal of marriage, and that, mainly for my sake, she had decided to accept. I palpitated with anxiety, having only one thought, that of you. 'We shall stay here, shan't we?' I stammered out. 'No, we are going to Innsbruck, where Ferdinand has a fine villa.' I heard no more. Everything seemed to turn black before my eyes. I learnt afterwards that I had fainted. I clasped my hands convulsively, and fell like a lump of lead. I cannot tell you all that happened in the next few days; how I, a powerless child, vainly revolted against the mighty elders. Even now, as I think of it, my hand shakes so that I can scarcely write. I could not disclose the real secret, and therefore my opposition seemed ill-tempered obstinacy. No one told me anything more. All the arrangements were made behind my back. The hours when I was at school were turned to account. Each time I came home some new article had been removed or sold. My life seemed to be falling to pieces, and at last one day, when I returned to dinner, the furniture removers had cleared the flat. In the empty rooms there were some packed trunks, and two camp-beds for Mother and myself. We were to sleep there one night more, and were then to go to Innsbruck.

On this last day I suddenly made up my mind that I could not live without being near you. You were all the world to me. It is difficult to say what I was thinking of, and whether in this hour of despair I was able to think at all. My mother was out of the house. I stood up, just as I was, in my school dress, and went over to your door. Yet I can hardly say that I went. With stiff limbs and trembling joints, I seemed to be drawn towards your door as by a magnet. It was in my mind to throw myself at your feet, and to beg you to keep me as a maid, as a slave. I cannot help feeling afraid that you will laugh at this infatuation of a girl of fifteen. But you would not laugh if you could realise how I stood there on the chilly landing, rigid with apprehension, and yet drawn onward by an irresistible force; how my arm seemed to lift itself in spite of me. The struggle appeared to last for endless, terrible seconds, and then I rang the bell. The shrill noise still sounds in my ears. It was followed by a silence in which my heart well-nigh stopped beating, and my blood stagnated, while I listened for your coming.

But you did not come. No one came. You must have been out that afternoon, and John must have been away too. With the dead note of the bell still sounding in my ears, I stole back into our empty dwelling and threw myself exhausted upon a rug, tired out by these few paces as if I had been wading through deep snow for hours. Yet beneath this exhaustion there still glowed the determination to see you, to speak to you, before they carried me away. I can assure you that there were no sensual longings in my mind; I was still ignorant, just because I never thought of anything but you. All I wanted was to see you once more, to cling to you. Throughout that dreadful night I waited for you. Directly my mother had gone to sleep, I crept into the hall to listen for your return. It was a bitterly cold night in January. I was tired, my limbs ached and there was no longer a chair on which I could sit, so I lay upon the floor, scourged by the draught that came under the door. In my thin dress I lay there, without any covering. I did not want to be warm, lest I should fall asleep and miss your footstep. Cramps seized me, so cold was it in the horrible darkness; again and again I had to stand up. But I waited, waited, waited for you, as for my fate.

At length (it must have been two or three in the morning) I heard the house door open, and footsteps on the stair. The sense of cold vanished, and a rush of heat passed over me. I softly opened the door, meaning to run out, to throw myself at your feet … I cannot tell what I should have done in my frenzy. The steps drew nearer. A candle flickered. Trembling, I held the door handle. Was it you coming up the stairs?

Yes, it was you, beloved, but you were not alone. I heard a gentle laugh, the rustle of silk, and your voice, speaking in low tones. There was a woman with you.

I cannot tell how I lived through the rest of the night. At eight next morning, they took me with them to Innsbruck. I had no strength left to resist.

My boy died last night. I shall be alone once more, if I really have to go on living. Tomorrow, strange men will come, black-clad and uncouth, bringing with them a coffin for the body of my only child. Perhaps friends will come as well, with wreaths—but what is the use of flowers on a coffin? They will offer consolation in one phrase or another. Words, words, words! What can words help? All I know is that I shall be alone again. There is nothing more terrible than to be alone among human beings. That is what I came to realise during those interminable two years in Innsbruck, from my sixteenth to my eighteenth year, when I lived with my people as a prisoner and an outcast. My stepfather, a quiet, taciturn man, was kind to me. My mother, as if eager to atone for an unwitting injustice, seemed ready to meet all my wishes. Those of my own age would have been glad to befriend me. But I repelled their advances with angry defiance. I did not wish to be happy, I did not wish to live content away from you, so I buried myself in a gloomy world of self-torment and solitude. I would not wear the new and gay dresses they bought for me. I refused to go to concerts or to the theatre, and I would not take part in cheerful excursions. I rarely left the house. Can you believe me when I tell you that I hardly got to know a dozen streets in this little town where I lived for two years? Mourning was my joy; I renounced society and every pleasure, and was intoxicated with delight at the mortification I thus super-added to the lack of seeing you. Moreover, I would let nothing divert me from my passionate longing to live only for you.

Sitting alone at home, hour after hour and day after day, I did nothing but think of you, turning over in my mind unceasingly my hundred petty memories of you, renewing every movement and every time of waiting, rehearsing these episodes in the theatre of my mind. The countless repetitions of the years of my childhood from the day on which you came into my life have so branded their details on my memory that I can recall every minute of those long-passed years as if they were yesterday. Thus my life was still entirely centred in you. I bought all your books. If your name was mentioned in the newspaper, the day was a red-letter day … Will you believe me when I tell you that I have read your books so often that I know them by heart? Were anyone to wake me in the night and quote a detached sentence, I could continue the passage unfalteringly even today, after thirteen years. Your every word was Holy Writ to me. The world existed for me only in relation to you. In the Viennese newspapers I read the reports of concerts and first nights, wondering which would interest you most. When evening came, I accompanied you in imagination, saying to myself: 'Now he is entering the hall; now he is taking his seat.' Such were my fancies a thousand times, simply because I had once seen you at a concert.

Why should I recount these things? Why recount the tragic hopelessness of a forsaken child? Why tell it to you, who have never dreamt of my admiration or of my sorrow? But was I still a child? I was seventeen; I was eighteen; young fellows would turn to look after me in the street, but they only made me angry. To love anyone but you, even to play with the thought of loving anyone but you, would have been so utterly impossible to me, that the mere tender of affection on the part of another man seemed to me a crime. My passion for you remained just as intense, but it changed in character as my body grew and my senses awakened, becoming more ardent, more physical, more unmistakably the love of a grown woman. What had been hidden from the thoughts of the uninstructed child, of the girl who had rung your door bell, was now my only longing. I wanted to give myself to you.

My associates believed me to be shy and timid. But I had an absolute fixity of purpose. My whole being was directed towards one end—back to Vienna, back to you. I fought successfully to get my own way, unreasonable, incomprehensible though it seemed to others. My stepfather was well-to-do, and looked upon me as his daughter. I insisted, however, that I would earn my own living, and at length got him to agree to my returning to Vienna as an employee in a dressmaking establishment belonging to a relative of his.

Need I tell you whither my steps first led me that foggy autumn evening when, at last, at last, I found myself back in Vienna? I left my trunk in the cloakroom and hurried to a tram. How slowly it moved! Every stop was a renewed vexation to me. In the end, I reached the house. My heart leapt when I saw a light in your window. The town, which had seemed so alien, so dreary, grew suddenly alive for me. I myself lived once more, now that I was near you, you who were my unending dream. When nothing but the thin, shining pane of glass was between you and my uplifted eyes, I could ignore the fact that in reality I was as far from your mind as if I had been separated by mountains and valleys and rivers. Enough that I could go on looking at your window. There was a light in it; that was your dwelling; you were there; that was my world. For two years I had dreamt of this hour, and now it had come. Throughout that warm and cloudy evening I stood in front of your windows, until the light was extinguished. Not until then did I seek my own quarters.

Evening after evening I returned to the same spot. Up to six o'clock I was at work. The work was hard, and yet I liked it: for the turmoil of the showroom masked the turmoil in my heart. The instant the shutters were rolled down, I flew to the beloved spot. To see you once more, to meet you just once, was all I wanted; simply from a distance to devour your face with my eyes. At length, after a week, I did meet you, and then the meeting took me by surprise. I was watching your window, when you came across the street. In an instant, I was a child once more, the girl of thirteen. My cheeks flushed. Although I was longing to meet your eyes, I hung my head and hurried past you as if someone had been in pursuit. Afterwards I was ashamed of having fled like a schoolgirl, for now I knew what I really wanted. I wanted to meet you; I wanted you to recognise me after all these weary years, to notice me, to love me.

For a long time you failed to notice me, although I took up my post outside your house every night, even when it was snowing, or when the keen wind of the Viennese winter was blowing. Sometimes I waited for hours in vain. Often, in the end, you would leave the house in the company of friends. Twice I saw you with a woman, and the fact that I was now awakened, that there was something new and different in my feeling towards you, was disclosed by the sudden heart-pang when I saw a strange woman walking confidently with you arm-in-arm. It was no surprise to me, for I had known since childhood how many such visitors came to your house, but now the sight aroused in me a definite bodily pain. I had a mingled feeling of enmity and desire when I witnessed this open manifestation of fleshly intimacy with another woman. For a day, animated by the youthful pride from which, perhaps, I am not yet free, I abstained from my usual visit; but how horrible was this empty evening of defiance and renunciation! The next night I was standing, as usual, in all humility, in front of your window; waiting, as I have ever waited, in front of your closed life.

At length came the hour when you noticed me. I marked your coming from a distance and collected all my forces to prevent myself shrinking out of your path. As chance would have it, a loaded dray filled the street, so that you had to pass quite close to me. Involuntarily your eyes encountered my figure, and immediately, though you had hardly noticed the attentiveness in my gaze, there came into your face that expression with which you were wont to look at women. The memory of it darted through me like an electric shock—that caressive and alluring glance, at once enfolding and disclothing, with which, years before, you had awakened the girl to become a woman and a lover. For a moment or two your eyes thus rested on me, for a space during which I could not turn my own eyes away, and then you had passed. My heart was beating so furiously that I had to slacken my pace, and when, moved by irresistible curiosity, I turned to look back, I saw that you were standing and watching me. The inquisitive interest of your expression convinced me that you had not recognised me. You did not recognise me, either then or later. How can I describe my disappointment? This was the first of such disappointments: the first time I had to endure what has always been my fate; that you have never recognised me. I must die, unrecognised. Ah, how can I make you understand my disappointment? During the years at Innsbruck I had never ceased to think of you. Our next meeting in Vienna was always in my thoughts. My fancies varied with my mood, ranging from the wildest possibilities to the most delightful. Every conceivable variation had passed through my mind. In gloomy moments it had seemed to me that you would repulse me, would despise me, for being of no account, for being plain or importunate. I had had a vision of every possible form of disfavour, coldness, or indifference. But never, in the extremity of depression, in the utmost realisation of my own insignificance, had I conceived this most abhorrent of possibilities—that you had never become aware of my existence. I understand now (you have taught me!) that a girl's or a woman's face must be for a man something extraordinarily mutable. It is usually nothing more than the reflection of moods which pass as swiftly as an image vanishes from a mirror. A man can readily forget a woman's face, because age modifies its lights and shades, and because at different times the dress gives it so different a setting. Resignation comes to a woman as her knowledge grows. But I, who was still a girl, was unable to understand your forgetfulness. My whole mind had been full of you ever since I had first known you, and this had produced in me the illusion that you must have often thought of me and waited for me. How could I have borne to go on living had I realised that I was nothing to you, that I had no place in your memory? Your glance that evening, showing me as it did that on your side there was not even a gossamer thread connecting your life with mine, meant for me a first plunge into reality, conveyed to me the first intimation of my destiny.

You did not recognise me. Two days later, when our paths again crossed, and you looked at me with an approach to intimacy, it was not in recognition of the girl who had loved you so long and whom you had awakened to womanhood; it was simply that you knew the face of the pretty ingénue of eighteen whom you had encountered at the same spot two evenings before. Your expression was one of friendly surprise, and a smile fluttered about your lips. You passed me as before, and as before you promptly slackened your pace. I trembled, I exulted, I longed for you to speak to me. I felt that for the first time I had become alive for you; I, too, walked slowly, and did not attempt to evade you. Suddenly, I heard your step behind me. Without turning round, I knew that I was about to hear your beloved voice directly addressing me. I was almost paralysed by the expectation, and my heart beat so violently that I thought I should have to stand still. You were at my side. You greeted me cordially, as if we were old acquaintances—though you did not really know me, though you have never known anything about my life. So simple and charming was your manner that I was able to answer you without hesitation. We walked along the street, and you asked me whether we could not have supper together. I agreed. What was there I could have refused you?

We supped in a little restaurant. You will not remember where it was. To you it will be one of many such. For what was I? One among hundreds; one adventure, one link in an endless chain. What happened that evening to keep me in your memory? I said very little, for I was so intensely happy to have you near me and to hear you speak to me. I did not wish to waste a moment upon questions or foolish words. I shall never cease to be thankful to you for that hour, for the way in which you justified my ardent admiration. I shall never forget the gentle tact you displayed. There was no undue eagerness, no hasty offer of a caress. Yet from the first moment you displayed so much friendly confidence that you would have won me even if my whole being had not long ere this been yours. Can I make you understand how much it meant to me that my five years of expectation were so perfectly fulfilled?

The hour grew late, and we came away from the restaurant. At the door you asked me whether I was in any hurry, or still had time to spare. How could I hide from you that I was yours? I said I had plenty of time. With a momentary hesitation, you asked me whether I would not come to your rooms for a talk. 'I shall be delighted,' I answered with alacrity, thus giving frank expression to my feelings. I could not fail to notice that my ready assent surprised you. I am not sure whether your feeling was one of vexation or pleasure, but it was obvious to me that you were surprised. Today, of course, I understand your astonishment. I know now that it is usual for a woman, even though she may ardently desire to give herself to a man, to feign reluctance, to simulate alarm or indignation. She must be brought to consent by urgent pleadings, by lies, adjurations and promises. I know that only professional prostitutes are accustomed to answer such an invitation with a perfectly frank assent—prostitutes, or simple-minded, immature girls. How could you know that, in my case, the frank assent was but the voicing of an eternity of desire, the uprush of yearnings that had endured for a thousand days and more?

In any case, my manner aroused your attention; I had become interesting to you. As we were walking along together, I felt that during our conversation you were trying to test me in some way. Your perceptions, your assured touch in the whole gamut of human emotions, made you realise instantly that there was something unusual here; that this pretty, complaisant girl carried a secret about with her. Your curiosity had been awakened and your discreet questions showed that you were trying to pluck the heart out of my mystery. But my replies were evasive. I would rather seem a fool than disclose my secret to you.

We went up to your flat. Forgive me, beloved, for saying that you cannot possibly understand all that it meant to me to go up those stairs with you—how I was mad, tortured, almost suffocated with happiness. Even now I can hardly think of it without tears, but I have no tears left. Everything in that house had been steeped in my passion; everything was a symbol of my childhood and its longing. There was the door behind which a thousand times I had awaited your coming; the stairs on which I had heard your footstep, and where I had first seen you through the judas where I had watched your comings and goings; the doormat on which I had once knelt; the sound of a key in the lock, which had always been a signal to me. My childhood and its passions were nested within these few yards of space. Here was my whole life, and it surged around me like a great storm, for all was being fulfilled, and I was going with you, I with you, into your, into our house. Think (the way I am phrasing it sounds trivial, but I know no better words) that up to your door was the world of reality, the dull everyday world which had been that of all my previous life. At this door began the magic world of my childish imaginings, Aladdin's realm. Think how, a thousand times, I had had my burning eyes fixed upon this door through which I was now passing, my head in a whirl, and you will have an inkling—no more—of all that this tremendous minute meant to me.

I stayed with you that night. You did not dream that before you no man had ever touched or seen my body. How could you fancy it, when I made no resistance, and when I suppressed every trace of shame, fearing lest I might betray the secret of my love? That would certainly have alarmed you; you care only for what comes and goes easily, for that which is light of touch, is imponderable. You dread being involved in anyone else's destiny. You like to give yourself freely to all the world—but not to make any sacrifices. When I tell you that I gave myself to you as a virgin, do not misunderstand me. I am not making any charge against you. You did not entice me, deceive me, seduce me. I threw myself into your arms; went out to meet my fate. I have nothing but thankfulness towards you for the blessedness of that night. When I opened my eyes in the darkness and you were beside me, I felt that I must be in heaven, and I was amazed that the stars were not shining on me. Never, beloved, have I repented giving myself to you that night. When you were sleeping beside me, when I listened to your breathing, touched your body and felt myself so near you, I shed tears for happiness.

I went away early in the morning. I had to go to my work, and I wanted to leave before your servant came. When I was ready to go, you put your arm round me and looked at me for a very long time. Was some obscure memory stirring in your mind, or was it simply that my radiant happiness made me seem beautiful to you? You kissed me on the lips, and I moved to go. You asked me: 'Would you not like to take a few flowers with you?' There were four white roses in the blue crystal vase on the writing table (I knew it of old from that stolen glance of childhood), and you gave them to me. For days they were mine to kiss.

We had arranged to meet on a second evening. Again it was full of wonder and delight. You gave me a third night. Then you said that you were called away from Vienna for a time— oh, how I had always hated those journeys of yours!—and promised that I should hear from you as soon as you came back. I would only give you a poste-restante address, and did not tell you my real name. I guarded my secret. Once more you gave me roses at parting—at parting.

Day after day for two months I asked myself ... no, I will not describe the anguish of my expectation and despair. I make no complaint. I love you just as you are, ardent and forgetful, generous and unfaithful. I love you just as you have always been. You were back long before the two months were up. The light in your windows showed me that, but you did not write to me. In my last hours I have not a line in your handwriting, not a line from you to whom my life was given. I waited, waited despairingly. You did not call me to you, did not write a word, not a word ...

My boy who died yesterday was yours too. He was your son, the child of one of those three nights. I was yours, and yours only from that time until the hour of his birth. I felt myself sanctified by your touch, and it would not have been possible for me then to accept any other man's caresses. He was our boy, dear; the child of my fully conscious love and of your careless, spendthrift, almost unwitting tenderness. Our child, our son, our only child. Perhaps you will be startled, perhaps merely surprised. You will wonder why I never told you of this boy, and why, having kept silence throughout the long years, I only tell you of him now, when he lies in his last sleep, about to leave me for all time—never, never to return. How could I have told you? I was a stranger, a girl who had shown herself only too eager to spend those three nights with you. Never would you have believed that I, the nameless partner in a chance encounter, had been faithful to you, the unfaithful. You would never, without misgivings, have accepted the boy as your own. Even if, to all appearance, you had trusted my word, you would still have cherished the secret suspicion that I had seized an opportunity of fathering upon you, a man of means, the child of another lover. You would have been suspicious. There would always have been a shadow of mistrust between you and me. I could not have borne it. Besides, I know you. Perhaps I know you better than you know yourself. You love to be carefree, light of heart, perfectly at ease, and that is what you understand by love. It would have been repugnant to you to find yourself suddenly in the position of father; to be made responsible, all at once, for a child's destiny. The breath of freedom is the breath of life to you, and you would have felt me to be a tie. Inwardly, even in defiance of your conscious will, you would have hated me as an embodied claim. Perhaps only now and again, for an hour or for a fleeting minute, should I have seemed a burden to you, should I have been hated by you. But it was my pride that I should never be a trouble or a care to you all my life long. I would rather take the whole burden on myself than be a burden to you; I wanted to be the one among all the women you had intimately known of whom you would never think except with love and thankfulness. In actual fact, you never thought of me at all. You forgot me.

I am not accusing you. Believe me, I am not complaining. You must forgive me if for a moment, now and again, it seems as if my pen had been dipped in gall. You must forgive me; for my boy, our boy, lies dead there beneath the flickering candles. I have clenched my fists against God, and have called him a murderer, for I have been almost beside myself with grief. Forgive me for complaining. I know that you are kind-hearted, and always ready to help. You will help the merest stranger at a word. But your kindliness is peculiar. It is unbounded. Anyone may have of yours as much as he can grasp with both hands. And yet, I must own, your kindliness works sluggishly. You need to be asked. You help those who call for help; you help from shame, from weakness and not from sheer joy in helping. Let me tell you openly that those who are in affliction and torment are not dearer to you than your brothers in happiness. Now, it is hard, very hard, to ask anything from such as you, even of the kindest among you. Once, when I was still a child, I watched through the judas in our door how you gave something to a beggar who had rung your bell. You gave quickly and freely, almost before he spoke. But there was a certain nervousness and haste in your manner, as if your chief concern were to be speedily rid of him; you seemed to be afraid to meet his eye. I have never forgotten this uneasy and timid way of giving help, this shunning of a word of thanks.

That is why I never turned to you in my difficulty. Oh, I know that you would have given me all the help I needed, in spite of a doubt that my child was yours. You would have offered me comfort and have given me money, an ample supply of money, but always with a masked impatience, a secret desire to shake off trouble. I even believe that you would have advised me to rid myself of the coming child. This was what I dreaded above all, for I knew that I should do whatever you wanted. But the child was all in all to me. It was yours; it was you reborn—not the happy and carefree you, whom I could never hope to keep, but you, given to me for my very own, flesh of my flesh, intimately intertwined with my own life. At length I held you fast; I could feel your life-blood flowing through my veins; I could nourish you, caress you, kiss you, as often as my soul yearned. That was why I was so happy when I knew that I was with child by you, and that is why I kept the secret from you. Henceforward you could not escape me; you were mine.

But you must not suppose that the months of waiting passed so happily as I had dreamt in my first transports. They were full of sorrow and care, full of loathing for the baseness of mankind. Things went hard with me. I could not stay at work during the later months, for my stepfather's relatives would have noticed my condition and would have sent the news home. Nor would I ask my mother for money; so until my time came I managed to live by the sale of some trinkets. A week before my confinement, the few crownpieces that remained to me were stolen by my laundress, so I had to go to the maternity hospital. The child, your son, was born there, in that asylum of wretchedness, among the very poor, the outcast and the abandoned. It was a deadly place. Everything was strange, was alien. We were all alien to one another, as we lay there in our loneliness, filled with mutual hatred, thrust together only by our kinship of poverty and distress into this crowded ward, reeking of chloroform and blood, filled with cries and moaning. A patient in these wards loses all individuality, except such as remains in the name at the head of the clinical record. What lies in the bed is merely a piece of quivering flesh, an object of study …

I ask your forgiveness for speaking of these things. I shall never speak of them again. For eleven years I have kept silence, and shall soon be dumb for evermore. Once, at least, I had to cry aloud, to let you know how dearly bought was this child, this boy who was my delight, and who now lies dead. I had forgotten those dreadful hours, forgotten them in his smiles and his voice, forgotten them in my happiness. Now, when he is dead, the torment has come to life again, and I had, this once, to give it utterance. But I do not accuse you; only God, only God who is the author of such purposeless affliction. Never have I cherished an angry thought of you. Not even in the utmost agony of giving birth did I feel any resentment against you; never did I repent the nights when I enjoyed your love; never did I cease to love you or to bless the hour when you came into my life. Were it necessary for me, fully aware of what was coming, to relive that time in hell, I would do it gladly, not once, but many times.

Our boy died yesterday, and you never knew him. His bright little personality has never come into the most fugitive contact with you, and your eyes have never rested on him. For a long time after our son was born, I kept myself hidden from you. My longing for you had become less overpowering. Indeed, I believe I loved you less passionately. Certainly, my love for you did not hurt so much, now that I had the boy. I did not wish to divide myself between you and him, and so I did not give myself to you, who were happy and independent of me, but to the boy who needed me, whom I had to nourish, whom I could kiss and fondle. I seemed to have been healed of my restless yearning for you. The doom seemed to have been lifted from me by the birth of this other you, who was truly my own. Rarely, now, did my feelings reach out towards you in your dwelling. One thing only—on your birthday I have always sent you a bunch of white roses, like the roses you gave me after our first night of love. Has it ever occurred to you, during these ten or eleven years, to ask yourself who sent them? Have you ever recalled having given such roses to a girl? I do not know, and never shall know. For me it was enough to send them to you out of the darkness; enough, once a year, to revive my own memory of that hour.

You never knew our boy. I blame myself today for having hidden him from you, for you would have loved him. You have never seen him smile when he first opened his eyes after sleep, his dark eyes that were your eyes, the eyes with which he looked merrily forth at me and the world. He was so bright, so lovable. All your light-heartedness and your mobile imagination were his likewise—in the form in which these qualities can show themselves in a child. He would spend entranced hours playing with things as you play with life, and then, grown serious, would sit long over his books. He was you, reborn. The mingling of sport and earnest, which is so characteristic of you, was becoming plain in him, and the more he resembled you, the more I loved him. He was good at his lessons, so that he could chatter in French like a magpie. His exercise books were the tidiest in the class. And what a fine, upstanding little man he was! When I took him to the seaside in the summer, at Grado, women used to stop and stroke his fair hair. At Semmering, when he was tobogganing, people would turn round to gaze after him. He was so handsome, so gentle, so appealing. Last year when he went to college as a boarder, he began to wear the collegiates' uniform of an eighteenth-century page, with a little dagger stuck in his belt—now he lies here in his shift, with pallid lips and crossed hands.

You will wonder how I could manage to give the boy so costly an upbringing, how it was possible for me to provide for him an entry into this bright and cheerful life of the well-to-do. Dear one, I am speaking to you from the darkness. Unashamed, I will tell you. Do not shrink from me. I sold myself. I did not become a street-walker, a common prostitute, but I sold myself. My friends, my lovers, were wealthy men. At first I sought them out, but soon they sought me, for I was (did you ever notice it?) a beautiful woman. Everyone to whom I gave myself was devoted to me. They all became my grateful admirers. They all loved me—except you, except you whom I loved.

Will you despise me now that I have told you what I did? I am sure you will not. I know you will understand everything, will understand that what I did was done only for you, for your other self, for your boy. In the lying-in hospital I had tasted the full horror of poverty. I knew that, in the world of the poor, those who are downtrodden are always the victims. I could not bear to think that your son, your lovely boy, was to grow up in that abyss, amid the corruptions of the street, in the poisoned air of a slum. His delicate lips must not learn the speech of the gutter; his fine, white skin must not be chafed by the harsh and sordid underclothing of the poor. Your son must have the best of everything, all the wealth and all the light-heartedness of the world. He must follow your footsteps through life, must dwell in the sphere in which you had lived.

That is why I sold myself. It was no sacrifice to me, for what are conventionally termed 'honour' and 'disgrace' were unmeaning words to me. You were the only one to whom my body could belong, and you did not love me, so what did it matter what I did with that body? My companions' caresses, even their most ardent passion, never sounded my depths, although many of them were persons I could not but respect, and although the thought of my own fate made me sympathise with them in their unrequited love. All these men were kind to me; they all petted and spoilt me; they all paid me every deference. One of them, a widower, an elderly man of title, used his utmost influence until he secured your boy's nomination to the college. This man loved me like a daughter. Three or four times he urged me to marry him. I could have been a Countess today, mistress of a lovely castle in the Tyrol. I could have been free from care, for the boy would have had a most affectionate father and I should have had a sedate, distinguished, and kind-hearted husband. But I persisted in my refusal, though I knew it gave him pain. It may have been foolish of me. Had I yielded, I should have been living a safe and retired life somewhere, and my child would still have been with me. Why should I hide from you the reason for my refusal? I did not want to bind myself. I wanted to remain free—for you. In my innermost self, in the unconscious, I continued to dream the dream of my childhood. Some day, perhaps, you would call me to your side, were it only for an hour. For the possibility of this one hour I rejected everything else, simply that I might be free to answer your call. Since my first awakening to womanhood, what had my life been but waiting, a waiting upon your will?

In the end, the expected hour came. And still you never knew that it had come! When it came, you did not recognise me. You have never recognised me, never, never. I met you often enough, in theatres, at concerts, in the Prater, and elsewhere. Always my heart leapt, but always you passed me by, unheeding. In outward appearance I had become a different person. The timid girl was a woman now; beautiful, it was said; decked out in fine clothes; surrounded by admirers. How could you recognise in me one whom you had known as a shy girl in the subdued light of your bedroom? Sometimes my companion would greet you, and you would acknowledge the greeting as you glanced at me. But your look was always that of a courteous stranger, a look of deference, but not of recognition—distant, hopelessly distant. Once, I remember, this non-recognition, familiar as it had become, was a torture to me. I was in a box at the opera with a friend, and you were in the next box. The lights were lowered when the Overture began. I could no longer see your face, but I could feel your breathing quite close to me, just as when I was with you in your room, and on the velvet-covered partition between the boxes your slender hand was resting. I was filled with an infinite longing to bend down and kiss this hand, whose loving touch I had once known. Amid the turmoil of sound from the orchestra, the craving grew even more intense. I had to hold myself back convulsively, to keep my lips away from your dear hand. At the end of the first act, I told my friend I wanted to leave. It was intolerable to me to have you sitting there beside me in the darkness, so near and so estranged.

But the hour came once more, only once more. It was all but a year ago, on the day after your birthday. My thoughts had been dwelling on you more than ever, for I used to keep your birthday as a festival. Early in the morning I had gone to buy the white roses which I sent you every year in commemoration of an hour you had forgotten. In the afternoon I took my boy for a drive and we had tea together. In the evening we went to the theatre. I wanted him to look upon this day as a sort of mystical anniversary of his youth, though he could not know the reason. The next day I spent with my intimate of that epoch, a young and wealthy manufacturer of Brunn, with whom I had been living for two years. He was passionately fond of me, and he too wanted me to marry him. I refused, for no reason he could understand although he loaded me and the child with presents, and was lovable enough in his rather stupid and slavish devotion. We went together to a concert, where we met a lively company. We all had supper at a restaurant in the Ringstrasse. Amid talk and laughter, I proposed that we should move on to a dancing hall. In general, such places, where the cheerfulness is always an expression of partial intoxication, are repulsive to me, and I would seldom go to them. But on this occasion some elemental force seemed at work in me, leading me to make the proposal, which was hailed with acclamation by the others. I was animated by an inexplicable longing, as if some extraordinary experience were awaiting me. As usual, everyone was eager to accede to my whims. We went to the dancing hall, drank some champagne, and I had a sudden access of almost frenzied cheerfulness such as I had never known. I drank one glass of wine after another, joined in the chorus of a suggestive song, and was in a mood to dance with glee. Then, all in a moment, I felt as if my heart had been seized by an icy or a burning hand. You were sitting with some friends at the next table, regarding me with an admiring and covetous glance, that glance which had always thrilled me beyond expression. For the first time in ten years you were looking at me again under the stress of all the unconscious passion in your nature. I trembled, and my hand shook so violently that I nearly let my wineglass fall. Fortunately my companions did not notice my condition, for their perceptions were confused by the noise of laughter and music.

Your look became continually more ardent, and touched my own senses to fire. I could not be sure whether you had at last recognised me, or whether your desires had been aroused by one whom you believed to be a stranger. My cheeks were flushed, and I talked at random. You could not help noticing the effect your glance had on me. You made an inconspicuous movement of the head, to suggest my coming into the ante-room for a moment. Then, having settled your bill, you took leave of your associates and left the table, after giving me a further sign that you intended to wait for me outside. I shook like one in the cold stage of a fever. I could no longer answer when spoken to, could no longer control the tumult of my blood.

At this moment, as chance would have it, a couple of Negroes with clattering heels began a barbaric dance to the accompaniment of their own shrill cries. Everyone turned to look at them, and I seized my opportunity. Standing up, I told my friend that I would be back in a moment and followed you.

You were waiting for me in the lobby, and your face lit up when I came. With a smile on your lips, you hastened to meet me. It was plain that you did not recognise me, neither the child nor the girl of the old days. Again, to you, I was a new acquaintance. 'Have you really got an hour to spare for me?' you asked in a confident tone, which showed that you took me for one of the women whom anyone can buy for a night. 'Yes,' I answered; the same tremulous but perfectly acquiescent 'Yes' that you had heard from me in my girlhood, more than ten years earlier, in the darkling street. 'Tell me when we can meet,' you said. 'Whenever you like,' I replied, for I knew nothing of shame where you were concerned. You looked at me with a little surprise, with a surprise which had in it the same flavour of doubt mingled with curiosity which you had shown before when you were astonished at the readiness of my acceptance. 'Now?' you enquired, after a moment's hesitation. 'Yes,' I replied, 'let us go.'

I was about to fetch my wrap from the cloakroom, when I remembered that my Brunn friend had handed in our things together, and that he had the ticket. It was impossible to go back and ask him for it, and it seemed to me even more impossible to renounce this hour with you to which I had been looking forward for years. My choice was instantly made. I gathered my shawl around me, and went forth into the misty night, regardless not only of my cloak, but regardless, likewise, of the kind-hearted man with whom I had been living for years—regardless of the fact that in this public way, before his friends, I was putting him into the ludicrous position of one whose mistress abandons him at the first nod of a stranger. Inwardly, I was well aware how basely and ungratefully I was behaving towards a good friend. I knew that my outrageous folly would alienate him from me for ever, and that I was playing havoc with my life. But what was his friendship, what was my own life, to me when compared with the chance of again feeling your lips on mine, of again listening to the tones of your voice. Now that all is over and done with I can tell you this, can let you know how I loved you. I believe that were you to summon me from my deathbed, I should find strength to rise in answer to your call.

There was a taxi at the door, and we drove to your rooms. Once more I could listen to your voice, once more I felt the ecstasy of being near you, and was almost as intoxicated with joy and confusion as I had been so long before. I cannot describe it all to you, how what I had felt ten years earlier was now renewed as we went up the well-known stairs together; how I lived simultaneously in the past and in the present, my whole being fused as it were with yours. In your rooms, little was changed. There were a few more pictures, a great many more books, one or two additions to your furniture—but the whole had the friendly look of an old acquaintance. On the writing table was the vase with the roses—my roses, the ones I had sent you the day before as a memento of the woman whom you did not remember, whom you did not recognise, not even now when she was close to you, when you were holding her hand and your lips were pressed on hers. But it comforted me to see my flowers there, to know that you had cherished something that was an emanation from me, was the breath of my love for you.

You took me in your arms. Again I stayed with you for the whole of one glorious night. But even then you did not recognise me. While I thrilled to your caresses, it was plain to me that your passion knew no difference between a

114

loving mistress and a harlot, that your spendthrift affections were wholly concentrated in their own expression. To me, the stranger picked up at a dancing hall, you were at once affectionate and courteous. You would not treat me lightly, and yet you were full of an enthralling ardour. Dizzy with the old happiness, I was again aware of the two-sidedness of your nature, of that strange mingling of intellectual passion with sensual, which had already enslaved me to you in my childhood. In no other man have I ever known such complete surrender to the sweetness of the moment. No other has for the time being given himself so utterly as did you who, when the hour was past, were to relapse into an interminable and almost inhuman forgetfulness. But I too forgot myself. Who was I, lying in the darkness beside you? Was I the impassioned child of former days; was I the mother of your son; was I a stranger? Everything in this wonderful night was at one and the same time entrancingly familiar and entrancingly new. I prayed that the joy might last for ever.

But morning came. It was late when we rose, and you asked me to stay to breakfast. Over the tea, which an unseen hand had discreetly served in the dining room, we talked quietly. As of old, you displayed a cordial frankness; and, as of old, there were no tactless questions, there was no curiosity about myself. You did not ask my name, nor where I lived. To you I was, as before, a casual adventure, a nameless woman, an ardent hour which leaves no trace when it is over. You told me that you were about to start on a long journey, that you were going to spend two or three months in northern Africa. The words broke in upon my happiness like a knell: 'Past, past, past and forgotten!' I longed to throw myself at your feet, crying: 'Take me with you, that you may at length come to know me, at length after all these years!' But I was timid, cowardly, slavish, weak. All I could say was: 'What a pity!' You looked at me with a smile: 'Are you really sorry?'

For a moment I was as if frenzied. I stood up and looked at you fixedly. Then I said: 'The man I love has always gone on a journey.' I looked you straight in the eyes. 'Now, now,' I thought, 'now he will recognise me!' You smiled, and said consolingly: 'One comes back after a time.' I answered: 'Yes, one comes back... but one has forgotten by then.'

I must have spoken with strong feeling, for my tone moved you. You too rose, and looked at me wonderingly and tenderly. You put your hands on my shoulders: 'Good things are not forgotten, and I shall not forget you.' Your eyes studied me attentively, as if you wished to form an enduring image of me in your mind. When I felt this penetrating glance, this exploration of my whole being, I could not but fancy that the spell of your blindness would at last be broken. 'He will recognise me! He will recognise me!' My soul trembled with expectation.

But you did not recognise me. No, you did not recognise me. Never had I been more of a stranger to you than I was at that moment, for had it been otherwise you could not possibly have done what you did a few minutes later. You had kissed me again, had kissed me passionately. My hair had been ruffled, and I had to tidy it once more. Standing at the glass, I saw in it—and as I saw, I was overcome with shame and horror—that you were surreptitiously slipping a couple of banknotes into my muff. I could hardly refrain from crying out; I could hardly refrain from slapping your face. You were paying me for the night I had spent with you, me who had loved you since childhood, me the mother of your son. To you I was only a prostitute picked up at a dancing hall. It was not enough that you should forget me; you had to pay me, and to debase me by doing so.

I hastily gathered up my belongings, that I might escape as quickly as possible; the pain was too great. I looked round for my hat. There it was, on the writing table, beside the vase with the white roses, my roses. I had an irresistible desire to make a last effort to awaken your memory. 'Will you give me one of your white roses?'—'Of course,' you answered, lifting them all out of the vase. 'But perhaps they were given you by a woman, a woman who loves you?'—'Maybe,' you replied, 'I don't know. They were a present, but I don't know who sent them; that's why I'm so fond of them.' I looked at you intently: 'Perhaps they were sent you by a woman whom you have forgotten!'

You were surprised. I looked at you yet more intently. 'Recognise me, only recognise me at last!' was the clamour of my eyes. But your smile, though cordial, had no recognition in it. You kissed me yet again, but you did not recognise me.

I hurried away, for my eyes were filling with tears, and I did not want you to see. In the entry, as I precipitated myself from the room, I almost cannoned into John, your servant. Embarrassed but zealous, he got out of my way and opened the front door for me. Then, in this fugitive instant, as I looked at him through my tears, a light suddenly flooded the old man's face. In this fugitive instant, I tell you, he recognised me, the man who had never seen me since my childhood. I was so grateful that I could have knelt before him and kissed his hands. I tore from my muff the banknotes with which you had scourged me, and thrust them upon him. He glanced at me in alarm—for in this instant I think he understood more of me than you have understood in your whole life. Everyone, everyone, has been eager to spoil me; everyone has loaded me with kindness. But you, only you, forgot me. You, only you, never recognised me.

My boy, our boy, is dead. I have no one left to love; no one in the world, except you. But what can you be to me—you who have never, never recognised me, you who stepped across me as you might step across a stream, you who trod on me as you might tread on a stone, you who went on your way unheeding, while you left me to wait for all eternity? Once I fancied that I could hold you for my own; that I held you, the elusive, in the child. But he was your son! In the night, he cruelly slipped away from me on a journey; he has forgotten me, and will never return. I am alone once more, more utterly alone than ever. I have nothing, nothing from you. No child, no word, no line of writing, no place in your memory. If anyone were to mention my name in your presence, to you it would be the name of a stranger. Shall I not be glad to die, since I am dead to you? Glad to go away, since you have gone away from me?

Beloved, I am not blaming you. I do not wish to intrude my sorrows into your joyful life. Do not fear that I shall ever trouble you further. Bear with me for giving way to the longing to cry out my heart to you this once, in the bitter hour when the boy lies dead. Only this once I must talk to you. Then I shall slip back into obscurity, and be dumb towards you as I have ever been. You will not even hear my cry so long as I continue to live. Only when I am dead will this heritage come to you; from one who has loved you more fondly than any other has loved you; from one whom you have never recognised; from one who has always been waiting your summons and whom you have never summoned. Perhaps, perhaps, when you receive this legacy you will call to me, and for the first time I shall be unfaithful to you, for I shall not hear you in the sleep of death. Neither picture nor token do I leave you, just as you tell me nothing, for never will you recognise me now. That was my fate in life, and it shall be my fate in death likewise. I shall not summon you in my last hour; I shall go my way leaving you ignorant of my name and my appearance. Death will be easy for me, for you will not feel it from afar. I could not die if my death were going to give you pain.

I cannot write any more. My head is so heavy; my limbs ache; I am feverish. I must lie down. Perhaps all will soon be over. Perhaps, this once, fate will be kind to me, and I shall not have to see them take away my boy … I cannot write any more. Farewell dear one, farewell. All my thanks go out to you. What happened was good in spite of everything. I shall be thankful to you till my last breath. I am so glad that I have told you all. Now you will know, though you can never fully understand, how much I have loved you, and yet my love will never be a burden to you. It is my solace that I shall not fail you. Nothing will be changed in your bright and lovely life. Beloved, my death will not harm you. This comforts me.

But who, ah who, will now send you white roses on your birthday? The vase will be empty. No longer will come that breath, that aroma, from my life, which once a year was breathed into your room. I have one last request—the first, and the last. Do it for my sake. Always on your birthday— a day when one thinks of oneself—get some roses and put them in the vase. Do it just as others, once a year, have a mass said for the beloved dead. I no longer believe in God, and therefore I do not want a mass said for me. I believe in you alone. I love none but you. Only in you do I wish to go on living—just one day in the year, softly, quietly, as I have always lived near you. Please do this, my darling, please do it … My first request, and my last … Thanks, thanks … I love you, I love you … Farewell … "

The letter fell from his nerveless hands. He thought long and deeply. Yes, he had vague memories of a neighbour's child, of a girl, of a woman in a dancing hall—all was dim and confused, like a flickering and shapeless view of a stone in the bed of a swiftly running stream. Shadows chased one another across his mind, but would not fuse into a picture. There were stirrings of memory in the realm of feeling, and still he could not remember. It seemed to him that he must have dreamt all these figures, must have dreamt often and vividly—and yet they had only been the phantoms of a dream. His eyes wandered to the blue vase on the writing table. It was empty. For years it had not been empty on his birthday. He shuddered, feeling as if an invisible door had been suddenly opened, a door through which a chill breeze from another world was blowing into his sheltered room. An intimation of death came to him, and an intimation of deathless love. Something welled up within him, and the thought of the dead woman stirred in his mind, bodiless and passionate, like the sound of distant music.

THE FOWLER SNARED

Translated from the German by Eden and Cedar Paul

LAST SUMMER I spent a month at Cadenabbia—one of those little places on Lake Como, where white villas are so prettily bowered amid dark trees. The town is quiet enough even during the spring season, when the narrow strand is thronged with visitors from Bellagio and Menaggio, but in these hot weeks of August it was an aromatic and sunny solitude. The hotel was almost empty. The few stragglers that remained looked at one another quizzically each morning, surprised to see anyone else staying on in so forsaken a spot. For my part, I was especially astonished by the persistence of an elderly gentleman, carefully dressed and of cultivated demeanour, who might have been a cross between an English statesman and a Parisian man-about-town. Why, I wondered, did he not go away to some seaside resort? He spent his days meditatively watching the smoke that rose from his cigarette, and occasionally fluttering the pages of a book. There came a couple of rainy days, and in these we struck up acquaintance. He made such cordial advances that the difference between our ages was soon bridged over, and we became quite intimate. Born in Livonia, educated in France and England, he had never had either a fixed occupation or a fixed place of abode. A homeless wanderer, he was, as it were, a pirate or viking—a rover who took his toll of beauty from every place where he chanced to set his foot. An amateur of all the arts, he disdained to practise any. They had given him a thousand happy hours, and he had never given them a moment's creative force. His life was one of those that seem utterly superfluous, for with his last breath the accumulated store of his experiences would be scattered without finding an heir.

I hinted as much one evening, when we sat in front of the hotel after dinner, watching the darkness steal across the lake.

"Perhaps you are right," he said with a smile. "I have no interest in memories. Experience is experienced once for all; then it is over and done with. The fancies of fiction, too—do they not fade after a time, do they not perish in twenty, fifty or a hundred years? But I will tell you an incident which might be worked up into a good story. Let us take a stroll. I can talk better when I am on the move."

We walked along the lovely road bordering the lake, beneath the cypresses and chestnut trees. The water, ruffled by the night breeze, gleamed through the foliage.

"Let me begin with a confession; I was in Cadenabbia last year, in August, and staying at the same hotel. No doubt that will surprise you, for I remember having told you that I make a point of avoiding these repetitions. But you will understand why I have broken my rule as soon as you have heard my story.

Of course the place was just as deserted as it is now. The man from Milan was here, that fellow who spends the whole day fishing, to throw his catch back into the lake when evening comes, in order to angle for the same fish next morning. There were two Englishmen, whose existence was so tranquil, so vegetative, that one hardly knew they were there. Besides these, there was a handsome stripling, and with him a charming though rather pale girl. I have my doubts whether she was his wife—they seemed much too fond of one another for that.

Last of all, there was a German family, typical North Germans. A lean, elderly woman, a faded blonde, all elbows and gawkiness; she had piercing blue eyes, and her peevish mouth looked like a slit cut by a knife. The other woman was unmistakably her sister, for she had the same traits, though somewhat softened. The two were always together, silently bent over their needlework, into which they seemed to be stitching all the vacancy of their minds—the pitiless Grey Sisters of a world of tedium and restraints. With them was a girl, sixteen or

126

seventeen years old, the daughter of one or the other. In her, the harshness of the family features was softened, for the delicate contours of budding womanhood were beginning to show themselves. All the same she was distinctly plain, being too lean and still immature. Moreover, she was unbecomingly dressed, and yet there was something wistful about her appearance.

Her eyes were large, and full of subdued fire, but she was so bashful that she could not look anyone in the face. Like the mother and the aunt, she always had some needlework with her, though she was not as industrious as they; from time to time the movements of her hands would grow sluggish, her fingers would doze, and she would sit motionless, gazing dreamily across the lake. I don't know what it was that I found so attractive in her aspect on these occasions. Was it no more than the commonplace but inevitable impression aroused by the sight of a withered mother beside a daughter in the fresh bloom of youth, the shadow behind the substance; the thought that in every cheek there lurks a fold; in every laugh, weariness; in every dream, disillusionment? Was it the ardent but aimless yearning that was so plainly manifest in her expression, the yearning of those wonderful hours in a girl's life when her eyes look covetously forth into the universe because she has not yet found the one thing to which in due time she will cling—to rot there as algae cling to and rot on a floating log? Whatever the cause, I found it pathetic to watch her, to note the loving way in which she would caress a dog or a cat, and the restlessness with which she would begin one task after another only to abandon it. Touching, too, was the eagerness with which she would scan the shabby books in the hotel library, or turn the well-thumbed pages of a volume or two of verse she had brought with her, would muse over the poems of Goethe or Baumbach."

He broke off for a moment, to say: "What are you laughing at?"

I apologised. "You must admit that the juxtaposition of Goethe and Baumbach is rather quaint."

"Quaint? Perhaps it is. But it's not so funny after all. A girl at that age doesn't care whether the poetry she reads is good or bad, whether the verses ring true or false. The metrical lines are only the vessels in which there can be conveyed something to quench thirst, and the quality of the wine matters nothing, for she is already drunken before she puts her lips to the cup.

That's how it was with this girl. She was brimful of longing. It peeped forth from her eyes, made her fingers wander tremulously over the table, gave to her whole demeanour an awkward and yet attractive appearance of mingled timidity and impulsiveness. She was in a fever to talk, to give expression to the teeming life within her, but there was no one to talk to. She was quite alone as she sat there between those two chill and circumspect elders, whose needles were plied so busily on either side of her. I was full of compassion for her, but I could not make any advances. What interest has such a girl in a man of my age? Besides, I detest opening up acquaintance with a family circle, and have a particular dislike for these philistine women of a certain age.

A strange fancy seized me. 'Here,' I thought to myself, 'is a girl fresh from school, unfledged and inexperienced, doubtless paying her first visit to Italy. All Germans read Shakespeare, and thanks to Shakespeare (who never set foot in Italy!) this land will be to her the land of romance and love—of Romeos, secret adventures, fans dropped as signals, flashing daggers, masks, duennas and billets-doux. Beyond question she must be dreaming of such things, and what limits are there to a girl's dreams, those streams of white cloud floating aimlessly in the blue, flashing red and gold when evening falls? Nothing will seem to her improbable or impossible.' I made up my mind to find her a lover.

That evening I wrote a long letter, a tender epistle, yet full of humility and respect. It was in German, but I managed to impart an exotic flavour to the phrasing. There was no signature. The writer asked nothing and offered nothing. It was the sort of love letter you will find in a novel—not too long—and characterised, if I may use the term, by a reserved extravagance. Knowing that, driven by the urge of her inner restlessness, she was always the first to enter the breakfast room, I rolled this letter inside her table napkin.

Next morning, I took up a post of observation in the garden. Watching her through the window, I marked her incredulous surprise. She was more than surprised, she was startled; her pale cheeks were tinted with a sudden flush, which spread down the neck. She looked round in alarm; her hands twitched; furtively, she hid the missive. Throughout breakfast she was restless, and could hardly eat a morsel, for her one desire was to get away into an unfrequented alley where she could pore over the mysterious letter—did you speak?"

I had made an involuntary movement, and had to account for it.

"You were taking a big risk. Did you not foresee that she might make enquiries, might ask the waiter how the letter found its way into her table napkin? Or that she might show it to her mother?"

"Of course I thought of such possibilities. But if you had seen the girl, had noted how she was scared if anyone spoke loudly, you would have had no anxiety at all. There are some young women who are so shamefaced that a man can take with them any liberties he pleases. They will endure the uttermost because they cannot bear to complain about such a thing.

I was delighted to watch the success of my device. She came back from her walk in the garden, and my own temples throbbed at the sight of her. She was a new girl, with a more sprightly gait. She did not know what to do with herself; her cheeks were burning once more, and she was adorably awkward in her embarrassment. So it went on throughout the day. She glanced at one window after another as if hoping to find there the clue to the enigma, and looked searchingly at every passer-by. Once her eyes met mine, and I averted my gaze, being careful not to betray myself by the flicker of an eyelid. But in that fugitive instant I became aware that a volcano of passionate enquiry was raging within her; I was, indeed, almost alarmed at the realisation, for I remembered what I had learnt long years before, that no pleasure is more seductive and more dangerous. than that which comes to a man when he is the first to awaken such a spark in a girl's eyes.

I watched her as she sat with idle fingers between the two stitching elders, and I saw how from time to time her hand moved towards a particular part of her dress where I was sure the letter lay hidden. The fascination of the sport grew. That evening I wrote a second letter, and continued to write to her night after night. It became more and more engrossing to instil into these letters the sentiments of a young man in love, to depict the waxing of an imaginary passion. No doubt one who sets snares for game has similar sensations; the deer-stalker must enjoy them to the full. Almost terrified at my own success, I was half in mind to discontinue the amusement, but the temptation to persevere in what had been so well begun was too much for me.

By now she seemed to dance as she walked; her features showed a hectic beauty. All her nights must have been devoted to expectation of the morning letter, for there were black rings beneath her eyes. She began to pay more attention to her appearance, and wore flowers in her hair. She touched everything more tenderly, and looked ever more questioningly at the things upon which her glance lit, for I had interwoven into the letters numerous indications that the writer was near at hand, was an Ariel who filled the air with music, watched all she did, but deliberately remained invisible.

So marked was the increase of cheerfulness, that even the dull old women noticed it, for they watched her springing gait with kindly inquisitiveness, noted the bloom on her cheeks, and exchanged meaning smiles with one another. Her voice became richer, more resonant, more confident; often it seemed as if she were on the point of bursting out into triumphant song, as if—But you're amused once more!"

"No, no, please go on with your story. I was only thinking how extraordinarily well you tell it. You have a real talent, and no novelist could better this recital."

"You seem to be hinting that I have the mannerisms of your German novelists, that I am lyrically diffuse, stilted, sentimental, tedious. I will try to be more concise. The marionette danced, and I pulled the strings skilfully. To avert suspicion from myself (for I sometimes felt her eyes rest on me dubiously), I had implied in the letter that the writer was not actually staying at Cadenabbia but at one of the neighbouring resorts, and that he came over here every day by boat. Thenceforward, whenever the bell rang to indicate the approach of the steamer, she would make some excuse for eluding maternal supervision, and from a corner of the pier would breathlessly watch the arrivals.

One day—the afternoon was overcast, and I had nothing better to do than to watch her—a strange thing happened. Among the passengers was a handsome young fellow, rather overdressed, after the Italian manner. As he surveyed the landing stage, he encountered the young girl's glance of eager enquiry. A smile involuntarily played round her lips, and her cheeks flamed. The young man started; his attention was riveted. Naturally enough, in answer to so ardent a look, full of so much unexpressed meaning, he smiled, and moved towards her. She took to flight, stopped for a moment, in the conviction that this was the long-expected lover, hurried on again, and then glanced back over her shoulder. The old interplay between desire and dread, yearning and shame, in which tender weakness always proves the stronger! Obviously encouraged, in spite of his surprise, the young man hastened after her. He had almost caught up with her, and I was feeling in my alarm that the edifice I had been building was about to be shattered, when the two elderly women came down the path. Like a frightened bird, the girl flew to seek their protection. The young man discreetly withdrew, but he and the girl exchanged another ardent glance before he turned away. I had had a warning to finish the game, but still the lure overpowered me, and I decided to enlist chance in my service. That evening I wrote her a letter that was longer than ever, in terms that could not fail to confirm her suspicion. To have two puppets to play with made the amusement twice as great.

Next morning I was alarmed to note signs of disorder; the charming restlessness had been replaced by an incomprehensible misery. Her eyes were tear-stained, and her silence was like the silence which preludes a fit of weeping. I had expected signs of joyous certainty, but her whole aspect was one of despair. I grew sick at heart. For the first time an intrusive force was at work; my marionette would not dance when I pulled the string. I racked my brains vainly in the attempt to discover what was amiss. Vexed and anxious at the turn things had taken, and determined to avoid the unconscious accusation of her looks, I went out for the whole day. When I returned, the matter was cleared up. Their table was not laid; the family had left. She had had to go away without saying a word to her lover. She could not dare to tell her mother and her aunt all that another day, another hour, might mean to her. They had snatched her out of this sweet dream to some pitiful little provincial town. I had never thought of such an end to my amusement. There still rises before my eyes the accusation of that last look of hers, instinct with anger, torment and hopelessness. I still think of all the suffering I brought into her young life, to cloud it perhaps for many years to come."

He had finished. But now it was quite dark, and the moon was shining fitfully through the clouds. We walked for some distance before my companion broke the silence.

"There is my story. Would it not be a good theme for a writer of fiction?"

"Perhaps. I shall certainly treasure it amid much more that you have told me. But one could hardly make a story of it, for it is merely a prelude. When people cross one another's paths like this without having their destinies intertwined, what more is there than a prelude? A story needs an ending."

"I see what you mean. You want to know what happened to the girl, her return home, the tragedy of her everyday life ... "

"No, I was not thinking of that. I have no further interest in the girl. Young girls are never interesting, however remarkable they may fancy themselves, for all their experiences are negative, and are therefore too much alike. The girl of your prelude will in due time marry some worthy citizen, and this affair will be to her nothing more than an ardent memory. I was not thinking of the girl."

"You surprise me. I don't know what can stir your interest in the young man. These glances, these sparks struck from flint, are such as everyone knows in his youth. Most of us hardly notice them at the time, and the rest forget them as soon as the spark is cold. Not until we grow old do we realise that these flashes are perhaps the noblest and deepest of all that happens to us, the most precious privilege of youth."

"I was not thinking of the young man either."

"What then?"

"I should like to tell the end of the older man's story, the letter-writer. I doubt if any man, even though well on in years, can write ardent letters and feign love in such a way without paying for it. I should try to show how the sport grew to earnest, and how the man who thought he was playing a game found that he had become a pawn in his own game. Let us suppose that the growing beauty of the girl, which he imagines he is contemplating dispassionately, charms him and holds him in thrall. Just when everything slips out of his hands, he feels a wild longing for the game—and the toy. It would delight me to depict that change in the love impulse which must make an ageing man's passion very like that of an immature youth, because both are aware of their own inadequacy. He should suffer from love's uneasiness and from the weariness of hope deferred. I should make him vacillate, follow up the girl to see her once more, but at the last moment lack courage to present himself in her sight. He should come back to the place where he had begun his sport, hoping to find her there again, wooing Fortune's favour only to find Fortune pitiless. That is the sort of end I should give the story, and it would be—"

"False, utterly false!"

I was startled. The voice at my ear was harsh and yet tremulous; it broke in upon my words like a threat. Never before had I seen my acquaintance moved by strong emotion. Instantly I realised that, in my thoughtless groping, I had laid my finger on a very sore spot. In his excitement he had come to a standstill, and when I turned to look at him the sight of his white hair was a distress to me.

I tried, rather lamely, to modify the significance of what I had said. But he turned this attempt aside. By now he had regained his composure, and he began to speak once more in a voice that was deep and tranquil but tinged with sadness:

"Perhaps, after all, you are right. That would certainly be an interesting way of ending the story. *L'amour coûte cher aux vieillards.* The phrase is Balzac's if I am not mistaken. I think it is the title of one of the most touching of his stories. Plenty more could be written under the same caption. But the old fellows, those who know most about it, would rather talk of their successes than of their failures. They think the failures will exhibit them in a ludicrous light, although these failures are but the inevitable swing of time's pendulum. Do you think it was merely by chance that the missing chapters of *Casanova's Memoirs* are those relating to the days when the adventurer was growing old, when the fowler was in danger of being caught in his own snare? Maybe his heart was too sore to write about it."

My friend offered me his hand. The thrill had quite passed out of his voice.

"Goodnight," he said. "I see it is dangerous to tell a young man tales on a summer evening. Foolish fancies, needless dreams, are so readily aroused at such times. Goodnight!"

He walked away into the darkness with a step which, though still elastic, was nevertheless a little slackened by age. It was already late. But the fatigue I might have felt this sultry night was kept at bay by the stir of the blood that comes when something strange has happened, or when sympathetic understanding makes one for an instant relive another's experiences. I wandered along the quiet and lonely road as far as the Villa Carlotta, where the marble stairs lead down to the lake, and seated myself on the cool steps. The night was wonderfully beautiful. The lights of Bellagio, which before had seemed close at hand, like fireflies flickering amid the leaves, now looked very far away across the water. The silent lake resembled a black jewel with sparkling edges. Like white hands, the rippling waves were playing up and down the lowest steps. The vault of heaven, radiant with stars, was infinite in its expanse. From time to time came a meteor, like one of these stars loosened from the firmament and plunging athwart the night sky; downwards into the dark, into the valleys, on to the hills, or into the distant water, driven by a blind force as our lives are driven into the abysses of unknown destinies.

THE INVISIBLE COLLECTION

An Episode of the Inflation Period in Germany

Translated from the German by Eden and Cedar Paul

A T THE FIRST JUNCTION *beyond Dresden, an elderly gentleman entered our compartment, smiled genially to the company, and gave me a special nod, as if to an old acquaintance. Seeing that I was at a loss, he mentioned his name. Of course I knew him! He was one of the most famous connoisseurs and art-dealers in Berlin. Before the war, I had often purchased autographs and rare books at his place. He took the vacant seat opposite me, and for a while we talked of matters not worth relating. Then, changing the conversation, he explained the object of the journey from which he was returning. It had, he said, been one of the strangest of his experiences in the thirty-seven years he had devoted to the occupation of art-dealer. Enough introduction. I will let him tell the story in his own words, without using quotation marks—to avoid the complication of wheels within wheels.*

You know (he said) what has been going on in my trade since the value of money began to diffuse into the void like gas. War-profiteers have developed a taste for old masters (Madonnas and so on), for manuscripts, for ancient tapestries. It is difficult to satisfy their craving, and a man like myself, who prefers to keep the best for his own use and enjoyment, is hard put to it not to have his house stripped bare. If I let them, they would buy the cufflinks from my shirt and the lamp from my writing table. Harder and harder to find goods to sell. I'm afraid the term 'goods' may grate upon you in this connection, but you must excuse me. I have picked it up from customers of the new sort. Evil communications … Through use and wont I have come to look upon an invaluable book from one of the early Venetian presses much as the philistine looks upon an overcoat that cost so or so many hundred dollars, and upon a sketch by Guercino as animated by nothing more worthy of reverence than the transmigrated soul of a banknote for a few thousand francs.

Impossible to resist the greed of these fellows with money to burn. As I looked round my place the other night, it seemed to me that there was so little left of any real value that I might as well put up the shutters. Here was a fine business which had come down to me from my father and my grandfather, but the shop was stocked with rubbish which, before 1914, a street-trader would have been ashamed to hawk upon a handcart.

In this dilemma, it occurred to me to flutter the pages of our old ledgers. Perhaps I should be put on the track of former customers who might be willing to resell what they had bought in prosperous days. True, such a list of sometime purchasers has considerable resemblance to a battlefield laden with the corpses of the slain, and in fact I soon realised that most of those people who had purchased from the firm when the sun was shining were dead or would be in such reduced circumstances that it was probable they must have sold anything of value among their possessions. However, I came across a bundle of letters from a man who was presumably the oldest yet alive—if he was alive. But he was so old that I had forgotten him, since he had bought nothing after the great explosion in the summer of 1914. Yes, very, very old. The earliest letters were dated more than half-a-century back, when my grandfather was head of the business. Yet I could not recall having had any personal relationships with him during the thirty-seven years in which I had been an active worker in the establishment.

All indications showed that he must have been one of those antiquated eccentrics, a few of whom survive in German provincial towns. His writing was copperplate, and every item in his orders was underlined in red ink. Each price was given in words as well as figures, so that there could be no mistake. These peculiarities, and his use of torn-out fly-leaves as writing paper, enclosed in a scratch assortment of envelopes, hinted at the miserliness of a confirmed backwoodsman. His signature was always followed by his style and title in full: *'Forest Ranger and Economic Councillor, Retired; Lieutenant, Retired; Holder of the Iron Cross First Class.*' Since he was obviously a veteran of the war of 1870-71, he must by now be close on eighty.

For all his cheese-paring and for all his eccentricities, he had manifested exceptional shrewdness, knowledge and taste as a collector of prints and engravings. A careful study of his orders, which had at first totalled very small sums indeed, disclosed that in the days when a taler could still pay for a pile of lovely German woodcuts, this country bumpkin had got together a collection of etchings and the like, outrivalling the widely trumpeted acquisitions of war profiteers. Merely those which, in the course of decades, he had bought from us for trifling sums would be worth a large amount of money today, and I had no reason to suppose that he had failed to pick up similar bargains elsewhere. Was his collection dispersed? I was too familiar with what had been going on in the art trade since the date of his last purchase not to feel confident that such a collection could scarcely have changed hands entirely without my getting wind of the event. If he was dead, his treasures had probably remained intact in the hands of his heirs.

The affair seemed so interesting that I set forth next day (yesterday evening) on a journey to one of the most out-of-the-way towns in Saxony. When I left the tiny railway station and strolled along the main street, it seemed to me impossible that anyone inhabiting one of these gimcrack houses, furnished in a way with which you are doubtless familiar, could possibly own a full set of magnificent Rembrandt etchings, together with an unprecedented number of Dürer woodcuts and a complete collection of Mantegnas. However, I went to the post office to enquire, and was astonished to learn that a sometime Forest Ranger and Economic Councillor of the name I mentioned was still living. They told me how to find his house, and I will admit that my heart beat faster than usual as I made my way there. It was well before noon.

The connoisseur of whom I was in search lived on the second floor of one of those jerry-built houses which were run up in such numbers by speculators during the sixties of the last century. The first floor was occupied by a master tailor. On the second landing to the left was the name-plate of the manager of the local post office, while the porcelain shield on the right-hand door bore the name of my quarry. I had run him to earth! My ring was promptly answered by a very old, white-haired woman wearing a black lace cap. I handed her my card and asked whether the master was at home. With an air of suspicion she glanced at me, at the card, and then back at my face once more. In this godforsaken little town a visit from an inhabitant of the metropolis was a disturbing event. However, in as friendly a tone as she could muster, she asked me to be good enough to wait a minute or two in the hall, and vanished through a doorway. I heard whispering, and then a loud, hearty, masculine voice: "Herr Rackner from Berlin, you say, the famous dealer in antiquities? Of course I shall be delighted to see him." Thereupon the old woman reappeared and invited me to enter.

I took off my overcoat, and followed her. In the middle of the cheaply furnished room was a man standing up to receive me. Old but hale, he had a bushy moustache and was wearing a semi-military frogged smoking jacket. In the most cordial way, he held out both hands towards me. But though this gesture was spontaneous and nowise forced, it was in strange contrast with the stillness of his attitude. He did not advance to meet me, so that I was compelled (I must confess I was a trifle piqued) to walk right up to him before I could shake his hand. Then I noticed that his hand, too, did not seek mine, but was waiting for mine to clasp it. At length I guessed what was amiss. He was blind.

Ever since I was a child I have been uncomfortable in the presence of the blind. It embarrasses me, produces in me a sense of bewilderment and shame to encounter anyone who is thoroughly alive, and yet has not the full use of his senses. I feel as if I were taking an unfair advantage, and I was keenly conscious of this sensation as I glanced into the fixed and sightless orbs beneath the bristling white eyebrows. The blind man, however, did not leave me time to dwell upon this discomfort. He exclaimed, laughing with boisterous delight: "A red-letter day, indeed! Seems almost a miracle that one of the big men of Berlin should drop in as you have done. There's need for us provincials to be careful, you know, when a noted dealer such as yourself is on the warpath. We've a saying in this part of the world: 'Shut your doors and button up your pockets if there are gypsies about!' I can guess why you've taken the trouble to call. Business doesn't thrive, I've gathered. No buyers or very few, so people are looking up their old customers. I'm afraid you'll draw a blank. We pensioners are glad enough to find there's still some dry bread for dinner. I've been a collector in my time, but now I'm out of the game. My buying days are over."

I hastened to tell him he was under a misapprehension, that I had not called with any thought of effecting sales. Happening to be in the neighbourhood, I felt loath to miss the chance of paying my respects to a long-standing customer who was at the same time one of the most famous among German collectors. Hardly had the phrase passed my lips when a remarkable change took place in the old man's expression. He stood stiffly in the middle of the room, but his face lit up and his whole aspect was suffused with pride. He turned in the direction where he fancied his wife to be, and nodded as if to say, "D'you hear that?" Then, turning back to me, he resumed—having dropped the brusque, drill-sergeant tone he had previously used, and speaking in a gentle, nay, almost tender voice:

"How charming of you … I should be sorry, however, if your visit were to result in nothing more than your making the personal acquaintanceship of an old buffer like myself. At any rate I've something worthwhile for you to see—more worthwhile than you could find in Berlin, in the Albertina at Vienna, or even in the Louvre (God's curse on Paris!). A man who has been a diligent collector for fifty years, with taste to guide him, gets hold of treasures that are not to be picked up at every street corner. Lisbeth, give me the key of the cupboard, please."

Now a strange thing happened. His wife, who had been listening with a pleasant smile, was startled. She raised her hands towards me, clasped them imploringly, and shook her head. What these gestures signified was a puzzle to me. Next she went up to her husband and touched his shoulder, saying:

"Franz, dear, you have forgotten to ask our visitor whether he may not have another appointment, and, anyhow, it is almost lunchtime. I am sorry," she went on, looking to me, "that we have not enough in the house for an unexpected guest. No doubt you will dine at the inn. If you will take a cup of coffee with us afterwards, my daughter Anna Maria will be here, and she is much better acquainted than I am with the contents of the portfolios."

Once more she glanced piteously at me. It was plain that she wanted me to refuse the proposal to examine the collection there and then. Taking my cue, I said that in fact I had a dinner engagement at the Golden Stag, but should be only too delighted to return at three, when there would be plenty of time to examine anything Herr Kronfeld wanted to show me. I was not leaving before six o'clock.

The veteran was as peeved as a child deprived of a favourite toy.

"Of course," he growled, "I know you mandarins from Berlin have extensive claims on your time. Still, I really think you will do well to spare me a few hours. It is not merely two or three prints I want to show you, but the contents of twenty-seven portfolios, one for each master, and all of them full to bursting. However, if you come at three sharp, I dare say we can get through by six."

The wife saw me out. In the entrance hall, before she opened the front door, she whispered: "Do you mind if Anna Maria comes to see you at the hotel before you return? It will be better for various reasons which I cannot explain just now."

"Of course, of course, a great pleasure. Really, I am dining alone, and your daughter can come along directly you have finished your own meal."

An hour later, when I had removed from the dining room to the parlour of the Golden Stag, Anna Maria Kronfeld arrived. An old maid, wizened and diffident, plainly dressed, she contemplated me with embarrassment. I did my best to put her at her ease, and expressed my readiness to go back with her at once, if her father was impatient, though it was short of the appointed hour. At this she reddened, grew even more confused, and then stammered a request for a little talk before we set out.

"Please sit down," I answered. "I am entirely at your service."

She found it difficult to begin. Her hands and her lips trembled. At length:

"My mother sent me. We have to ask a favour of you. Directly you get back, Father will want to show you his collection, and the collection ... the collection. Well, there's very little of it left."

She panted, almost sobbed, and continued:

"I must be frank ... You know what troubled times we are passing through, and I am sure you will understand. Soon after the war broke out, my father became completely blind. His sight had already been failing. Agitation, perhaps, contributed. Though he was over seventy, he wanted to go to the front, remembering the fight in which he had taken part so long ago. Naturally there was no use for his services. Then, when the advance of our armies was checked, he took the matter very much to heart, and the doctor thought that may have precipitated the oncoming of blindness. In other respects, as you will have noticed, he is vigorous. Down to 1914 he could take long walks, and go out shooting. Since the failure of his eyes, his only pleasure is in his collection. He looks at it every day. 'Looks at it,' I say, though he sees nothing. Each afternoon he has the portfolios on the table, and fingers the prints one by one, in the order which many years have rendered so familiar. Nothing else interests him. He makes me read reports of auctions, and the higher the prices, the more enthusiastic does he become.

"There's the dreadful feature of the situation. Father knows nothing about the inflation; that we are ruined; that his monthly pension would not provide us with a day's food. Then we have others to support. My sister's husband was killed at Verdun, and there are four children. These money troubles have been kept from him. We cut down expenses as much as we could, but it is impossible to make ends meet. We began to sell things, trinkets and so on, without interfering with his beloved collection. There was very little to sell, since Father had always spent whatever he could scrape together upon woodcuts, copperplate engravings and the like. The collector's mania! Well, at length it was a question whether we were to touch the collection or to let him starve. We didn't ask permission. What would have been the use? He hasn't the ghost of a notion how hard food is to come by, at any price; he has never heard that Germany was defeated and has surrendered Alsace-Lorraine. We don't read him items of that sort from the newspapers!

"The first piece we sold was a very valuable one, a Rembrandt etching, and the dealer paid us a good price, a good many thousand marks. We thought it would last us for years. But you know how money was melting away in 1922 and 1923. After we had provided for our immediate needs, we put the rest in a bank. In two months it was gone! We had to sell another engraving, and then another. That was during the worst days of inflation, and each time the dealer delayed settlement until the price was not worth a tenth or a hundredth of what he had promised to pay. We tried auction rooms. and were cheated there too, though the bids were raised by millions. The million- or milliard-mark notes were wastepaper by the time we got them. The collection was scattered to provide daily bread, and little of that.

"That was why Mother was so much alarmed when you turned up today. Directly the portfolios are opened, our well-intentioned fraud will be disclosed. He knows each item by touch. You see, every print we disposed of was immediately replaced by a sheet of blank cartridge paper of the same size and thickness, so that he would notice no difference when he handled it. Feeling them one by one, and counting them, he derives almost as much pleasure as if he could actually see them. He never tries to show them to anyone here, where there is no connoisseur, no one worthy to look at them, but he loves each of them so ardently that I think his heart would break if he knew they had been dispersed. The last time he asked someone to look at them, it was the curator of the copperplate engravings in Dresden, who died years ago.

"I beseech you"—her voice broke—"not to shatter his illusion, not to undermine his faith, that the treasures he will describe to you are there for the seeing. He would not survive the knowledge of their loss. Perhaps we have wronged him; yet what could we do? One must live. Orphaned children are more valuable than old prints. Besides, it has been life and happiness to him to spend three hours every afternoon going through his imaginary collection, and talking to each specimen as if it were a friend. Today may be the most enthralling experience since his sight failed. How he has longed for the chance of exhibiting his treasures to an expert! If you will lend yourself to the deception ... "

In my cold recital, I cannot convey to you how poignant was this appeal. I have seen many a sordid transaction in my business career; have had to look on supinely while persons ruined by inflation have been cheated out of cherished heirlooms which they were compelled to sacrifice for a crust. But my heart has not been utterly calloused, and this tale touched me to the quick. I need hardly tell you that I promised to play up.

We went to her house together. On the way I was grieved (though not surprised) to learn for what preposterously small amounts these ignorant though kind-hearted women had parted with prints, many of which were extremely valuable and some of them unique. This confirmed my resolve to give all the help in my power. As we mounted the stairs we heard a jovial shout: "Come in! Come in!" With the keen hearing of the blind, he had recognised the footsteps for which he had been eagerly waiting.

"Franz usually takes a siesta after lunch, but excitement kept him awake today," said the old woman with a smile as she let us in. A glance at her daughter showed her that all was well. The stack of portfolios was on the table. The blind collector seized me by the arm and thrust me into a chair which was placed ready for me.

"Let's begin at once. There's a lot to see, and time presses. The first portfolio contains Dürers. Nearly a full set, and you'll think each cut finer than the others. Magnificent specimens. Judge for yourself."

He opened the portfolio as he spoke, saying:

"We start with the *Apocalypse* series, of course."

Then, tenderly, delicately (as one handles fragile and precious objects), he picked up the first of the blank sheets of cartridge paper and held it admiringly before my sighted eyes and his blind ones. So enthusiastic was his gaze that it was difficult to believe he could not see. Though I knew it to be fancy, I found it difficult to doubt that there was a glow of recognition in the wrinkled face.

"Have you ever come across a finer print? How sharp the impression. Every detail crystal-clear. I compared mine with the one at Dresden; a good one, no doubt, but 'fuzzy' in contrast with the specimen you are looking at. Then I have the whole pedigree."

He turned the sheet over and pointed at the back so convincingly that involuntarily I leant forwards to read the non-existent inscriptions.

"The stamp of the Nagler collection, followed by those of Remy and Esdaille. My famous predecessors never thought that their treasure would come to roost in this little room."

I shuddered as the unsuspecting enthusiast extolled the blank sheet of paper; my flesh crept when he placed a fingernail on the exact spot where the alleged imprints had been made by long-dead collectors. It was as ghostly as if the disembodied spirits of the men he named had risen from the tomb. My tongue cleaved to the roof of my mouth—until once more I caught sight of the distraught countenances of Kronfeld's wife and daughter. Then I pulled myself together and resumed my role. With forced heartiness, I exclaimed:

"Certainly you are right. This specimen is peerless."

He swelled with triumph.

"But that's nothing," he went on. "Look at these two, the *Melancholia*, and the illuminated print of *The Passion*. The latter, beyond question, has no equal. The freshness of the tints! Your colleagues in Berlin and the custodians of the public galleries would turn green with envy at the sight."

I will not bore you with details. Thus it went on, a paean, for more than two hours, as he ransacked portfolio after portfolio. An eerie business to watch the handling of these two or three hundred blanks, to chime in at appropriate moments with praise of merits which for the blind collector were so eminently real that again and again (this was my salvation) his faith kindled my own.

Once only did disaster loom. He was 'showing' me a first proof of Rembrandt's *Antiope*, which must have been of inestimable value and which had doubtless been sold for a song. Again he commented on the sharpness of the print, but as he passed his fingers lightly over it the sensitive tips missed some familiar indentation. His face clouded, his mouth trembled, and he said:

"Surely, surely it's the *Antiope*? No one touches the woodcuts and etchings but myself. How can it have got misplaced?"

"Of course it's the *Antiope*, Herr Kronfeld," I said, hastening to take the 'print' from his hand and to expatiate upon various details which my own remembrance enabled me to conjure up upon the blank surface.

His bewilderment faded. The more I praised, the more gratified he became, until at last he said exultantly to the two women:

"Here's a man who knows what's what! You have been inclined to grumble at my 'squandering' money upon the collection. It's true that for half-a-century and more I denied myself beer, wine, tobacco, travelling, visits to the theatre, books, devoting all I could spare to these purchases you have despised. Well, Herr Rackner confirms my judgment. When I am dead and gone, you'll be richer than anyone in the town, as wealthy as the wealthiest folk in Dresden, and you'll have good reason for congratulating yourself on my 'craze'. But so long as I'm alive, the collection must be kept together. After I'm dead and buried, this expert or another will help you to sell. You'll have to, since my pension dies with me."

As he spoke, his fingers caressed the despoiled portfolios. It was horrible and touching. Not for years, not since 1914, had

I witnessed an expression of such unmitigated happiness on the face of a German. His wife and daughter watched him with tear-dimmed eyes, yet ecstatically, like those women of old who—fearful and rapturous—found the stone rolled away and the sepulchre empty in the garden outside the wall of Jerusalem. But the man could not have enough of my appreciation. He went on from portfolio to portfolio, from 'print' to 'print', drinking in my words, until, exhausted, I was glad when the false blanks were replaced in their cases and room was made to serve coffee on the table.

My host, far from being tired, looked rejuvenated. He had story after story to tell concerning the way he had chanced upon his multifarious treasures, wanting, in this connection, to take out each relevant piece once more. He grew peevish when I insisted, when his wife and daughter insisted, that I should miss my train if he delayed me any longer …

In the end he was reconciled to my going, and we said good-bye. His voice mellowed; he took both my hands in his and fondled them with the tactile appreciation of the blind.

"Your visit has given me immense pleasure," he said with a quaver in his voice. "What a joy to have been able at long last to show my collection to one competent to appreciate it. I can do something to prove my gratitude, to make your visit to a blind old man worthwhile. A codicil to my will shall stipulate that your firm, whose probity everyone knows, will be entrusted with the auctioning of my collection."

He laid a hand lovingly upon the pile of worthless port-folios.

"Promise me they shall have a handsome catalogue. I could ask no better monument."

I glanced at the two women, who were exercising the utmost control, fearful lest the sound of their trembling should reach his keen ears. I promised the impossible, and he pressed my hand in response.

Wife and daughter accompanied me to the door. They did not venture to speak, but tears were flowing down their cheeks. I myself was in little better condition. An art-dealer, I had come in search of bargains. Instead, as events turned out, I had been a sort of angel of good luck, lying like a trooper in order to assist in a fraud which kept an old man happy. Ashamed of lying, I was glad that I had lied. At any rate I had aroused an ecstasy which seems foreign to this period of sorrow and gloom.

As I stepped forth into the street, I heard a window open, and my name called. Though the old fellow could not see me, he knew in which direction I should walk, and his sightless eyes were turned thither. He leant out so far that his anxious relatives put their arms round him lest he should fall. Waving a handkerchief, he shouted:

"A pleasant journey to you, Herr Rackner."

His voice rang like a boy's. Never shall I forget that cheerful face, which contrasted so grimly with the careworn aspect of the passers-by in the street. The illusion I had helped to sustain made life good for him. Was it not Goethe who said:

"Collectors are happy creatures!"

BUCHMENDEL

Translated from the German by Eden and Cedar Paul

BUCHWINKEL

HAVING JUST GOT BACK to Vienna, after a visit to an out-of-the-way part of the country, I was walking home from the station when a heavy shower came on, such a deluge that the passers-by hastened to take shelter in doorways, and I myself felt it expedient to get out of the downpour. Luckily there is a café at almost every street corner in the metropolis, and I made for the nearest, though not before my hat was dripping wet and my shoulders were drenched to the skin. An old-fashioned suburban place, lacking the attractions copied from Germany of music and a dance floor to be found in the centre of the town; full of small shopkeepers and working folk who consumed more newspapers than coffee and rolls. Since it was already late in the evening, the air, which would have been stuffy anyhow, was thick with tobacco-smoke. Still, the place was clean and brightly decorated, had new satin-covered couches and a shining cash register, so that it looked thoroughly attractive. In my haste to get out of the rain, I had not troubled to read its name—but what matter? There I rested, warm and comfortable, though looking rather impatiently through the blue-tinted window panes to see when the shower would be over, and I should be able to get on my way.

Thus I sat unoccupied, and began to succumb to that inertia which results from the narcotic atmosphere of the typical Viennese café. Out of this void, I scanned various individuals whose eyes, in the murky room, had a greyish look in the artificial light; I mechanically contemplated the young woman at the counter as, like an automaton, she dealt out sugar and a teaspoon to the waiter for each cup of coffee; with half an eye and a wandering attention I read the uninteresting advertisements on the walls—and there was something agreeable about these dull occupations. But suddenly, and in a peculiar fashion, I was aroused from what had become almost a doze. A vague internal movement had begun; much as a toothache sometimes begins, without one being able to say whether it is on the right side or the left, in the upper jaw or the lower. All I became aware of was a numb tension, an obscure sentiment of spiritual unrest. Then, without knowing why, I grew fully conscious. I must have been in this café once before, years ago, and random associations had awakened memories of the walls, the tables, the chairs, the seemingly unfamiliar smoke-filled room.

The more I endeavoured to grasp this lost memory, the more obstinately did it elude me; a sort of jellyfish glistening in the abysses of consciousness, slippery and unseizable. Vainly did I scrutinise every object within the range of vision. Certainly when I had been here before the counter had had neither marble top nor cash register; the walls had not been panelled with imitation rosewood; these must be recent acquisitions. Yet I had indubitably been here, more than twenty years back. Within these four walls, as firmly fixed as a nail driven up to the head in a tree, there clung a part of my ego, long since overgrown. Vainly I explored, not only the room, but my own inner man, to grapple the lost links. Curse it all, I could not plumb the depths!

It will be seen that I was becoming vexed, as one is always out of humour when one's grip slips in this way, and reveals the inadequacy, the imperfections, of one's spiritual powers. Yet I still hoped to recover the clue. A slender thread would suffice, for my memory is of a peculiar type, both good and bad; on the one hand stubbornly untrustworthy, and on the other incredibly dependable. It swallows the most important details, whether in concrete happenings or in faces, and no voluntary exertion will induce it to regurgitate them from the gulf. Yet the most trifling indication—a picture postcard, the address on an envelope, a newspaper cutting—will suffice to hook up what is wanted as an angler who has made a strike and successfully imbedded his hook reels in a lively, struggling, and reluctant fish. Then I can recall the features of a man seen once only, the shape of his mouth and the gap to the left where he had an upper eye tooth knocked out, the falsetto tone of his laugh and the twitching of the moustache when he chooses to be merry, the entire change of expression which hilarity effects in him. Not only do these physical traits rise before my mind's eye, but I remember, years afterwards, every word the man said to me, and the tenor of my replies. But if I am to see and feel the past thus vividly, there must be some material link to start the current of associations. My memory will not work satisfactorily on the abstract plane.

I closed my eyes to think more strenuously, in the attempt to forge the hook which would catch my fish. In vain! In vain! There was no hook, or the fish would not bite. So fierce waxed my irritation with the inefficient and mulish thinking apparatus between my temples that I could have struck myself a violent blow on the forehead, much as an irascible man will shake and kick a penny-in-the-slot machine which, when he has inserted his coin, refuses to render him his due.

So exasperated did I become at my failure, that I could no longer sit quiet, but rose to prowl about the room. The instant I moved, the glow of awakening memory began. To the right of the cash-register, I recalled, there must be a doorway leading into a windowless room, where the only light was artificial. Yes, the place actually existed. The decorative scheme was different, but the proportions were unchanged. A square box of a place, behind the bar—the card room. My nerves thrilled as I contemplated the furniture, for I was on the track, I had found the clue, and soon I should know all. There were two small billiard tables, looking like silent ponds covered with green scum. In the corners, card tables, at one of which two bearded men of professorial type were

playing chess. Beside the iron stove, close to a door labelled
'*Telephone*', was another small table. In a flash, I had it! That
was Mendel's place, Jacob Mendel's. That was where Mendel
used to hang out, Buchmendel. I was in the Café Gluck! How
could I have forgotten Jacob Mendel. Was it possible that I
had not thought about him for ages, a man so peculiar as well-
nigh to belong to the Land of Fable, the eighth wonder of the
world, famous at the university and among a narrow circle
of admirers, magician of book-fanciers, who had been wont
to sit there from morning till night, an emblem of bookish
lore, the glory of the Café Gluck? Why had I had so much
difficulty in hooking my fish? How could I have forgotten
Buchmendel?

I allowed my imagination to work. The man's face and form
pictured themselves vividly before me. I saw him as he had
been in the flesh, seated at the table with its grey marble top,
on which books and manuscripts were piled. Motionless he
sat, his spectacled eyes fixed upon the printed page. Yet not
altogether motionless, for he had a habit (acquired at school in
the Jewish quarter of the Galician town from which he came)
of rocking his shiny bald pate backwards and forwards and
humming to himself as he read. There he studied catalogues
and tomes, crooning and rocking, as Jewish boys are taught to
do when reading the Talmud. The rabbis believe that, just as
a child is rocked to sleep in its cradle, so are the pious ideas of
the holy text better instilled by this rhythmical and hypnotising
movement of head and body. In fact, as if he had been in
a trance, Jacob Mendel saw and heard nothing while thus
occupied. He was oblivious to the click of billiard balls, the
coming and going of waiters, the ringing of the telephone bell;
he paid no heed when the floor was scrubbed and when the
stove was refilled. Once a red-hot coal fell out of the latter, and
the flooring began to blaze a few inches from Mendel's feet; the
room was full of smoke, and one of the guests ran for a pail of

water to extinguish the fire. But neither the smoke, the bustle, nor the smell, diverted his attention from the volume before him. He read as others pray, as gamblers follow the spinning of the roulette wheel, as drunkards stare into vacancy; he read with such profound absorption that ever since I first watched him the reading of ordinary mortals has seemed a pastime. This Galician second-hand book dealer, Jacob Mendel, was the first to reveal to me in my youth the mystery of absolute concentration which characterises the artist and the scholar, the sage and the imbecile; the first to make me acquainted with the tragical happiness and unhappiness of complete absorption.

A senior student introduced me to him. I was studying the life and doings of a man who is even today too little known, Mesmer the magnetiser. My researches were bearing scant fruit, for the books I could lay my hands on conveyed sparse information, and when I applied to the university librarian for help he told me, uncivilly, that it was not his business to hunt up references for a freshman. Then my college friend suggested taking me to Mendel.

"He knows everything about books, and will tell you where to find the information you want. The ablest man in Vienna, and an original to boot. The man is a saurian of the book world, an antediluvian survivor of an extinct species."

We went, therefore, to the Café Gluck, and found Buchmendel in his usual place, bespectacled, bearded, wearing a rusty black suit, and rocking as I have described. He did not notice our intrusion, but went on reading, looking like a nodding mandarin. On a hook behind him hung his ragged black overcoat, the pockets of which bulged with manuscripts, catalogues and books. My friend coughed loudly, to attract his attention, but Mendel ignored the sign. At length Schmidt rapped on the table top, as if knocking at a door, and at this Mendel glanced up, mechanically pushed his spectacles on to his forehead, and from beneath his thick and untidy ashen grey brows there glared at us two dark, alert little eyes. My friend introduced me, and I explained my quandary, being careful (as Schmidt had advised) to express great annoyance at the librarian's unwillingness to assist me. Mendel leant back, laughed scornfully, and answered with a strong Galician accent:

"Unwillingness, you think? Incompetence, that's what's the matter with him. He's a jackass, I've known him (for my sins) twenty years at least, and he's learnt nothing in the whole of that time. Pocket their wages—that's all such fellows can do. They should be mending the road, instead of sitting over books."

This outburst served to break the ice, and with a friendly wave of the hand the bookworm invited me to sit down at his table. I reiterated my object in consulting him; to get a list of all the early works on animal magnetism, and of contemporary and subsequent books and pamphlets for and against Mesmer. When I had said my say, Mendel closed his left eye for an instant, as if excluding a grain of dust. This was, with him, a sign of concentrated attention. Then, as though reading from an invisible catalogue, he reeled out the names of two or three dozen titles, giving in each case place and date of publication and approximate price. I was amazed, though Schmidt had warned me what to expect. His vanity was tickled by my surprise, for he went on to strum the keyboard of his marvellous memory, and to produce the most astounding bibliographical marginal notes. Did I want to know about sleepwalkers, Perkins's metallic tractors, early experiments in hypnotism, Braid, Gassner, attempts to conjure up the Devil, Christian Science, theosophy, Madame Blavatsky? In connection with each item there was a hailstorm of book names, dates and appropriate details. I was beginning to understand that Jacob Mendel was a living lexicon, something like the general catalogue of the British Museum Reading Room, but able to walk about on two legs. I stared dumbfounded at this bibliographical phenomenon, which masqueraded in the sordid and rather unclean appearance of a Galician second-hand book dealer, who, after rattling off some eighty titles (with assumed indifference, but really with the satisfaction of one who plays an unexpected trump), proceeded to wipe his spectacles with a handkerchief which might long before have been white.

Hoping to conceal my astonishment, I enquired:

"Which among these works do you think you could get for me without too much trouble?"

"Oh, I'll have a look round," he answered. "Come here tomorrow and I shall certainly have some of them. As for the others, it's only a question of time, and of knowing where to look."

"I'm greatly obliged to you," I said and, then, wishing to be civil, moved in haste, proposing to give him a list of the books I wanted. Schmidt nudged me warningly, but too late. Mendel had already flashed a look at me—such a look, at once triumphant and affronted, scornful and overwhelmingly superior—the royal look with which Macbeth answers Macduff when summoned to yield without a blow. He laughed curtly. His Adam's apple moved excitedly. Obviously he had gulped down a choleric, an insulting epithet.

Indeed he had good reason to be angry. Only a stranger, an ignoramus, could have proposed to give him, Jacob Mendel, a memorandum, as if he had been a bookseller's assistant or an underling in a public library. Not until I knew him better did I fully understand how much my would-be politeness must have galled this aberrant genius—for the man had, and knew himself to have, a titanic memory, wherein, behind a dirty and undistinguished-looking forehead, was indelibly recorded a picture of the title-page of every book that had been printed. No matter whether it had issued from the press yesterday or hundreds of years ago, he knew its place of publication, its author's name and its price. From his mind, as if from the printed page, he could read off the contents, could reproduce the illustrations, could visualise, not only what he had actually held in his hands, but also what he had glanced at in a bookseller's window, could see it with the same vividness as an artist sees the creations of fancy which he has not yet reproduced upon canvas. When a book was offered for six marks by a Regensburg dealer, he could remember that, two years before, a copy of the same work had changed hands for four crowns at a Viennese auction, and he recalled the name of the purchaser. In a word, Jacob Mendel never forgot a title or a figure; he knew every plant, every animal, every star, in the continually revolving and incessantly changing cosmos of the book universe. In each literary specialty, he knew more than the specialists; he knew the contents of the libraries better than the librarians: he knew the book lists of most publishers better than the heads of the firms concerned—though he had nothing to guide him except the magical powers of his inexplicable but invariably accurate memory.

True, this memory owed its infallibility to the man's limitations, to his extraordinary power of concentration. Apart from books, he knew nothing of the world. The phenomena of existence did not begin to become real for him until they had been set in type, arranged upon a composing stick, collected and, so to say, sterilised in a book. Nor did he read books for their meaning, to extract their spiritual or narrative substance.

What aroused his passionate interest, what fixed his attention, was the name, the price, the format, the title page. Though in the last analysis unproductive and uncreative, this specifically antiquarian memory of Jacob Mendel, since it was not a printed book catalogue but was stamped upon the grey matter of a mammalian brain, was, in its unique perfection, no less remarkable a phenomenon than Napoleon's gift for physiognomy, Mezzofanti's talent for languages, Lasker's skill at chess openings, Busoni's musical genius. Given a public position as teacher, this man with so marvellous a brain might have taught thousands and hundreds of thousands of students, have trained others to become men of great learning and of incalculable value to those communal treasure houses we call libraries. But to him, a man of no account, a Galician Jew, a book-dealer whose only training had been received in a Talmudic school, this upper world of culture was a fenced precinct he could never enter, and his amazing faculties could only find application at the marble-topped table in the inner room of the Café Gluck. When, some day, there arises a great psychologist who shall classify the types of that magical power we term memory, as effectively as Buffon classified the genus and species of animals, a man competent to give a detailed description of all the varieties, he will have to find a pigeon-hole for Jacob Mendel, forgotten master of the lore of book prices and book titles, the ambulatory catalogue alike of incunabula and the modern commonplace.

In the book trade and among ordinary persons, Jacob Mendel was regarded as nothing more than a second-hand book dealer in a small way of business. Sunday after Sunday, his stereotyped advertisement appeared in the *Neue Freie Presse* and the *Neues Wiener Tagblatt*. It ran as follows:

Best prices paid for old books, Mendel, Obere Alserstrasse.

A telephone number followed, really that of the Café Gluck. He rummaged every available corner for his wares, and once a week, with the aid of a bearded porter, conveyed fresh booty to his headquarters and got rid of old stock—for he had no proper bookshop. Thus he remained a petty trader, and his business was not lucrative. Students sold him their textbooks, which year by year passed through his hands from one generation to another, and for a small percentage on the price he would procure any additional book that was wanted. He charged little or nothing for advice. Money seemed to have no standing in his world. No one had ever seen him better dressed than in the threadbare black coat. For breakfast and supper he had a glass of milk and a couple of rolls, while at midday a modest meal was brought to him from a neighbouring restaurant. He did not smoke; he did not play cards; one might almost say he did not live, were it not that his eyes were alive behind his spectacles, and unceasingly fed his enigmatic brain with words, tides, names. The brain, like a fertile pasture, greedily sucked in this abundant irrigation. Human beings did not interest him, and of all human passions perhaps one only moved him, the most universal—vanity.

When someone, wearied by a futile hunt in countless other places, applied to him for information, and was instantly put on the track, his self-gratification was overwhelming, and it was unquestionably a delight to him that in Vienna and elsewhere there existed a few dozen persons who respected him for his knowledge and valued him for the services he could render. In every one of these large conurbations we call towns, there are here and there facets which reflect one and the same universe in miniature—unseen by most, but highly prized by connoisseurs, by brethren of the same craft, by devotees of the same passion. The fans of the book market knew Jacob Mendel. Just as anyone encountering a difficulty in deciphering a score would apply to Eusebius Mandyczewski of the Musical Society, who would be found wearing a grey skullcap and seated among multifarious musical manuscripts, ready, with a friendly smile, to solve the most obstinate problem; and just as, today, anyone in search of information about the Viennese theatrical and cultural life of earlier times will unhesitatingly look up the scholar Father Glossy, so, with equal confidence did the bibliophiles of Vienna, when they had a particularly hard nut to crack, make a pilgrimage to the Café Gluck and lay their difficulty before Jacob Mendel.

To me, young and eager for new experiences, it became enthralling to watch such a consultation. Whereas ordinarily, when a would-be seller brought him some ordinary book, he would contemptuously clap the cover to and mutter, "Two crowns", if shown a rare or unique volume, he would sit up and take notice, lay the treasure upon a clean sheet of paper, and, on one such occasion, he was obviously ashamed of his dirty, ink-stained fingers and filthy fingernails. Tenderly, cautiously, respectfully, he would turn the pages of the treasure. One would have been as loath to disturb him at such a moment as to break in upon the devotions of a man at prayer, and in very truth there was a flavour of solemn ritual and religious observance about the way in which contemplation, palpation, smelling and weighing in the hand followed one another in orderly succession. His rounded back waggled while he was thus engaged, he muttered to himself, exclaimed "Ah" now and again to express wonder or admiration, or "Oh, dear" when a page was missing or another had been mutilated by the larva of a book beetle. His weighing of the tome in his hand was as circumspect as if books were sold by the ounce, and his sniffing at it as sentimental as a girl's smelling of a rose. Of course it would have been the height of bad form for the owner to show impatience during this ritual of examination.

When it was over, he willingly, nay enthusiastically, tendered all the information at his disposal, not forgetting relevant anecdotes, and dramatised accounts of the prices which other specimens of the same work had fetched at auctions or in sales by private treaty. He looked brighter, younger, more lively at such times, and only one thing could put him seriously out of humour. This was when a novice offered him money for his expert opinion. Then he would draw back with an affronted air, looking for all the world like the skilled custodian of a museum gallery to whom an American traveller has offered a tip—for to Jacob Mendel contact with a rare book was something sacred, as is contact to a young man with a woman who has not had the bloom rubbed off. Such moments were his platonic love affairs. Books exerted a spell on him, never money. Vainly, therefore, did great collectors (among them one of the notables of Princeton University) try to recruit Mendel as librarian or book-buyer. The offer was declined with thanks. He could not forsake his familiar headquarters at the Café Gluck. Thirty-three years before, an awkward youngster with black down sprouting on his chin and black ringlets hanging over his temples, he had come from Galicia to Vienna, intending to adopt the calling of rabbi, but before long he forsook the worship of the harsh and jealous Jehovah to devote himself to the more lively and polytheistic cult of books. Then he happened upon the Café Gluck, by degrees making it his workshop, headquarters, post office—his world. Just as an astronomer, alone in an observatory, watches night after night through a telescope the myriads of stars, their mysterious movements, their changeful medley, their extinction and their flaming-up anew, so did Jacob Mendel, seated at his table in the Café Gluck, look through his spectacles into the universe of books, a universe that lies above the world of our everyday life, and, like the stellar universe, is full of changing cycles.

It need hardly be said that he was highly esteemed in the Café Gluck, whose fame seemed to us to depend far more upon his unofficial professorship than upon the godfathership of the famous musician, Christoph Willibald Gluck, composer of *Alceste* and *Iphigenie*. He belonged to the outfit quite as much as did the old cherry-wood counter, the two billiard tables with their cloth stitched in many places, and the copper coffee urn. His table was guarded as a sanctuary. His numerous clients and customers were expected to take a drink 'for the good of the house', so that most of the profit of his far-flung knowledge

flowed into the big leather pouch slung round the waist of
Deubler, the waiter. In return for being a centre of attraction,
Mendel enjoyed many privileges. The telephone was at his
service for nothing. He could have his letters directed to the
café, and his parcels were taken in there. The excellent old
woman who looked after the toilet brushed his coat, sewed
on buttons and carried a small bundle of underlinen every
week to the wash. He was the only guest who could have a
meal sent in from the restaurant, and every morning Herr
Standhartner, the proprietor of the café, made a point of
coming to his table and saying "Good morning!"—though
Jacob Mendel, immersed in his books, seldom noticed the
greeting. Punctually at half-past seven he arrived, and did
not leave till the lights were extinguished. He never spoke to
the other guests, never read a newspaper, noticed no changes,
and once, when Herr Standhartner civilly asked him whether
he did not find the electric light more agreeable to read by
than the malodorous and uncertain kerosene lamps they had
replaced, he stared in astonishment at the new incandescents.
Although the installation had necessitated several days'
hammering and bustle, the introduction of the glow-lamps
had escaped his notice. Only through the two round apertures
of the spectacles, only through these two shining lenses, did
the thousands of black infusorians which were the letters filter
into his brain. Whatever else happened in his vicinity was
disregarded as unmeaning noise. He had spent more than
thirty years of his waking life at this table, reading, comparing,
calculating, in a continuous waking dream, interrupted only
by intervals of sleep.

A sense of horror overcame me when, looking into the inner
room behind the bar of the Café Gluck, I saw that the marble
top of the table where Jacob Mendel used to deliver his
oracles was now as bare as a tombstone. Grown older since
those days, I understood how much disappears when such a

man drops out of his place in the world, were it only because, amid the daily increase in hopeless monotony, the unique grows continually more precious. Besides, in my callow youth a profound intuition had made me exceedingly fond of Buchmendel. It was through the observation of him that I had first become aware of the enigmatic fact that supreme achievement and outstanding capacity are only rendered possible by mental concentration, by a sublime monomania that verges on lunacy. Through the living example of this obscure genius of a second-hand book dealer, far more than through the flashes of insight in the works of our poets and other imaginative writers, had been made plain to me the persistent possibility of a pure life of the spirit, of complete absorption in an idea, an ecstasy as absolute as that of an Indian yogi or a medieval monk, and I had learnt that this was possible in an electric-lit café and adjoining a telephone box. Yet I had forgotten him, during the war years and through a kindred immersion in my own work. The sight of the empty table made me ashamed of myself, and at the same time curious about the man who used to sit there.

What had become of him? I called the waiter and enquired. "No, Sir," he answered, "I'm sorry, but I never heard of Herr Mendel. There is no one of that name among the frequenters of the Café Gluck. Perhaps the head waiter will know."

"Herr Mendel?" said the head waiter dubiously, after a moment's reflection. "No, Sir, never heard of him. Unless you mean Herr Mendl, who has a hardware store in the Florianigasse?"

I had a bitter taste in the mouth, the taste of an irrecoverable past. What is the use of living, when the wind obliterates our footsteps in the sand directly we have gone by? Thirty years, perhaps forty, a man had breathed, read, thought and spoken within this narrow room; three or four years had elapsed, and there had arisen a new king over Egypt, which knew not

Joseph. No one in the Café Gluck had ever heard of Jacob Mendel, of Buchmendel. Somewhat pettishly I asked the head waiter whether I could have a word with Herr Standhartner, or with one of the old staff.

"Herr Standhartner, who used to own the place? He sold it years ago, and has died since. The former head waiter? He saved up enough to retire, and lives upon a little property at Krems. No, Sir, all of the old lot are scattered. All except one, indeed, Frau Sporschil, who looks after the toilet. She's been here for ages, worked under the late owner, I know. But she's not likely to remember your Herr Mendel. People like her hardly know one guest from another."

I dissented in thought:

"One does not forget a Jacob Mendel so easily!" What I said was:

"Still, I should like to have a word with Frau Sporschil, if she has a moment to spare."

The *Toilettenfrau* (known in the Viennese vernacular as the *Schocoladefrau)* soon emerged from the basement, white-haired, run-to-seed, heavy-footed, wiping her chapped hands upon a towel as she came. She had been called away from her task of cleaning up, and was obviously uneasy at being summoned into the strong light of the guest rooms, for common folk in Vienna, where an authoritarian tradition has lingered on after the revolution, always think it must be a police matter where their 'superiors' want to question them. She eyed me suspiciously, though humbly. But as soon as I asked her about Jacob Mendel, she relaxed, and at the same time her eyes filled with tears.

"Poor Herr Mendel ... so there's still someone who bears him in mind?"

Old people are commonly much moved by anything which recalls the days of their youth and revives the memory of past companionships. I asked if he was still alive.

"Good Lord, no. Poor Herr Mendel must have died five or six years ago. Indeed, I think it's fully seven since he passed away. Dear, good man that he was; and how long I knew him, more than twenty-five years; he was already sitting every day at his table when I began to work here. It was a shame, it was, the way they let him die."

Growing more and more excited, she asked if I was a relative. No one had ever enquired about him before. Didn't I know what had happened to him?

"No," I replied, "and I want you to be good enough to tell me all about it."

She looked at me timidly, and continued to wipe her damp hands. It was plain to me that she found it embarrassing, with her dirty apron and her tousled white hair, to be standing in the full glare of the café. She kept looking round anxiously, to see if one of the waiters might be listening.

"Let's go into the card room," I said, "Mendel's old room. You shall tell me your story there."

She nodded appreciatively, thankful that I understood, and led the way to the inner room, a little shambling in her gait. As I followed, I noticed that the waiters and the guests were staring at us as a strangely assorted pair. We sat down opposite one another at the marble-topped table, and there she told me the story of Jacob Mendel's ruin and death. I will give the tale as nearly as possible in her own words, supplemented here and there by what I learnt afterwards from other sources.

"Down to the outbreak of war, and after the war had begun, he continued to come here every morning at half-past seven, to sit at this table and study all day just as before. We had the feeling that the fact of a war going on had never entered his mind. Certainly he didn't read the newspapers, and didn't talk to anyone except about books. He paid no attention when (in the early days of the war, before the authorities put a stop to such things) the newspaper-vendors ran through the streets shouting, "*Great Battle on the Eastern Front*," (or wherever it might be), "*Horrible Slaughter*," and so on; when people gathered in knots to talk things over, he kept himself to himself; he did not know that Fritz, the billiard-marker, who fell in one of the first battles, had vanished from this place; he did not know that Herr Standhartner's son had been taken prisoner by the Russians at Przemysl; never said a word when the bread grew more and more uneatable and when he was given bean coffee to drink at breakfast and supper instead of hot milk. Once only did he express surprise at the changes, wondering why so few students came to the café. There was nothing in the world that mattered to him except his books.

"Then disaster befell him. At eleven one morning, two police-men came, one in uniform, and the other a plain-clothes man. The latter showed the red rosette under the lapel of his coat and asked whether there was a man named Jacob Mendel in the house. They went straight to Herr Mendel's table. The poor man, in his innocence, supposed they had books to sell, or wanted some information, but they told him he was under arrest, and took him away at once. It was a scandal for the café. All the guests flocked round Herr Mendel, as he stood between the two police officers, his spectacles pushed up under his hair, staring from each to the other, bewildered. Some ventured a protest, saying there must be a mistake—that Herr Mendel was a man who would not hurt a fly, but the detective was furious, and told them to mind their own business. They took him away, and none of us at the Café Gluck saw him again for two years. I never found out what they had against him, but I would take my dying oath that they must have made a mistake. Herr Mendel could never have done anything wrong. It was a crime to treat an innocent man so harshly."

The excellent Frau Sporschil was right. Our friend Jacob Mendel had done nothing wrong. He had merely (as I subsequently learnt) done something incredibly stupid, only explicable to those who knew the man's peculiarities. The military censorship board, whose function it was to supervise correspondence passing into and out of neutral lands, one day got its hands upon a postcard written and signed by a certain Jacob Mendel, properly stamped for transmission abroad.

This postcard was addressed to Monsieur Jean Labourdaire, Libraire, Quai de Grenelle, Paris—to an enemy country, therefore. The writer complained that the last eight issues of the monthly *Bulletin bibliographique de la France* had failed to reach him, although his annual subscription had been duly paid in advance. The pedantic official who read this missive (a high-school teacher with a bent for the study of the Romance languages, called up for war service and sent to employ his talents at the censorship board instead of wasting them in the trenches) was astonished by its tenor. "Must be a joke," he thought. He had to examine some two thousand letters and postcards every week, always on the alert to detect anything that might savour of espionage, but never yet had he chanced upon anything so absurd as that an Austrian subject should unconcernedly drop into one of the imperial and royal letter boxes a postcard addressed to someone in an enemy land, regardless of the trifling detail that since August 1914 the Central Powers had been cut off from Russia on one side and from France on the other by barbed-wire entanglements and a network of ditches in which men armed with rifles and bayonets, machine guns and artillery, were doing their utmost to exterminate one another like rats. Our schoolmaster enrolled in the *Landsturm* did not treat this first postcard seriously, but pigeon-holed it as a curiosity not worth talking about to his chief. But a few weeks later there turned up another card, again from Jacob Mendel, this time to John Aldridge, Bookseller, Golden Square, London, asking whether the addressee could send the last few numbers of the *Antiquarian* to an address in Vienna which was clearly stated on the card.

The censor in the blue uniform began to feel uneasy. Was his correspondent trying to trick the schoolmaster? Were the cards written in cipher? Possible, anyhow; so the subordinate went over to the major's desk, clicked his heels together, saluted and laid the suspicious documents before the 'properly constituted authority'. A strange business, certainly. The police were instructed by telephone to see if there actually was a Jacob Mendel at the specified address, and, if so, to bring the fellow along. Within the hour, Mendel had been arrested, and (still stupefied by the shock) brought before the major, who showed him the postcards and asked him with drill-sergeant roughness whether he acknowledged their authorship. Angered at being spoken to so sharply, and still more annoyed because his perusal of an important catalogue had been interrupted, Mendel answered tardily:

"Of course I wrote the cards. That's my handwriting and signature. Surely one has a right to claim the delivery of a periodical to which one has subscribed?"

The major swung half-round in his swivel chair and exchanged a meaning glance with the lieutenant seated at the adjoining desk.

"The man must be a double-distilled idiot", was what they mutely conveyed to one another.

Then the chief took counsel within himself whether he should discharge the offender with a caution, or whether he should treat the case more seriously. In all offices, when such doubts arise, the usual practice is not to spin a coin, but to send in a report. Thus Pilate washes his hands of responsibility. Even if the report does no good, it can do no harm, and is merely one useless manuscript or typescript added to a million others.

In this instance, however, the decision to send in a report did much harm, alas, to an inoffensive man of genius, for it involved asking a series of questions, and the third of them brought suspicious circumstances to light.

"Your full name?"

"Jacob Mendel."

"Occupation?"

"Book-pedlar."(For, as already explained, Mendel had no shop, but only a pedlar's licence.)

"Place of birth?" Now came the disaster. Mendel's birthplace was not far from Petrikau. The major raised his eyebrows. Petrikau, or Piotrkov, was across the frontier in Russian Poland.

"You were born a Russian subject. When did you acquire Austrian nationality? Show me your papers."

Mendel gazed at the officer uncomprehendingly through his spectacles.

"Papers? Identification papers? I have nothing but my pedlar's licence."

"What's your nationality, then? Was your father Austrian or Russian?"

Undismayed, Mendel answered:

"A Russian, of course."

"What about yourself?"

"Wishing to evade Russian military service, I slipped across the frontier thirty-three years ago, and ever since I have lived in Vienna."

The matter seemed to the major to be growing worse and worse.

"But didn't you take steps to become an Austrian subject?"

"Why should I?" countered Mendel. "I never troubled my head about such things."

"Then you are still a Russian subject?"

Mendel, who was bored by this endless questioning, answered simply:

"Yes, I suppose I am."

The startled and indignant major threw himself back in his chair with such violence that the wood cracked protestingly.

So this was what it had come to! In Vienna, the Austrian capital, at the end of 1915, after Tarnow, when the war was in full blast, after the great offensive, a Russian could walk about unmolested, could write letters to France and England, while the police ignored his machinations. And then the fools who wrote in the newspapers wondered why Conrad von Hötzendorf had not advanced in seven-league boots to Warsaw, and the general staff was puzzled because every movement of the troops was immediately blabbed to the Russians.

The lieutenant had sprung to his feet and crossed the room to his chief's table. What had been an almost friendly conversation took a new turn, and degenerated into a trial.

"Why didn't you report as an enemy alien directly the war began?"

Mendel, still failing to realise the gravity of his position, answered in his singing Jewish jargon:

"Why should I report? I don't understand."

The major regarded this enquiry as a challenge, and asked threateningly:

"Didn't you read the notices that were posted up everywhere?"

"No."

"Didn't you read the newspapers?"

"No."

The two officers stared at Jacob Mendel (now sweating with uneasiness) as if the moon had fallen from the sky into their office. Then the telephone buzzed, the typewriters clacked, orderlies ran hither and thither, and Mendel was sent under guard to the nearest barracks, where he was to await transfer to a concentration camp. When he was ordered to follow the two soldiers, he was frankly puzzled, but not seriously perturbed. What could the man with the gold-lace collar and the rough voice have against him? In the upper world of books, where Mendel lived and breathed and had his being, there was no warfare, there were no misunderstandings, only an ever-increasing knowledge of words and figures, of book titles and authors' names. He walked good-humouredly enough downstairs between the soldiers, whose first charge was to take him to the police station. Not until he was there, when the books were taken out of his overcoat pockets, and the police impounded the portfolio containing a hundred important memoranda and customers' addresses, did he lose his temper, and begin to resist and strike blows. They had to tie his hands. In the struggle, his spectacles fell off, and these magical telescopes, without which he could not see into the wonder world of books, were smashed into a thousand pieces. Two days later, insufficiently clad (for his only wrap was a light summer cloak) he was sent to the internment camp for Russian civilians at Komorn.

I have no information as to what Jacob Mendel suffered during these two years of internment, cut off from his beloved books, penniless, among roughly nurtured men, few of whom could read or write, in a huge human dunghill. This must be left to the imagination of those who can grasp the torments of a caged eagle. By degrees, however, our world, grown sober after its fit of drunkenness, has become aware that, of all the cruelties and wanton abuses of power during the war, the most needless and therefore the most inexcusable was this herding together behind barbed-wire fences of thousands upon thousands of persons who had outgrown the age of military service, who had made homes for themselves in a foreign land, and who (believing in the good faith of their hosts) had refrained from exercising the sacred right of hospitality granted even by the Tunguses and Araucanians—the right to flee while time permits. This crime against civilisation was committed with the same unthinking harshness in France, Germany and Britain, in every belligerent country of our crazy Europe.

Probably Jacob Mendel would, like thousands as innocent as he, have perished in this cattle-pen, have gone stark mad; have succumbed to dysentery, asthenia, softening of the brain, had it not been that, before the worst happened, a chance (typically Austrian) recalled him to the world in which a spiritual life became again possible. Several times after his disappearance, letters from distinguished customers were delivered for him at the Café Gluck. Count Schonberg, sometime lord-lieutenant of Styria, an enthusiastic collector of works on heraldry; Siegenfeld, the former dean of the theological faculty, who was writing a commentary on the works of St Augustine; Edler von Pisek, an octogenarian admiral on the retired list, engaged in writing his memoirs—these and other persons of note, wanting information from Buchmendel, had repeatedly addressed communications to him at his familiar haunt, and some of these were duly forwarded to the concentration camp at Komorn. There they fell into the hands of the commanding officer, who happened to be a man of humane disposition, and who was astonished to find what notables were among the correspondents of this 'dirty little Russian Jew', who, half-blind now that his spectacles were broken and with no money to buy new ones, crouched in a corner like a mole, grey, eyeless, and dumb. A man who had such patrons must be a person of importance, whatever he looked like. The CO therefore read the letters to the shortsighted Mendel, and penned answers for him to sign—answers which were mainly requests that influence should be exercised on his behalf. The spell worked, for these correspondents had the solidarity of collectors. Joining forces and pulling strings they were able (giving guarantees for the 'enemy alien's' good behaviour) to secure leave for Buchmendel's return to Vienna in 1917, after more than two years at Komorn—on the condition that he should report daily to the police. The proviso mattered little. He was a free man once more, free to take up his quarters in his old attic, free to handle books again, free (above all) to return to his table in the Café Gluck. I can best describe the return from the underworld of the camp in the good Frau Sporschil's own words:

"One day—Jesus, Mary, Joseph; I could hardly believe my eyes—the door opened little wider than a crack, and through this opening he sidled, poor Herr Mendel. He was wearing a tattered and much-darned military cloak, and his head was covered by what had perhaps once been a hat thrown away by the owner as past use. No collar. His face looked like a death's head, so haggard it was, and his hair was pitifully thin. But he came in as if nothing had happened, went straight to his table and took off his cloak, not briskly as of old, for he panted with the exertion. Nor had he any books with him. He just sat there without a word, staring straight in front of him with hollow, expressionless eyes. Only by degrees, after we had brought him the big bundle of printed matter which had arrived for him from Germany, did he begin to read again. But he was never the same man."

No, he was never the same man, not now the *miraculum mundi*, the magical walking book catalogue. All who saw him in those days told me the same pitiful story. Something had gone irrecoverably wrong; he was broken; the blood-red comet of the war had burst into the remote, calm atmosphere of his bookish world. His eyes, accustomed for decades to look at nothing but print, must have seen terrible sights in the wire-fenced human stockyard, for the eyes that had formerly been so alert and full of ironical gleams were now almost completely veiled by the inert lids, and looked sleepy and red-bordered behind the carefully repaired spectacle frames. Worse still, a cog must have broken somewhere in the marvellous machinery of his memory, so that the working of the whole was impaired; for so delicate is the structure of the brain (a sort of switchboard made of the most fragile substances, and as easily jarred as are all instruments of precision) that a blocked arteriole, a congested bundle of nerve fibres, a fatigued group of cells, even a displaced molecule, may put the apparatus out of gear and make harmonious working impossible. In Mendel's memory, the keyboard of knowledge, the keys were stiff, or—to use psychological terminology—the associations were impaired. When, now and again, someone came to ask for information, Jacob stared blankly at the enquirer, failing to understand the question, and even forgetting it before he had found the answer. Mendel was no longer Buchmendel, just as the world was no longer the world. He could not now become wholly absorbed in his reading, did not rock as of old when he read, but sat bolt upright, his glasses turned mechanically towards the printed page, but perhaps not reading at all, and only sunk in a reverie. Often, said Frau Sporschil, his head would drop on to his book and he would fall asleep in the daytime, or he would gaze hour after hour at the stinking acetylene lamp which (in the days of the coal famine) had replaced the electric lighting. No, Mendel was no longer Buchmendel, no longer the eighth wonder of the world, but a weary, worn-out, though still-breathing, useless bundle of beard and ragged garments, who sat, as futile as a potato, where of old the Pythian oracle had sat; no longer the glory of the Café Gluck, but a shameful scarecrow, evil-smelling, a parasite.

That was the impression he produced upon the new proprietor, Horian Gurtner from Retz, who, a successful profiteer in flour and butter, had cajoled Standhartner into selling him the Café Gluck for eighty thousand rapidly depreciating paper crowns. He took everything into his hard peasant grip, hastily arranged to have the old place redecorated, bought fine-looking satin-covered seats, installed a marble porch, and was in negotiation with his next-door neighbour to buy a place where he could extend the café into a dance hall. Naturally while he was making these embellishments, he was not best pleased by the parasitic encumbrance of Jacob Mendel, a filthy old Galician Jew, who had been in trouble with the authorities during the war, who was still to be regarded as an 'enemy alien', and, while occupying a table from morning till night, consumed no more than two cups of coffee and four or five rolls. Standhartner, indeed, had put in a word for this guest of long standing, had explained that Mendel was a person of note, and, in the stock-taking, had handed him over as having a permanent lien upon the establishment, but as an asset rather than a liability. Horian Gurtner, however, had brought into the café not only new furniture and an up-to-date cash register, but also the profit-making and hard temper of the post-war era, and awaited the first pretext for ejecting from his smart coffee house the last troublesome vestige of suburban shabbiness.

A good excuse was not slow to present itself. Jacob Mendel was impoverished to the last degree. Such banknotes as had been left to him had crumbled away to nothing during the inflation period; his regular clientele had been killed, ruined, or dispersed. When he tried to resume his early trade of book-dealer, calling from door to door to buy and to sell, he found that he lacked the strength to carry books up and down stairs. A hundred little signs showed him to be a pauper. Seldom, now, did he have a midday meal sent in from the restaurant, and he began to run up a score at the Café Gluck for his modest breakfast and supper. Once his payments were as much as three weeks overdue. Were it only for this reason, the head waiter wanted Gurtner to "give Mendel the sack". But Frau Sporschil intervened, and stood surety for the debtor. What was due could be stopped out of her wages! This staved off disaster for a while, but worse was to come. For some time the head waiter had noticed that rolls were disappearing faster than the tally would account for. Naturally suspicion fell upon Mendel, who was known to be six months in debt to the tottering old porter whose services he still needed. The head waiter, hidden behind the stove, was able, two days later to catch Mendel red-handed. The unwelcome guest had stolen from his seat in the card-room, crept behind the counter in the front room, taken two rolls from the bread basket, returned to the card-room, and hungrily devoured them. When settling up at the end of the day, he said he had only had coffee—no rolls. The source of wastage had been traced, and the waiter reported his discovery to the proprietor. Herr Gurtner, delighted to have so good an excuse for getting rid of Mendel, made a scene, openly accused him of theft, and declared that nothing but the goodness of his own heart prevented his sending for the police.

"But after this," said Florian, "you'll kindly take yourself off for good and all. We don't want to see your face again at the Café Gluck."

Jacob Mendel trembled, but made no reply. Abandoning his poor belongings, he departed without a word.

"It was ghastly," said Frau Sporschil. "Never shall I forget the sight. He stood up, his spectacles pushed on to his forehead, and his face white as a sheet. He did not even stop to put on his cloak although it was January, and very cold. You'll remember that severe winter, just after the war. In his fright, he left the book he was reading open upon the table. I did not notice it at first, and then, when I wanted to pick it up and take it after him, he had already stumbled out through the doorway. I was afraid to follow him into the street, for Herr Gurtner was standing at the door and shouting at him, so that a crowd had gathered. Yet I felt ashamed to the depths of my soul. Such a thing would never have happened under the old master. Herr Standhartner would not have driven Herr Mendel away for pinching one or two rolls when he was hungry, but would have let him have as many as he wanted for nothing, to the end of his days. Since the war, people seem to have grown heartless. Drive away a man who had been a guest daily for so many, many years. Shameful! I should not like to have to answer before God for such cruelty!"

The good woman had grown excited and, with the passionate garrulousness of old age, she kept on repeating how shameful it was, and that nothing of the sort would have happened if Herr Standhartner had not sold the business. In the end I tried to stop the flow by asking her what had happened to Mendel, and whether she had ever seen him again. These questions excited her yet more.

"Day after day, when I passed his table, it gave me the creeps, as you will easily understand. Each time I thought to myself: 'Where can he have got to, poor Herr Mendel?' Had I known where he lived, I would have called and taken him something nice and hot to eat—for where could he get the money to cook food and warm his room? As far as I knew, he had no family in the whole world. When, after a long time, I had heard nothing about him, I began to believe that it must be all up with him, and that I should never see him again. I had made up my mind to have a mass said for the peace of his soul, knowing him to be a good man, after twenty-five years' acquaintance.

"At length one day in February, at half-past seven in the morning, when I was cleaning the windows, the door opened, and in came Herr Mendel. Generally, as you know, he sidled in, looking confused, and not quite all there, but this time, somehow, it was different. I noticed at once the strange look in his eyes; they were sparkling, and he rolled them this way and that, as if to see everything at once; as for his appearance, he seemed nothing but beard and skin and bone. Instantly it crossed my mind: 'He's forgotten all that happened last time he was here; it's his way to go about like a sleepwalker noticing nothing; he doesn't remember about the rolls, and how shamefully Herr Gurtner ordered him out of the place, half in mind to set the police on him.' Thank goodness, Herr Gurtner hadn't come yet, and the head waiter was drinking coffee. I ran up to Herr Mendel, meaning to tell him he'd better make himself scarce, for otherwise that ruffian"—she looked round timidly to see if

184

we were overheard, and hastily amended her phrase—"Herr Gurtner, I mean, would only have him thrown into the street once more. 'Herr Mendel,' I began. He started, and looked at me. In that very moment (it was dreadful), he must have remembered the whole thing, for he almost collapsed, and began to tremble, not his fingers only, but to shiver and shake from head to foot. Hastily he stepped back into the street, and fell in a heap on the pavement as soon as he was outside the door. We telephoned for the ambulance and they carried him off to hospital, the nurse who came saying he had a high fever directly she touched him. He died that evening. 'Double pneumonia,' the doctor said, and that he never recovered consciousness—could not have been fully conscious when he came to the Café Gluck. As I said, he had entered like a man walking in his sleep. The table where he had sat day after day for thirty-six years drew him back to it like a home."

Frau Sporschil and I went on talking about him for a long time, the two last persons to remember this strange creature, Buchmendel: I to whom in my youth the book-dealer from Galicia had given the first revelation of a life wholly devoted to the things of the spirit; she, the poor old woman who was caretaker of a café toilet, who had never read a book in her life, and whose only tie with this strangely matched comrade in her subordinate, poverty-stricken world had been that for twenty-five years she had brushed his overcoat and had sewn on buttons for him. We too might have been considered strangely assorted, but Frau Sporschil and I got on very well together, linked, as we sat at the forsaken marble-topped table, by our common memories that our talk had conjured up— for joint memories, and above all loving memories, always establish a tie. Suddenly, while in the full stream of talk, she exclaimed:

"Lord Jesus, how forgetful I am. I still have the book he left on the table the evening Herr Gurtner gave him the key of the street. I didn't know where to take it. Afterwards, when no one appeared to claim it, I ventured to keep it as a souvenir. You don't think it wrong of me, Sir?"

She went to a locker where she stored some of the requisites for her job, and produced the volume for my inspection. I found it hard to repress a smile, for I was face to face with one of life's little ironies. It was the second volume of Hayn's *Bibliotheca Germanorum erotica et curiosa*, a compendium of gallant literature known to every book-collector. *Habent sua fata libelli*—Books have their own destiny! This scabrous publication, a legacy of the vanished magician, had fallen into toilworn hands which had perhaps never held any other printed work than a prayer book. Maybe I was not wholly successful in controlling my mirth, for the expression of my face seemed to perplex the worthy soul, and once more she said:

"You don't think it wrong of me to keep it, Sir?"

I shook her cordially by the hand.

"Keep it, and welcome," I said. "I am absolutely sure that our old friend Mendel would be only too delighted to know that someone among the many thousands he has provided with books cherishes his memory."

Then I took my departure, feeling a trifle ashamed when I compared myself with this excellent old woman, who, so simply and so humanely, had fostered the memory of the dead scholar. For she, uncultured though she was, had at least preserved a book as a memento; whereas I, a man of education and a writer, had completely forgotten Buchmendel for years—I, who at least should have known that one only makes books in order to keep in touch with one's fellows after one has ceased to breathe, and thus to defend oneself against the inexorable fate of all that lives—transitoriness and oblivion.

TWENTY-FOUR HOURS IN THE LIFE OF A WOMAN

Translated from the German by Anthea Bell

IN THE LITTLE GUEST HOUSE on the Riviera where I was staying at the time, ten years before the war, a heated discussion had broken out at our table and unexpectedly threatened to degenerate into frenzied argument, even rancour and recrimination. Most people have little imagination. If something doesn't affect them directly, does not drive a sharp wedge straight into their minds, it hardly excites them at all, but if an incident, however slight, takes place before their eyes, close enough for the senses to perceive it, it instantly rouses them to extremes of passion. They compensate for the infrequency of their sympathy, as it were, by exhibiting disproportionate and excessive vehemence.

Such was the case that day among our thoroughly bourgeois company at table, where on the whole we just made equable small talk and cracked mild little jokes, usually parting as soon as the meal was over: the German husband and wife to go on excursions and take snapshots, the portly Dane to set out on tedious fishing expeditions, the distinguished English lady to return to her books, the Italian married couple to indulge in escapades to Monte Carlo, and I to lounge in a garden chair or get some work done. This time, however, our irate discussion left us all still very much at odds, and if someone suddenly rose it was not, as usual, to take civil leave of the rest of us, but in a mood of heated irascibility that, as I have said, was assuming positively frenzied form.

The incident obsessing our little party, admittedly, was odd enough. From outside, the guest house where the seven of us were staying might have been an isolated villa—with a wonderful view of the rock-strewn beach from its windows—but in fact it was only the cheaper annexe of the Grand Palace Hotel to which it was directly linked by the garden, so that we in the guest house were in constant touch with the hotel guests.

And that same hotel had been the scene of an outright scandal the day before, when a young Frenchman had arrived by the midday train, at twenty-past twelve (I can't avoid giving the time so precisely because it was of importance to the incident itself, and indeed to the subject of our agitated conversation), and took a room with a view of the sea, opening straight on to the beach, which in itself indicated that he was in reasonably easy circumstances. Not only his discreet elegance but, most of all, his extraordinary and very appealing good looks made an attractive impression. A silky blond moustache surrounded sensuously warm lips in a slender, girlish face; soft, wavy brown hair curled over his pale forehead; every glance of his melting eyes was a caress—indeed everything about him was soft, endearing, charming, but without any artifice or affectation. At a distance he might at first remind you slightly of those pink wax dummies to be seen adopting dandified poses in the window displays of large fashion stores, walking-stick in hand and representing the ideal of male beauty, but closer inspection dispelled any impression of foppishness, for—most unusually— his charm was natural and innate, and seemed an inseparable part of him. He greeted everyone individually in passing, in a manner as warm as it was modest, and it was a pleasure to see his unfailingly graceful demeanour unaffectedly brought into play on every occasion. When a lady was going to the cloakroom he made haste to fetch her coat, he had a friendly glance or joke for every child, he was both affable and discreet—in short, he seemed to be one of those happy souls who, secure in the knowledge that their bright faces and youthful attractions are pleasing to others, transmute that security anew into yet more charm. His presence worked wonders among the hotel guests, most of whom were elderly and sickly, and he irresistibly won everyone's liking with the victorious bearing of youth, that flush of ease and liveliness with which charm so delightfully endows some human beings. Only a couple of hours

192

after his arrival he was playing tennis with the two daughters of the stout, thick-set manufacturer from Lyon—twelve-year-old Annette and thirteen-year-old Blanche—and their mother, the refined, delicate and reserved Madame Henriette, smiled slightly to see her inexperienced daughters unconsciously flirting with the young stranger. That evening he watched for an hour as we played chess, telling a few amusing anecdotes now and then in an unobtrusive style, strolled along the terrace again with Madame Henriette while her husband played dominoes with a business friend as usual; and late in the evening I saw him in suspiciously intimate conversation with the hotel secretary in the dim light of her office. Next morning he went fishing with my Danish chess partner, showing a remarkable knowledge of angling, and then held a long conversation about politics with the Lyon manufacturer in which he also proved himself an entertaining companion, for the stout Frenchman's hearty laughter could be heard above the sound of the breaking waves. After lunch he spent an hour alone with Madame Henriette in the garden again, drinking black coffee, played another game of tennis with her daughters and chatted in the lobby to the German couple. At six o'clock I met him at the railway station when I went to post a letter. He strode quickly towards me and said, as if apologetically, that he had been suddenly called away but would be back in two days' time. Sure enough, he was absent from the dining room that evening, but only in person, for he was the sole subject of conversation at every table, and all the guests praised his delightful, cheerful nature.

That night, I suppose at about eleven o'clock, I was sitting in my room finishing a book when I suddenly heard agitated shouts and cries from the garden coming in through my open window. Something was obviously going on over at the hotel. Feeling concerned rather than curious, I immediately hurried across—it was some fifty paces—and found the guests and staff milling around in great excitement. Madame Henriette, whose husband had been playing dominoes with his friend from Namur as usual, had not come back from her evening walk on the terrace by the beach, and it was feared that she had suffered an accident. The normally ponderous, slow-moving manufacturer kept charging down to the beach like a bull, and when he called: "Henriette! Henriette!" into the night, his voice breaking with fear, the sound conveyed something of the terror and the primeval nature of a gigantic animal wounded to death. The waiters and pageboys ran up and down the stairs in agitation, all the guests were woken and the police were called. The fat man, however, trampled and stumbled his way through all this, waistcoat unbuttoned, sobbing and shrieking as he pointlessly shouted the name "Henriette! Henriette!" into the darkness. By now the children were awake upstairs, and stood at the window in their night dresses, calling down for their mother. Their father hurried upstairs again to comfort them.

And then something so terrible happened that it almost defies retelling, for a violent strain on human nature, at moments of extremity, can often give such tragic expression to a man's bearing that no images or words can reproduce it with the same lightning force. Suddenly the big, heavy man came down the creaking stairs with a changed look on his face, very weary and yet grim. He had a letter in his hand. "Call them all back!" he told the hotel major-domo, in a barely audible voice. "Call everyone in again. There's no need. My wife has left me."

Mortally wounded as he was, the man showed composure, a tense, superhuman composure as he faced all the people standing around, looking at him curiously as they pressed close and then suddenly turned away again, each of them feeling alarmed, ashamed and confused. He had just enough strength left to make his way unsteadily past us, looking at no one, and switch off the light in the reading room. We heard the sound of his ponderous, massive body dropping heavily into an armchair, and then a wild, animal sobbing, the weeping of a man who has never wept before. That elemental pain had a kind of paralysing power over every one of us, even the least of those present. None of the waiters, none of the guests who had joined the throng out of curiosity, ventured either a smile or a word of condolence. Silently, one by one, as if put to shame by so shattering an emotional outburst, we crept back to our rooms, while that stricken specimen of mankind shook and sobbed alone with himself in the dark as the building slowly laid itself to rest, whispering, muttering, murmuring and sighing.

You will understand that such an event, striking like lightning before our very eyes and our perceptions, was likely to cause considerable turmoil in persons usually accustomed to an easygoing existence and carefree pastimes. But while this extraordinary incident was certainly the point of departure for the discussion that broke out so vehemently at our table, almost bringing us to blows, in essence the dispute was more fundamental, an angry conflict between two warring concepts of life. For it soon became known from the indiscretion of a chambermaid who had read the letter—in his helpless fury, the devastated husband had crumpled it up and dropped it on the floor somewhere—that Madame Henriette had not left alone but, by mutual agreement, with the young Frenchman (for whom most people's liking now swiftly began to evaporate). At first glance, of course, it might seem perfectly understandable for this minor Madame Bovary to exchange her stout, provincial husband for an elegant and handsome young fellow. But what aroused so much indignation in all present was the circumstance that neither the manufacturer nor his daughters, nor even Madame Henriette herself, had ever set eyes on this Lovelace before, and consequently their evening conversation for a couple of hours on the terrace, and the one-hour session in the garden over black coffee, seemed to have sufficed to make a woman about thirty-three years old and of blameless reputation abandon her husband and two children overnight, following a young dandy previously unknown to her without a second thought. This apparently evident fact was unanimously condemned at our table as perfidious deceit and a cunning manoeuvre on the part of the two lovers: of course Madame Henriette must have been conducting a clandestine affair with the young man long before, and he had come here, Pied Piper that he was, only to settle the final details of their flight, for—so our company deduced—it was out of the question for a decent woman who had known a man a mere couple of hours to run off just like that when he first whistled her up. It amused me to take a different view, and I energetically defended such an eventuality as possible, even probable in a woman who at heart had perhaps been ready to take some decisive action through all the years of a tedious, disappointing marriage. My unexpected opposition quickly made the discussion more general, and it became particularly agitated when both married couples, the Germans and the Italians alike, denied the existence of the *coup de foudre* with positively scornful indignation, condemning it as folly and tasteless romantic fantasy.

Well, it's of no importance here to go back in every detail over the stormy course of an argument conducted between soup and dessert: only professionals of the table d'hôte are witty, and points made in the heat of a chance dispute at table are usually banal, since the speakers resort to them clumsily and in haste. It is also difficult to explain how our discussion came to assume the form of insulting remarks so quickly; I think it grew so vehement in the first place because of the instinctive wish of both husbands to reassure themselves that their own wives were incapable of such shallow inconstancy. Unfortunately they could find no better way of expressing their feelings than to tell me that no one could speak as I did except a man who judged the feminine psyche by a bachelor's random conquests, which came only too cheap. This accusation rather annoyed me, and when the German lady added her mite by remarking instructively that there were real

women on the one hand and 'natural-born tarts' on the other,
and in her opinion Madame Henriette must have been one of
the latter, I lost patience entirely and became aggressive myself.
Such a denial of the obvious fact that at certain times in her life
a woman is delivered up to mysterious powers beyond her own
will and judgement, I said, merely concealed fear of our own
instincts, of the demonic element in our nature, and many people seemed to take pleasure in feeling themselves stronger, purer
and more moral that those who are 'easily led astray'. Personally,
I added, I thought it more honourable for a woman to follow her
instincts freely and passionately than to betray her husband in
his own arms with her eyes closed, as so many did. Such, roughly,
was the gist of my remarks, and the more the others attacked
poor Madame Henriette in a conversation now rising to fever
pitch, the more passionately I defended her (going far beyond
what I actually felt in the case). My enthusiasm amounted to
what in student circles might have been described as a challenge
to the two married couples, and as a not very harmonious quar-
tet they went for me with such indignant solidarity that the old
Dane, who was sitting there with a jovial expression, much like
the referee at a football match with stopwatch in hand, had to tap
his knuckles on the table from time to time in admonishment.
"Gentlemen, please!" But it never worked for long. One of the
husbands had jumped up from the table three times already,
red in the face, and could be calmed by his wife only with difficulty—in short, a dozen minutes more and our discussion would
have ended in violence, had not Mrs C suddenly poured oil on
the stormy waters of the conversation.

Mrs C, the white-haired, distinguished old English lady,
presided over our table as unofficial arbiter. Sitting very upright in her place, turning to everyone with the same uniform
friendliness, saying little and yet listening with the most grati-
fying interest, she was a pleasing sight from the purely physical viewpoint, and an air of wonderfully calm composure

emanated from her aristocratically reserved nature. Up to a certain point she kept her distance from the rest of us, although she could also show special kindness with tactful delicacy: she spent most of her time in the garden reading books, and sometimes played the piano, but she was seldom to be seen in company or deep in conversation. You scarcely noticed her, yet she exerted a curious influence over us all, for no sooner did she now, for the first time, intervene in our discussion than we all felt, with embarrassment, that we had been too loud and intemperate.

Mrs C had made use of the awkward pause when the German gentleman jumped brusquely up and was then induced to sit quietly down again. Unexpectedly, she raised her clear, grey eyes, looked at me indecisively for a moment, and then, with almost objective clarity, took up the subject in her own way.

"So you think, if I understand you correctly, that Madame Henriette—that a woman can be cast unwittingly into a sudden adventure, can do things that she herself would have thought impossible an hour earlier, and for which she can hardly be held responsible?"

"I feel sure of it, ma'am."

"But then all moral judgements would be meaningless, and any kind of vicious excess could be justified. If you really think that a *crime passionnel*, as the French call it, is no crime at all, then what is the state judiciary for? It doesn't take a great deal of good will—and you yourself have a remarkable amount of that," she added, with a slight smile, "to see passion in every crime, and use that passion to excuse it."

The clear yet almost humorous tone of her words did me good, and instinctively adopting her objective stance I answered half in jest, half in earnest myself: "I'm sure that the state judiciary takes a more severe view of such things than I do; its duty is to protect morality and convention without regard for pity, so it is obliged to judge and make no excuses. But as a private person I don't see why I should voluntarily assume the role of public prosecutor. I'd prefer to appear for the defence. Personally, I'd rather understand others than condemn them."

Mrs C looked straight at me for a while with her clear grey eyes, and hesitated. I began to fear she had failed to understand what I said, and was preparing to repeat it in English. But with a curious gravity, as if conducting an examination, she continued with her questions.

"Don't you think it contemptible or shocking, though, for a woman to leave her husband and her children to follow some chance-met man, when she can't even know if he is worth her love? Can you really excuse such reckless, promiscuous conduct in a woman who is no longer in her first youth, and should have disciplined herself to preserve her self-respect, if only for the sake of her children?"

"I repeat, ma'am," I persisted, "that I decline to judge or condemn her in this case. To you, I can readily admit that I was exaggerating a little just now—poor Madame Henriette is certainly no heroine, not even an adventuress by nature, let alone a *grande amoureuse*. So far as I know her, she seems to me just an average, fallible woman. I do feel a little respect for her because she bravely followed the dictates of her own will, but even more pity, since tomorrow, if not today, she is sure to be deeply unhappy. She may have acted unwisely and certainly too hastily, but her conduct was not base or mean, and I still challenge anyone's right to despise the poor unfortunate woman."

"And what about you yourself; do you still feel exactly the same respect and esteem for her? Don't you see any difference between the woman you knew the day before yesterday as a respectable wife, and the woman who ran off with a perfect stranger a day later?"

"None at all. Not the slightest, not the least difference."

"*Is that so?*" She instinctively spoke those words in English; the whole conversation seemed to be occupying her mind to a remarkable degree. After a brief moment's thought, she raised her clear eyes to me again, with a question in them.

"And suppose you were to meet Madame Henriette tomorrow, let's say in Nice on the young man's arm, would you still greet her?"

"Of course."

"And speak to her?"

"Of course."

"If … if you were married, would you introduce such a woman to your wife as if nothing had happened?"

"Of course."

"*Would you really?*" she said, in English again, speaking in tones of incredulous astonishment.

"*Indeed I would,*" I answered, unconsciously falling into English too.

Mrs C was silent. She still seemed to be thinking hard, and suddenly, looking at me as if amazed at her own courage, she said: "I don't know if I would. Perhaps I might." And with the indefinable and peculiarly English ability to end a conversation firmly but without brusque discourtesy, she rose and offered me her hand in a friendly gesture. Her intervention had restored peace, and we were all privately grateful to her for ensuring that although we had been at daggers drawn a moment ago, we could speak to each other with tolerable civility again. The dangerously charged atmosphere was relieved by a few light remarks.

Although our discussion seemed to have been courteously resolved, its irate bitterness had none the less left a faint, lingering sense of estrangement between me and my opponents in argument. The German couple behaved with reserve, while over the next few days the two Italians enjoyed asking me ironically, at frequent intervals, whether I had heard anything of '*la cara signora Henrietta*'. Urbane as our manners might appear, something of the equable, friendly good fellowship of our table had been irrevocably destroyed.

The chilly sarcasm of my adversaries was made all the more obvious by the particular friendliness Mrs C had shown me since our discussion. Although she was usually very reserved, and hardly ever seemed to invite conversation with her table companions outside meal times, she now on several occasions found an opportunity to speak to me in the garden and—I might almost say—distinguish me by her attention, for her upper-class reserve made a private talk with her seem a special favour. To be honest, in fact, I must say she positively sought me out and took every opportunity of entering into conversation with me, in so marked a way that had she not been a white-haired elderly lady I might have entertained some strange, conceited ideas. But when we talked our conversation inevitably and without fail came back to the same point of departure, to Madame Henriette: it seemed to give her some mysterious pleasure to accuse the errant wife of weakness of character and irresponsibility. At the same time, however, she seemed to enjoy my steadfast defence of that refined and delicate woman, and my insistence that nothing could ever make me deny my sympathy for her. She constantly steered our conversation the same way, and in the end I hardly knew what to make of her strange, almost eccentric obsession with the subject.

This went on for a few days, maybe five or six, and she never said a word to suggest why this kind of conversation had assumed importance for her. But I could not help realising that it had when I happened to mention, during a walk, that my stay here would soon be over, and I thought of leaving the day after tomorrow. At this her usually serene face suddenly assumed a curiously intense expression, and something like the shadow of a cloud came into her clear grey eyes. "Oh, what a pity! There's still so much I'd have liked to discuss with you." And from then on a certain uneasy restlessness showed that while she spoke she was thinking of something else, something that occupied and distracted her mind a great deal. At last she herself seemed disturbed by this mental distraction, for in the middle of a silence that had suddenly fallen between us she unexpectedly offered me her hand.

"I see that I can't put what I really want to say to you clearly. I'd rather write it down." And walking faster than I was used to seeing her move, she went towards the house.

I did indeed find a letter in her energetic, frank handwriting in my room just before dinner that evening. I now greatly regret my carelessness with written documents in my youth, which means that I cannot reproduce her note word for word, and can give only the gist of her request: might she, she asked, tell me about an episode in her life? It lay so far back in the past, she wrote, that it was hardly a part of her present existence any more, and the fact that I was leaving the day after tomorrow made it easier for her to speak of something that had occupied and preyed on her mind for over twenty years. If I did not feel such a conversation was an importunity, she would like to ask me for an hour of my time.

The letter—I merely outline its contents here—fascinated me to an extraordinary degree: its English style alone lent it great clarity and resolution. Yet I did not find it easy to answer. I tore up three drafts before I replied:

I am honoured by your showing such confidence in me, and I promise you an honest response should you require one. Of course I cannot ask you to tell me more than your heart dictates. But whatever you tell, tell yourself and me the truth. Please believe me: I feel your confidence a special honour.

The note made its way to her room that evening, and I received the answer next morning:

You are quite right: half the truth is useless, only the whole truth is worth telling. I shall do my best to hide nothing from myself or from you. Please come to my room after dinner—at the age of sixty-seven, I need fear no misinterpretation, but I cannot speak freely in the garden, or with other people near by. Believe me, I did not find it easy to make my mind up to take this step.

During the day we met again at table and discussed indifferent matters in the conventional way. But when we encountered each other in the garden she avoided me in obvious confusion, and I felt it both painful and moving to see this white-haired old lady fleeing from me down an avenue lined with pine trees, as shy as a young girl.

At the appointed time that evening I knocked on her door, and it was immediately opened; the room was bathed in soft twilight, with only the little reading lamp on the table casting a circle of yellow light in the dusk. Mrs C came towards me without any self-consciousness, offered me an armchair and sat down opposite me. I sensed that she had prepared mentally for each of these movements, but then came a pause, obviously unplanned, a pause that grew longer and longer as she came to a difficult decision. I dared not inject any remark into this pause, for I sensed a strong will wrestling with great resistance here. Sometimes the faint notes of a waltz drifted up from the drawing room below, and I listened intently, as if to relieve the silence of some of its oppressive quality. She too seemed to feel the unnatural tension of the silence awkward, for she suddenly pulled herself together to take the plunge, and began.

"It's only the first few words that are so difficult. For the last two days I have been preparing to be perfectly clear and truthful; I hope I shall succeed. Perhaps you don't yet understand why I am telling all this to you, a stranger, but not a

day, scarcely an hour goes by when I do not think of this particular incident, and you can believe me, an old woman now,
when I say it is intolerable to spend one's whole life staring
at a single point in it, a single day. Everything I am about to
tell you, you see, happened within the space of just twenty-
four hours in my sixty-seven years of life, and I have often
asked myself, I have wondered to the point of madness, why
a moment's foolish action on a single occasion should matter. But we cannot shake off what we so vaguely call conscience, and when I heard you speak so objectively of Madame
Henriette's case I thought that perhaps there might be an
end to my senseless dwelling on the past, my constant self-
accusation, if I could bring myself to speak freely to someone, anyone, about that single day in my life. If I were not an
Anglican but a Catholic, the confessional would long ago have
offered me an opportunity of release by putting what I have
kept silent into words—but that comfort is denied us, and so I
make this strange attempt to absolve myself by speaking to you
today. I know all this sounds very odd, but you agreed unhesitatingly to my suggestion, and I am grateful.

As I said, I would like to tell you about just one day in my
life—all the rest of it seems to me insignificant and would be
tedious listening for anyone else. There was nothing in the least
out of the ordinary in the course of it until my forty-second year.
My parents were rich landlords in Scotland, we owned large fac-
tories and leased out land, and in the usual way of the gentry in
my country we spent most of the year on our estates but went
to London for the season. I met my future husband at a party
when I was eighteen. He was a second son of the well-known R
family, and had served with the army in India for ten years. We
soon married, and led the carefree life of our social circle: three
months of the year in London, three months on our estates, and
the rest of the time in hotels in Italy, Spain and France. Not the
slightest shadow ever clouded our marriage, and we had two sons

who are now grown up. When I was forty my husband suddenly died. He had returned from his years in the tropics with a liver complaint, and I lost him within the space of two terrible weeks. My elder son was already in the army, my younger son at university—so I was left entirely alone overnight, and used as I was to affectionate companionship, that loneliness was a torment to me. I felt I could not stay a day longer in the desolate house where every object reminded me of the tragic loss of my beloved husband, and so I decided that while my sons were still unmarried, I would spend much of the next few years travelling.

In essence, I regarded my life from that moment on as entirely pointless and useless. The man with whom I had shared every hour and every thought for twenty-three years was dead, my children did not need me, I was afraid of casting a cloud over their youth with my sadness and melancholy—but I wished and desired nothing any more for myself. I went first to Paris, where I visited shops and museums out of sheer boredom, but the city and everything else were strange to me, and I avoided company because I could not bear the polite sympathy in other people's eyes when they saw that I was in mourning. How those months of aimless, apathetic wandering passed I can hardly say now; all I know is that I had a constant wish to die, but not the strength to hasten the end I longed for so ardently.

In my second year of mourning, that is to say my forty-second year, I had come to Monte Carlo at the end of March in my unacknowledged flight from time that had become worthless and was more than I could deal with. To be honest, I came there out of tedium, out of the painful emptiness of the heart that wells up like nausea, and at least tries to nourish itself on small external stimulations. The less I felt in myself, the more strongly I was drawn to those places where the whirligig of life spins most rapidly. If you are experiencing nothing yourself, the passionate restlessness of others stimulates the nervous system like music or drama.

That was why I quite often went to the casino. I was intrigued to see the tide of delight or dismay ebbing and flowing in other people's faces, while my own heart lay at such a low ebb. In addition my husband, although never frivolous, had enjoyed visiting such places now and then, and with a certain unintentional piety I remained faithful to his old habits. And there in the casino began those twenty-four hours that were more thrilling than any game, and disturbed my life for years.

I had dined at midday with the Duchess of M, a relation of my family, and after supper I didn't feel tired enough to go to bed yet. So I went to the gaming hall, strolled among the tables without playing myself, and watched the mingled company in my own special way. I repeat, in my own special way, the way my dead husband had once taught me when, tired of watching, I complained of the tedium of looking at the same faces all the time: the wizened old women who sat for hours before venturing a single jetton, the cunning professionals, the *demi-mondaines* of the card table, all that dubious chance-met company which, as you'll know, is considerably less picturesque and romantic than it is always painted in silly novels, where you might think it the *fleur d'élégance* and aristocracy of Europe. Yet the casino of twenty years ago, when real money, visible and tangible, was staked and crackling banknotes, gold Napoleons and pert little five-franc pieces rained down, was far more attractive than it is today, with a solid set of folk on Cook's Tours tediously frittering their characterless gaming chips away in the grand, fashionably renovated citadel of gambling. Even then, however, I found little to stimulate me in the similarity of so many indifferent faces, until one day my husband, whose private passion was for chiromancy—that's to say, divination by means of the hand—showed me an unusual method of observation which proved much more interesting, exciting and fascinating than standing casually around. In this method you never look at a face, only at the rectangle of the

206

table, and on the table only at the hands of the players and the way they move. I don't know if you yourself ever happen to have looked at the green table, just that green square with the ball in the middle of it tumbling drunkenly from number to number, while fluttering scraps of paper, round silver and gold coins fall like seedcorn on the spaces of the board, to be raked briskly away by the croupier or shovelled over to the winner like harvest bounty. If you watch from that angle, only the hands change—all those pale, moving, waiting hands around the green table, all emerging from the ever-different caverns of the players' sleeves, each a beast of prey ready to leap, each varying in shape and colour, some bare, others laden with rings and clinking bracelets, some hairy like wild beasts, some damp and writhing like eels, but all of them tense, vibrating with a vast impatience. I could never help thinking of a racecourse where the excited horses are held back with difficulty on the starting line in case they gallop away too soon; they quiver and buck and rear in just the same way. You can tell everything from those hands, from the way they wait, they grab, they falter; you can see an avaricious character in a claw-like hand and a spendthrift in a relaxed one, a calculating man in a steady hand and a desperate man in a trembling wrist; hundreds of characters betray themselves instantly in their way of handling money, crumpling or nervously creasing notes, or letting it lie as the ball goes round, their hands now weary and exhausted. Human beings give themselves away in play—a cliché, I know, but I would say their own hands give them away even more clearly in gambling. Almost all gamblers soon learn to control their faces—from the neck up, they wear the cold mask of impassivity; they force away the lines around their mouths and hide their agitation behind clenched teeth, they refuse to let their eyes show uneasiness, they smooth the twitching muscles of the face into an artificial indifference, obeying the dictates of polite conduct. But just because their whole

207

attention is concentrated on controlling the face, the most visible part of the body, they forget their hands, they forget that some people are watching nothing but those hands, guessing from them what the lips curved in a smile, the intentionally indifferent glances wish to conceal. Meanwhile, however, their hands shamelessly reveal their innermost secrets. For a moment inevitably comes when all those carefully controlled, apparently relaxed fingers drop their elegant negligence. In the pregnant moment when the roulette ball drops into its shallow compartment and the winning number is called, in that second every one of those hundred or five hundred hands spontaneously makes a very personal, very individual movement of primitive instinct. And if an observer like me, particularly well-informed as I was because of my husband's hobby, is used to watching the hands perform in this arena, it is more exciting even than music or drama to see so many different temperaments suddenly erupt. I simply cannot tell you how many thousands of varieties of hands there are: wild beasts with hairy, crooked fingers raking in the money like spiders; nervous, trembling hands with pale nails that scarcely dare to touch it; hands noble and vulgar, hands brutal and shy, cunning hands, hands that seem to be stammering—but each of these pairs of hands is different, the expression of an individual life, with the exception of the four or five pairs of hands belonging to the croupiers. Those hands are entirely mechanical, and with their objective, businesslike, totally detached precision function like the clicking metal mechanism of a gas meter by comparison with the extreme liveliness of the gamblers' hands. But even those sober hands produce a surprising effect when contrasted with their racing, passionate fellows; you might say they were wearing a different uniform, like policemen in the middle of a surging, agitated riot. And then there is the personal incentive of getting to know the many different habits and passions of individual pairs of hands within a few days; by then I had always made acquaintances among them and divided them, as if they were human beings, into those I liked and those I did not. I found the greed and incivility of some so repulsive that I would always avert my gaze from them, as if from some impropriety. Every new pair of hands to appear on the table, however, was a fresh experience and a source of curiosity to me; I often quite forgot to look at the face which, surrounded by a collar high above them, was set impassively on top of an evening shirt or a glittering décolletage, a cold social mask.

When I entered the gaming hall that evening, passed two crowded tables, reached a third, and was taking out a few coins, I was surprised to hear a very strange sound directly opposite me in the wordless, tense pause that seems to echo with silence and always sets in as the ball, moving sluggishly, hesitates between two numbers. It was a cracking, clicking sound like the snapping of joints. I looked across the table in amazement. And then I saw—I was truly startled!—I saw two hands such as I had never seen before, left and right clutching each other like doggedly determined animals, bracing and extending together and against one another with such heightened tension that the fingers' joints cracked with a dry sound like a nut cracking open. They were hands of rare beauty, unusually long, unusually slender, yet taut and muscular—very white, the nails pale at their tips, gently curving and the colour of mother-of-pearl. I kept watching them all evening, indeed I kept marvelling at those extraordinary, those positively unique hands—but what surprised and alarmed me so much at first was the passion in them, their crazily impassioned expressiveness, the convulsive way they wrestled with and supported each other. I knew at once that I was seeing a human being overflowing with emotion, forcing his passion into his fingertips lest it tear him apart. And then—just as the ball, with a dry click, fell into place in the wheel and the croupier called out the number—at that very moment the two hands suddenly fell apart like a pair of animals struck by a single bullet. They dropped, both of them, truly dead and not just exhausted; they dropped with so graphic an expression of lethargy, disappointment, instant extinction, as if all was finally over, that I can find no words to describe it. For never before or since have I seen such speaking hands, hands in which every muscle was eloquent and passion broke almost tangibly from the pores of the skin. They lay on the green table for a moment like jellyfish cast up by the sea, flat and dead. Then one of them, the right hand, began laboriously raising itself again, beginning with the fingertips; it quivered, drew back, turned on itself, swayed, circled, and suddenly reached nervously for a jetton, rolling the token uncertainly like a little wheel between the tips of thumb and middle finger. And suddenly it arched, like a panther arching its back, and shot forwards, positively spitting the hundred-franc jetton out on the middle of the black space. At once, as if at a signal, the inactive, slumbering left hand was seized by excitement too; it rose, slunk, crawled over to its companion hand, which was trembling now as if exhausted by throwing down the jetton, and both hands lay there together trembling, the joints of their fingers working away soundlessly on the table, tapping slightly together like teeth chattering in a fever—no, I had never seen hands of such expressive eloquence, or such spasmodic agitation and tension. Everything else in this vaulted room, the hum from the other halls around it, the calls of the croupiers crying their wares like market traders, the movement of people and of the ball itself which now, dropped from above, was leaping like a thing possessed around the circular cage that was smooth as parquet flooring—all this diversity of whirling, swirling impressions flitting across the nerves suddenly seemed to me dead and dull compared to those two trembling, breathing, gasping, waiting, freezing, trembling hands, that extraordinary pair of hands which somehow held me spellbound.

But finally I could no longer refrain; I had to see the human being, the face to which those magical hands belonged, and fearfully—yes, I do mean fearfully, for I was afraid of those hands!—my gaze slowly travelled up the gambler's sleeves and narrow shoulders. And once again I had a shock, for his face spoke the same fantastically extravagant language of extremes as the hands, shared the same terrible grimness of expression and delicate, almost feminine beauty. I had never seen such a face before, a face so transported and utterly beside itself, and I had plenty of opportunity to observe it at leisure as if it were a mask, an unseeing sculpture: those possessed eyes did not turn to right or left for so much as a second, their pupils were fixed and black beneath the widely opened lids, dead glass balls reflecting that other mahogany-coloured ball rolling and leaping about the roulette wheel in such foolish high spirits. Never, I repeat, had I seen so intense or so fascinating a face. It belonged to a young man of perhaps twenty-four, it was fine-drawn, delicate, rather long and very expressive. Like the hands, it did not seem entirely masculine, but resembled the face of a boy passionately absorbed in a game—although I noticed none of that until later, for now the face was entirely veiled by an expression of greed and of madness breaking out. The thin mouth, thirsting and open, partly revealed the teeth: you could see them ten paces away, grinding feverishly while the parted lips remained rigid. A light-blond lock of hair clung damply to his forehead, tumbling forwards like the hair of a man falling, and a tic fluttered constantly around his nostrils as if little waves were invisibly rippling beneath the skin. The bowed head was moving instinctively further and further forwards; you felt it was being swept away with the whirling of the little ball, and now, for the first time, I understood the convulsive pressure of the hands. Only by the intense strain of pressing them together did the body, falling from its central axis, contrive to keep its balance. I had never—I must repeat it yet again—I had never seen a face in which passion showed so openly, with such shamelessly naked animal feeling, and I stared at that face, as fascinated and spellbound by its obsession as was its own gaze by the leaping, twitching movement of the circling ball. From that moment on I noticed nothing else in the room, everything seemed to me dull, dim and blurred, dark by comparison with the flashing fire of that face, and disregarding everyone else present I spent perhaps an hour watching that one man and every movement he made: the bright light that sparkled in his eyes, the convulsive knot of his hands loosening as if blown apart by an explosion, the parting of the shaking fingers as the croupier pushed twenty gold coins towards their eager grasp. At that moment the face looked suddenly bright and very young, the lines in it smoothed out, the eyes began to gleam, the convulsively bowed body straightened lightly, easily—he suddenly sat there as relaxed as a horseman, borne up by the sense of triumph, fingers toying lovingly, idly with the round coins, clinking them together, making them dance and jingle playfully. Then he turned his head restlessly again, surveyed the green table as if with the flaring nostrils of a young hound seeking the right scent, and suddenly, with one quick movement, placed all the coins on one rectangular space. At once the watchfulness, the tension returned. Once more the little waves, rippling galvanically, spread out from his lips, once again his hands were clasped, the boyish face disappeared behind greedy expectation until the spasmodic tension exploded and fell apart in disappointment: the face that had just looked boyish turned faded, wan and old, light disappeared from the burnt-out eyes, and all this within the space of a second as the ball came to rest on the wrong number. He had lost; he stared at the ball for a few seconds almost like an idiot, as if he did not understand, but as the croupier began calling to whip up interest, his fingers took out a few coins again. But his certainty was gone; first he put the coins on one space, then, thinking better of it, on another, and when the ball had begun to roll his trembling hand, on a sudden impulse, quickly added two crumpled banknotes.

This alternation of up and down, loss and gain, continued without a break for about an hour, and during that hour I did not, even for a moment, take my fascinated gaze from that ever-changing face and all the passions ebbing and flowing over it. I kept my eyes fixed on those magical hands, their every muscle graphically reflecting the whole range of the man's feelings as they rose and fell like a fountain. I had never watched the face of an actor in the theatre as intently as I watched this one, seeing the constant, changing shades of emotion flitting over it like light and shade moving over a landscape. I had never immersed myself so wholeheartedly in a game as I did in the reflection of this stranger's excitement. If someone had been observing me at that moment he would surely have taken my steely gaze for a state of hypnosis, and indeed my benumbed perception was something like that—I simply could not look away from the play of those features, and everything else in the room, the lights, the laughter, the company and its glances, merely drifted vaguely around me, a yellow mist with that face in the middle of it, a flame among flames. I heard nothing, I felt nothing, I did not notice people coming forwards beside me, other hands suddenly reaching out like feelers, putting down money or picking it up; I did not see the ball or hear the croupier's voice, yet I saw it all as if I were dreaming, exaggerated as in a concave mirror by the excitement and extravagance of those moving hands. For I did not have to look at the roulette wheel to know whether the ball had come to rest on red or black, whether it was still rolling or beginning to falter. Every stage of the game, loss and gain, hope and disappointment, was fierily reflected in the nerves and movements of that passionate face.

But then came a terrible moment—something that I had been vaguely fearing all this time, something that had weighed like a gathering thunderstorm on my tense nerves, and now suddenly ripped through them. Yet again the ball had fallen back into the shallow depression with that dry little click, yet again came the tense moment when two hundred lips held their breath until the croupier's voice announced the winning number—this time it was zero—while he zealously raked in the clinking coins and crackling notes from all sides. At that moment those two convulsively clasped hands made a particularly terrifying movement, leaping up as if to catch something that wasn't there and then dropping to the table again exhausted, with no strength in them, only the force of gravity flooding back. Then, however, they suddenly came to life yet again, feverishly retreating from the table to the man's own body, clambering up his torso like wild cats, up and down, left and right, nervously trying all his pockets to see if some forgotten coin might not have slipped into one of them. But they always came back empty, and the pointless, useless search began again ever more frantically, while the roulette wheel went on circling and others continued playing, while coins clinked, chairs were shifted on the floor, and all the small sounds, put together a hundredfold, filled the room with a humming note. I trembled, shaking with horror; I felt it all as clearly as if my own fingers were rummaging desperately for a coin in the pockets and folds of my creased garments. And suddenly, with a single abrupt movement, the man rose to his feet opposite me, like a man standing up when he suddenly feels unwell and must rise if he is not to suffocate. His chair crashed to the floor behind him. Without even noticing, without paying any attention to his surprised and abashed neighbours as they avoided his swaying figure, he stumbled away from the table.

The sight petrified me. For I knew at once where the man was going: to his death. A man getting to his feet like that was not on his way back to an inn, a wine bar, a wife, a railway carriage, to any form of life at all, he was plunging straight into the abyss. Even the most hardened spectator in that hellish gaming hall could surely have seen that the man had nothing to fall back on, not at home or in a bank or with a family, but had been sitting here with the last of his money, staking his life, and was now staggering away somewhere else, anywhere, but undoubtedly out of that life. I had feared all along, I had sensed from the first moment, as if by magic, that more than loss or gain was staked on the game, yet now it struck me like a bolt of dark lightning to see the life suddenly go out of his eyes and death cast its pale shadow over his still living face. Instinctively—affected as I was by his own graphic gestures—I clutched at myself while the man tore himself away from his place and staggered out, for his own uncertain gait was now transferred to my own body just as his tension had entered my veins and nerves. Then I was positively wrenched away, I had to follow him; my feet moved without my own volition. It was entirely unconscious, I did not do it of my own accord, it was something happening to me when, taking no notice of anyone, feeling nothing myself, I went out into the corridor leading to the doors.

He was standing at the cloakroom counter, and the attendant had brought him his coat. But his arms would no longer obey him, so the helpful attendant laboriously eased them into the sleeves, as if he were paralysed. I saw him automatically put his hand in his waistcoat pocket to give the man a tip, but his fingers emerged empty. Then he suddenly seemed to remember everything, awkwardly stammered something to the cloakroom attendant, and as before moved forwards abruptly and then stumbled like a drunk down the casino steps, where the attendant stood briefly watching him go, with a smile that was at first contemptuous and then understanding.

His bearing shook me so much that I felt ashamed to have seen it. Involuntarily I turned aside, embarrassed to have watched a stranger's despair as if I were in a theatre—but then that vague fear suddenly took me out of myself once again. Quickly, I retrieved my coat, and thinking nothing very definite, purely mechanically and compulsively I hurried out into the dark after the stranger."

Mrs C interrupted her story for a moment. She had been sitting calmly opposite me, speaking almost without a break with her characteristic tranquil objectivity, as only someone who had prepared and carefully organised the events of her tale in advance could speak. Now, for the first time, she stopped, hesitated, and then suddenly broke off and turned directly to me.

"I promised you and myself," she began, rather unevenly, "to tell you all the facts with perfect honesty. Now I must ask you to believe in my honesty, and not assume that my conduct had any ulterior motives. I might not be ashamed of them today, but in this case such suspicions would be entirely unfounded. And I must emphasise that, when I hurried after that ruined gambler in the street, I had certainly not fallen in love with him—I did not think of him as a man at all, and indeed I was over forty myself at the time and had never looked at another man since my husband's death. All that part of my life was finally over; I tell you this explicitly, and I must, or you would not understand the full horror of what happened later. On the other hand, it's true that I would find it difficult to give a clear name to the feeling that drew me so compulsively after the unfortunate man; there was curiosity in it, but above all a dreadful fear, or rather a fear of something dreadful, something I had felt invisibly enveloping the young man like a miasma from the first moment. But such feelings can't be dissected and taken apart, if only because they come over one too compulsively, too fast, too spontaneously—very likely mine expressed nothing but the instinct to help with which one snatches back a child about to run into the road in front of a motor car. How else can we explain why non-swimmers will jump off a bridge to help a drowning man? They are simply impelled to do it as if by magic, some other will pushes them off the bridge before they have time to consider the pointless bravery of their conduct properly; and in just the same way, without thinking, without conscious reflection, I hurried after the unfortunate young man out of the gaming room, to the casino doors, out of the doors and on to the terrace.

And I am sure that neither you nor any other feeling human being with his eyes open could have withstood that fearful curiosity, for a more disturbing sight can hardly be imagined than the way the gambler, who must have been twenty-four at the most but moved as laboriously as an old man and was swaying like a drunk, dragged himself shakily and disjointedly down the steps to the terrace beside the road. Once there, his body dropped on to a bench, limp as a sack. Again I shuddered as I sensed, from that movement, that the man had reached the end of his tether. Only a dead man or one with nothing left to keep him alive drops like that. His head, fallen to one side, leant back over the bench, his arms hung limp and shapeless to the ground, and in the dim illumination of the faintly flickering street lights any passer-by would have thought he had been shot. And it was like that—I can't explain why the vision suddenly came into my mind, but all of a sudden it was there, real enough to touch, terrifying and terrible—it was like that, as a man who had been shot, that I saw him before me at that moment, and I knew for certain that he had a revolver in his pocket, and tomorrow he would be found lying lifeless and covered with blood on this or some other bench. For he had dropped like a stone falling into a deep chasm, never to stop until it reaches the bottom: I never saw such a physical expression of exhaustion and despair.

So now, consider my situation: I was standing twenty or thirty paces from the bench and the motionless, broken man on it, with no idea what to do, on the one hand wishing to help, on the other restrained by my innate and inbred reluctance to speak to a strange man in the street. The gaslights flickered dimly in the overcast sky, few figures hurried past, for it was nearly midnight and I was almost entirely alone in the park with this suicidal figure. Five or ten times I had already pulled myself together and approached him, but shame or perhaps that deeper premonitory instinct, the idea that falling men are likely to pull those who come to their aid down with them, made me withdraw—and in this midst of this indecision I was clearly aware of the pointless, ridiculous aspect of the situation. Nonetheless, I could neither speak nor turn away, I could not do anything but I could not leave him. And I hope you will believe me when I say that for perhaps an hour, an endless hour, I walked indecisively up and down that terrace, while time was divided up by thousands of little sounds from the breaking waves of the invisible sea—so shaken and transfixed was I by the idea of the annihilation of a human being.

Yet I could not summon up the courage to say a word or make a move, and I would have waited like that half the night, or perhaps in the end my wiser self-interest would have prevailed on me to go home, and indeed I think I had already made up my mind to leave that helpless bundle of misery lying there—when a superior force put an end to my indecision. It began to rain. All evening the wind had been piling up heavy spring clouds full of moisture above the sea, lungs and heart felt the pressure of the lowering sky, and now drops suddenly began to splash down. Soon a heavy rain was falling in wet torrents blown about by the wind. I instinctively sheltered under the projecting roof of a kiosk, but although I put up my umbrella gusts of wind kept blowing the rain on my dress. I felt the cold mist thrown up by the falling raindrops spray my face and hands.

But—and it was such a terrible sight that even now, two decades later, the memory still constricts my throat—but in the middle of this cloudburst the unfortunate man stayed perfectly still on his bench, never moving. Water was gurgling and dripping from all the eaves; you could hear the rumble of carriages from the city; people with their coat collars turned up hurried past to right and to left; all living creatures ducked in alarm, fled, ran, sought shelter; man and beast felt universal fear of the torrential element—but that black heap of humanity on the bench did not stir or move. I told you before that he had the magical gift of graphically expressing everything he felt in movement and gesture. But nothing, nothing on earth could convey despair, total self-surrender, death in the midst of life to such shattering effect as his immobility, the way he sat there in the falling rain, not moving, feeling nothing, too tired to rise and walk the few steps to the shelter of the projecting roof, utterly indifferent to his own existence. No sculptor, no poet, not Michelangelo or Dante has ever brought that sense of ultimate despair, of ultimate human misery so feelingly to my mind as the sight of that living figure letting the watery element drench him, too weary and uncaring to make a single move to protect himself.

That made me act; I couldn't help it. Pulling myself together, I ran the gauntlet of the lashing rain and shook the dripping bundle of humanity to make him get up from the bench. 'Come along!' I seized his arm. Something stared up at me, with difficulty. Something in him seemed to be slowly preparing to move, but he did not understand. 'Come along!' Once again, almost angry now, I tugged at his wet sleeve. Then he slowly stood up, devoid of will and swaying. 'What do you want?' he asked, and I could not reply, for I myself had no idea where to take him— just away from the cold downpour where he had been sitting so senselessly, suicidally, in the grip of deep despair. I did not let go of his arm but dragged the man on, since he had no will of his own, to the sales kiosk where the narrow, projecting roof at least partly sheltered him from the raging attack of the stormy rain as the wind tossed it wildly back and forth. That was all I wanted, I had nothing else in mind, just to get him somewhere dry, under a roof. As yet I had thought no further.

So we stood side by side on that narrow strip of dry ground, the wall of the kiosk behind us and above us only the roof, which was not large enough, for the insatiable rain insidiously came in under it as sudden gusts of wind flung wet, chilly showers over our clothes and into our faces. The situation became intolerable. I could hardly stand there any longer beside this dripping wet stranger. On the other hand, having dragged him over here I couldn't just leave him and walk away without a word. Something had to be done, and gradually I forced myself to think clearly. It would be best, I thought, to send him home in a cab and then go home myself; he would be able to look after himself tomorrow. So as he stood beside me gazing fixedly out at the turbulent night I asked, 'Where do you live?'

'I'm not staying anywhere ... I only arrived from Nice this morning ... we can't go to my place.'

I did not immediately understand this last remark. Only later did I realise that the man took me for ... for a *demi-mondaine*, one of the many women who haunt the casino by night, hoping to extract a little money from lucky gamblers or drunks. After all, what else was he to think, for only now that I tell you about it do I feel all the improbability, indeed the fantastic nature of my situation—what else was he to think of me? The way I had pulled him off the bench and dragged him away as if it were perfectly natural was certainly not the conduct of a lady. But this idea did not occur to me at once. Only later, only too late did his terrible misapprehension dawn upon me, or I would never have said what I did next, in words that were bound to reinforce his impression. 'Then we'll just take a room in a hotel. You can't stay here. You must get under cover somewhere.'

Now I understood his painful misunderstanding, for he did not turn towards me but merely rejected the idea with a certain contempt in his voice: 'I don't need a room; I don't need anything now. Don't bother, you won't get anything out of me. You've picked the wrong man. I have no money.'

This too was said in a dreadful tone, with shattering indifference, and the way he stood there dripping wet and leaning against the wall, slack and exhausted to the bone, shook me so much that I had no time to waste on taking petty offence. I merely sensed, as I had from the first moment when I saw him stagger from the gaming hall, as I had felt all through this improbable hour, that here was a human being, a young, living, breathing human being on the very brink of death, and I must save him. I came closer.

'Never mind money, come along! You can't stay here. I'll get you under cover. Don't worry about anything, just come with me.'

He turned his head and I felt, while the rain drummed round us with a hollow sound and the eaves cast water down to splash at our feet, that for the first time he was trying to make out my face in the dark. His body seemed to be slowly shaking off its lethargy too.

'As you like,' he said, giving in. 'It's all one to me … after all, why not? Let's go.' I put up my umbrella, he moved to my side and took my arm. I felt this sudden intimacy uncomfortable; indeed, it horrified me. I was alarmed to the depths of my heart. But I did not feel bold enough to ask him to refrain, for if I rejected him now he would fall into the bottomless abyss, and everything I had tried to do so far would be in vain. We walked the few steps back to the casino, and only now did it strike me that I had no idea what to do with him. I had better take him to a hotel, I thought quickly, and give him money to spend the night there and go home in the morning. I was not thinking beyond that. And as the carriages were now rapidly drawing up outside the casino I hailed a cab and we got in. When the driver asked where to, I couldn't think what to say at first. But realising that the drenched, dripping man beside me would not be welcome in any of the best hotels—on the other hand, genuinely inexperienced as I was, with nothing else in mind—I just told the cabby, 'Some simple hotel, anywhere!'

The driver, indifferent, and wet with rain himself, drove his horses on. The stranger beside me said not a word, the wheels rattled, the rain splashed heavily against the windows, and I felt as if I were travelling with a corpse in that dark, lightless rectangular space, in a vehicle like a coffin. I tried to think of something to say to relieve the strange, silent horror of our presence there together, but I could think of nothing. After a few minutes the cab stopped. I got out first and paid the driver, who shut the door after us as if drunk with sleep. We were at the door of a small hotel that was unknown to me, with a glass porch above us providing a tiny area of shelter from the rain, which was still lashing the impenetrable night around us with ghastly monotony.

The stranger, giving way to his inertia, had instinctively leant against the wall, and water was dripping from his wet hat and crumpled garments. He stood there like a drunk who has been fished out of the river, still dazed, and a channel of water trickling down from him formed around the small patch of ground where he stood. But he made not the slightest effort to shake himself or take off the hat from which raindrops kept running over his forehead and face. He stood there entirely apathetically, and I cannot tell you how his broken demeanour moved me.

But something had to be done. I put my hand into my bag. 'Here are a hundred francs,' I said. 'Take a room and go back to Nice tomorrow.'

He looked up in astonishment.

'I was watching you in the gaming hall,' I continued urgently, noticing his hesitation. 'I know you've lost everything, and I fear you're well on the way to doing something stupid. There's no shame in accepting help—here, take it!'

But he pushed away my hand with an energy I wouldn't have expected in him. 'You are very good,' he said, 'but don't waste your money. There's no help for me now. Whether I sleep tonight or not makes not the slightest difference. It will all be over tomorrow anyway. There's no help for me.'

'No, you must take it,' I urged. 'You'll see things differently tomorrow. Go upstairs and sleep on it. Everything will look different in daylight.'

But when I tried to press the money on him again he pushed my hand away almost violently. 'Don't,' he repeated dully. 'There's no point in it. Better to do it out of doors than leave blood all over their room here. A hundred or even a thousand francs won't help me. I'd just go to the gaming hall again tomorrow with the last few francs, and I wouldn't stop until they were all gone. Why begin again? I've had enough.'

You have no idea how that dull tone of voice went to my heart, but think of it: a couple of inches from you stands a young, bright, living, breathing human being, and you know that if you don't do your utmost, then in a few hours time this thinking, speaking, breathing specimen of youth will be a corpse. And now I felt a desire like rage, like fury, to overcome his senseless resistance. I grasped his arm. 'That's enough stupid talk. You go up these steps now and take a room, and I'll come in the morning and take you to the station. You must get away from here, you must go home tomorrow, and I won't rest until I've seen you sitting in the train with a ticket. You can't throw your life away so young just because you've lost a couple of hundred francs, or a couple of thousand. That's cowardice, silly hysteria concocted from anger and bitterness. You'll see that I'm right tomorrow!'

'Tomorrow!' he repeated in a curiously gloomy, ironic tone. 'Tomorrow! If you knew where I'd be tomorrow! I wish I knew myself—I'm mildly curious to find out. No, go home, my dear, don't bother about me and don't waste your money.'

But I wasn't giving up now. It had become like a mania obsessing me. I took his hand by force and pressed the banknote into it. 'You will take this money and go in at once!' And so saying I stepped firmly up to the door and rang the bell. 'There, now I've rung, and the porter will be here in a minute. Go in and lie down. I'll be outside here at nine tomorrow to take you straight to the station. Don't worry about anything, I'll see to what's necessary to get you home. But now go to bed, have a good sleep, and don't think of anything else!'

At that moment the key turned inside the door and the porter opened it.

'Come on, then!' said my companion suddenly, in a harsh, firm embittered voice, and I felt his fingers span my wrist in an iron grip. I was alarmed ... so greatly alarmed, so paralysed, struck as if by lightning, that all my composure vanished. I wanted to resist, tear myself away, but my will seemed numbed, and I ... well, you will understand ... I was ashamed to struggle with a stranger in front of the porter, who stood there waiting impatiently. And so, suddenly, I was inside the hotel. I wanted to speak, say something, but my throat would not obey me ... and his hand lay heavy and commanding on my arm. I vaguely felt it draw me as if unawares up a flight of steps—a key clicked in a lock. And suddenly I was alone with this stranger in a strange room, in some hotel whose name I do not know to this day."

Mrs C stopped again, and suddenly rose to her feet. It seemed that her voice would not obey her any more. She went over to the window and looked out in silence for some minutes, or perhaps she was just resting her forehead on the cold pane; I did not have the courage to look closely, for I found it painful to see the old lady so agitated. So I sat quite still, asking no questions, making no sound, and waited until she came back, stepping firmly, and sat down opposite me.

"Well—now the most difficult part is told. And I hope you will believe me when I assure you yet again, when I swear by all that is sacred to me, by my honour and my children, that up to that moment no idea of any ... any relationship with the stranger had entered my mind, that I really had been suddenly plunged into this situation against my own will, indeed entirely unawares, as if I had fallen through a trapdoor from the level path of my existence. I have promised to be honest with you and with myself, so I repeat again that I embarked on this tragic venture merely through a rather overwrought desire to help, not through any other, any personal feeling, quite without any wishes or forebodings.

You must spare me the tale of what happened in that room that night; I myself have forgotten not a moment of it, and I never will. I spent it wrestling with another human being for his life, and I repeat, it was a battle of life and death. I felt only too clearly, with every fibre of my being, that this stranger, already half-lost, was clutching at his last chance with all the avid passion of a man threatened by death. He clung to me like one who already feels the abyss yawning beneath him. For my part, I summoned everything in me to save him by all the means at my command. A human being may know such an hour perhaps only once in his life, and out of millions, again, perhaps only one will know it—but for that terrible chance I myself would never have guessed how ardently, desperately, with what boundless greed a man given up for lost will still suck at every red drop of life. Kept safe for twenty years from all the demonic forces of existence, I would never have understood how magnificently, how fantastically Nature can merge hot and cold, life and death, delight and despair together in a few brief moments. And that night was so full of conflict and of talk, of passion and anger and hatred, with tears of entreaty and intoxication, that it seemed to me to last a thousand years, and we two human beings who fell entwined into its chasm, one of us in frenzy, the other unsuspecting, emerged from that mortal tumult changed, completely transformed, senses and emotions transmuted.

But I don't want to talk about that. I cannot and will not describe it. However, I must just tell you of the extraordinary moment when I woke in the morning from a leaden sleep, from nocturnal depths such as I had never known before. It took me a long time to open my eyes, and the first thing I saw was a strange ceiling over me, and then, looking further an entirely strange, unknown, ugly room. I had no idea how I came to be there. At first I told myself I must still be dreaming, an unusually lucid, transparent dream into which I had passed from my dull, confused slumber—but the sparkling bright sunshine outside the windows was unmistakably genuine, the light of morning, and the sounds of the street echoed from below, the rattle of carriages, the ringing of tram bells, the noise of people—so now I knew that I was awake and not dreaming. I instinctively sat up to get my bearings, and then—as my glance moved sideways—then I saw, and I can never describe my alarm to you, I saw a stranger sleeping in the broad bed beside me … a strange, perfectly strange, half-naked, unknown man … oh, I know there's no real way to describe the awful realisation; it struck me with such terrible force that I sank back powerless. But not in a kindly faint, not falling unconscious, far from it: with lightning speed, everything became as clear to me as it was inexplicable, and all I wanted was to die of revulsion and shame at suddenly finding myself in an unfamiliar bed in a decidedly shady hotel, with a complete stranger beside me. I still remember how my heart missed a beat, how I held my breath as if that would extinguish my life and above all my consciousness, which grasped everything yet understood none of it.

I shall never know how long I lay like that, all my limbs icy cold: the dead must lie rigid in their coffins in much the same way. All I know is that I had closed my eyes and was praying to God, to some heavenly power, that this might not be true, might not be real. But my sharpened senses would not let me deceive myself, I could hear people talking in the next room, water running, footsteps shuffling along the corridor outside, and each of these signs mercilessly proved that my senses were terribly alert.

How long this dreadful condition lasted I cannot say: such moments are outside the measured time of ordinary life. But suddenly another fear came over me, swift and terrible: the stranger whose name I did not know might wake up and speak to me. And I knew at once there was only one thing to do: I must get dressed and make my escape before he woke. I must not let him set eyes on me again, I must not speak to him again. I must save myself before it was too late, go away, away, away, back to some kind of life of my own, to my hotel, I must leave this pernicious place, leave this country, never meet him again, never look him in the eye, have no witnesses, no accusers, no one who knew. The idea dispelled my faintness: very cautiously, with the furtive movements of a thief, I inched out of bed (for I was desperate to make no noise) and groped my way over to my clothes. I dressed very carefully, trembling all the time lest he might wake up, and then I had finished, I had done it. Only my hat lay at the foot of the bed on the far side of the room, and then, as I tiptoed over to pick it up—I couldn't help it, at that moment I had to cast another glance at the face of the stranger who had fallen into my life like a stone dropping off a window sill. I meant it to be just one glance, but it was curious—the strange young man who lay sleeping there really was a stranger to me. At first I did not recognise his face from yesterday. The impassioned, tense, desperately distressed features of the mortally agitated man might have been entirely extinguished—this man's face was not the same, but was an utterly childlike, utterly boyish face that positively radiated purity and cheerfulness. The lips, so grim yesterday as he clenched his teeth on them, were dreaming, had fallen softly apart, half-curving in a smile; the fair hair curled gently over the smooth forehead, the breath passed from his chest over his body at repose like the mild rippling of waves.

Perhaps you may remember that I told you earlier I had never before seen greed and passion expressed with such outrageous extravagance by any human being as by that stranger at the gaming table. And I tell you now that I had never, even in children whose baby slumbers sometimes cast an angelic aura of cheerfulness around them, seen such an expression of brightness, of truly blissful sleep. The uniquely graphic nature of that face showed all its feelings, at present the paradisaical easing of all internal heaviness, a sense of freedom and salvation. At this surprising sight all my own fear and horror fell from me like a heavy black cloak—I was no longer ashamed, no, I was almost glad. The terrible and incomprehensible thing that had happened suddenly made sense to me; I was happy, I was proud to think that but for my dedicated efforts the beautiful, delicate young man lying here carefree and quiet as a flower would have been found somewhere on a rocky slope, his body shattered and bloody, his face ruined, lifeless, with staring eyes. I had saved him; he was safe. And now I looked—I cannot put it any other way—I looked with maternal feeling at the man I had reborn into life more painfully than I bore my own children. In the middle of that shabby, threadbare room in a distasteful, grubby house of assignation, I was overcome by the kind of emotion—ridiculous as you may find it put into words—the kind of emotion one might have in church, a rapturous sense of wonder and sanctification. From the most dreadful moment of a whole life there now grew a second life, amazing and overwhelming, coming in sisterly fashion to meet me.

Had I made too much noise moving about? Had I involuntarily exclaimed out loud? I don't know, but suddenly the sleeping man opened his eyes. I flinched back in alarm. He looked round in surprise—just as I had done before earlier, and now he in his own turn seemed to be emerging with difficulty from great depths of confusion. His gaze wandered intently round the strange, unfamiliar room and then fell on me in amazement. But before he spoke, or could quite pull himself together, I had control of myself. I did not let him say a word, I allowed no questions, no confidences; nothing of yesterday or of last night was to be explained, discussed or mulled over again.

228

'I have to go now,' I told him quickly. 'You stay here and get dressed. I'll meet you at twelve at the entrance to the casino, and I'll take care of everything else.'

And before he could say a word in reply I fled, to be rid of the sight of the room, and without turning back left the hotel whose name I did not know, any more than I knew the name of the stranger with whom I had just spent the night."

Mrs C interrupted her narrative for a moment again, but all the strain and distress had gone from her voice: like a carriage that toils uphill with difficulty but then, having reached the top, rolls swiftly and smoothly down the other side, her account now proceeded more easily:

"Well—so I made haste to my hotel through the morning light of the streets. The drop in the temperature had driven all the hazy mists from the sky above, just as my own distress had been dispelled. For remember what I told you earlier: I had given up my own life entirely after my husband's death. My children did not need me, I didn't care for my own company, and there's no point in a life lived aimlessly. Now, for the first time, a task had suddenly come my way: I had saved a human being, I had exerted all my powers to snatch him back from destruction. There was only a little left to do—for my task must be completed to the end. So I entered my hotel, ignoring the porter's surprise when he saw me returning at nine in the morning—no shame and chagrin over last night's events oppressed me now, I felt my will to live suddenly revive, and an unexpectedly new sense of the point of my existence flowed warmly through my veins. Once in my room I quickly changed my clothes, putting my mourning aside without thinking (as I noticed only later) and choosing a lighter colour instead, went to the bank to withdraw money, and made haste to the station to find out train times. With a determination that surprised me

I also made a few other arrangements. Now there was nothing left to do but ensure the departure from Monte Carlo and ultimate salvation of the man whom fate had cast in my way.

It is true that I needed strength to face him personally. Everything yesterday had taken place in the dark, in a vortex; we had been like two stones thrown out of a torrential stream suddenly striking together; we scarcely knew each other face to face, and I wasn't even sure whether the stranger would recognise me again. Yesterday had been chance, frenzy, a case of two confused people possessed; today I must be more open with him, since I must now confront him in the pitiless light of day with myself, my own face, as a living human being.

But it all turned out much easier than I expected. No sooner had I approached the casino at the appointed hour than a young man jumped up from a bench and made haste towards me. There was something so spontaneous, so childlike, unplanned and happy in his surprise and in each of his eloquent movements; he almost flew to me, the radiance of a joy that was both grateful and deferential in his eyes, which were lowered humbly as soon as they felt my confusion in his presence. Gratitude is so seldom found, and those who are most grateful cannot express it, are silent in their confusion, or ashamed, or sometimes seem ungracious just to conceal their feelings. But in this man, the expression of whose every feeling God, like a mysterious sculptor, had made sensual, beautiful, graphic, his gratitude glowed with radiant passion right through his body. He bent over my hand and remained like that for a moment, the narrow line of his boyish head reverently bowed, respectfully brushing kisses on my fingers; only then did he step back, ask how I was, and look at me most movingly. There was such courtesy in everything he said that within a few minutes the last of my anxiety had gone. As if reflecting the lightening of my own feelings, the landscape around was shining, the spell on it broken: the sea that had been disturbed and angry yesterday lay so calm and bright that every pebble beneath the gently breaking surf gleamed white, and the casino, that den of iniquity, looked up with Moorish brightness to the damask sky that was now swept clean. The kiosk with the projecting roof beneath which the pouring rain had forced us to shelter yesterday proved to be a flower stall; great bunches of flowers and foliage lay there in motley confusion, in white, red, other bright colours and green, and a young girl in a colourful blouse was offering them for sale.

I invited him to lunch with me in a small restaurant, and there the young stranger told me the story of his tragic venture. It confirmed my first presentiment when I had seen his trembling, nervously shaking hands on the green table. He came from an old aristocratic family in the Austrian part of Poland, was destined for a diplomatic career, had studied in Vienna and passed his first examination with great success a month ago. As a reward, and to celebrate the occasion, his uncle, a high-ranking general-staff officer, had taken him to the Prater in a cab, and they went to the races. His uncle was lucky with his bets and won three times running; then they ate supper in an elegant restaurant on the strength of the fat wad of banknotes that were the uncle's gains. Next day, again to mark his success in the examinations, the budding diplomat received a sum of money from his father which was as much as his usual monthly allowance. Two days earlier this would have seemed to him a large sum, but now, seeing how easily his uncle had won money, it struck him as trifling and left him indifferent. Directly after dinner, therefore, he went to the races again, laid wild, frenzied bets, and fortune—or rather misfortune—would have it that he left the Prater after the last race with three times the sum he had brought there. Now a mania for gambling infected him; sometimes he went to the races, sometimes to play in coffee houses and clubs, exhausting his time, his studies, his nerves, and above all his money. He was no longer able to think or to sleep peacefully, and he was quite unable to control himself; one night, coming home from a club where he had lost everything, he found a crumpled banknote forgotten in his waistcoat pocket as he was undressing. There was no holding him; he got dressed again and walked the streets until he found a few people playing dominoes in a coffee house, and sat with them until dawn. On one occasion his married sister came to his aid, paying his debts to moneylenders who were very ready to give credit to the heir of a great and noble name. For a while he was lucky at play again—but then matters went inexorably downhill, and the more he lost, the more urgently did unsecured obligations and fixed-term IOUs require him to find relief by winning. He had long ago pawned his watch and his clothes, and at last a terrible thing happened: he stole two large pearl earrings that she seldom wore from his old aunt's dressing table. He pawned one of the pearls for a large sum, which his gambling quadrupled that evening. But instead of redeeming the pearl he staked all his winnings and lost. At the time when he left Vienna the theft had not yet been discovered, so he pawned the second pearl and on a sudden impulse travelled by train to Monte Carlo to win the fortune he dreamt of at roulette. On arrival he had sold his suitcase, his clothes, his umbrella; he had nothing left but a revolver with four cartridges, and a small cross set with jewels given him by his godmother, Princess X. He did not want to part with the cross, but it too had been sold for fifty francs that afternoon, just to let him try to satisfy his urge by playing for life or death one last time that evening.

He told me all this with the captivating charm of his original and lively nature. And I listened shaken, gripped and much moved, but not for a moment did it occur to me to feel horror that the man at my table was in sober fact a thief. Yesterday, if someone had so much as suggested to me that I, a woman with a blameless past who expected the company she kept to be strictly and conventionally virtuous, would be sitting here on familiar terms with a perfectly strange young man, not much older than my son, who had stolen a pair of pearl earrings, I would have thought he had taken leave of his senses and such a thing was impossible. But I felt no horror at all as he told his tale, for he spoke so naturally and passionately that it seemed more like the account of a fever or illness than a crime. Moreover, the word 'impossible' had suddenly lost its meaning for a woman who had known such an unexpected, torrential experience as I had the night before. In those ten hours, I had come to know immeasurably more about reality than in my preceding forty respectable years of life.

Yet something else about his confession did alarm me, and that was the feverish glint in his eyes, which made all the nerves of his face twitch galvanically as he talked about his passion for gambling. Even speaking of it aroused him, and his face graphically and with terrible clarity illustrated that tension between pleasure and torment. His hands, those beautiful, nervous, slender-jointed hands, instinctively began to turn into preying, hunting, fleeing animal creatures again, just as they did at the gaming table. As he spoke I saw them suddenly trembling, beginning at the wrists, arching and clenching into fists, then opening up to intertwine their fingers once more. And when he confessed to the theft of the pearl earrings they suddenly performed a swift, leaping, quick, thieving movement—I involuntarily jumped. I could see his fingers pouncing on the jewels and swiftly stowing them away in the hollow of his clenched hand. And with nameless horror, I recognised that the very last drop of this man's blood was poisoned by his addiction.

That was the one thing that so shattered and horrified me about his tale, the pitiful enslavement of a young, light-hearted, naturally carefree man to a mad passion. I considered it my prime duty to persuade my unexpected protégé, in friendly fashion, that he must leave Monte Carlo, where the temptation was most dangerous, without delay, he must return to his family this very day, before anyone noticed that the pearl earrings were gone and his future was ruined for ever. I promised him money for his journey and to redeem the jewellery, though only on condition that he left today and swore to me, on his honour, never to touch a card or play any other game of chance again.

I shall never forget the passion of gratitude, humble at first, then gradually more ardent, with which that lost stranger listened to me, how he positively drank in my words as I promised him help, and then he suddenly reached both hands over the table to take mine in a gesture I can never forget, a gesture of what one might call adoration and sacred promise. There were tears in his bright but slightly confused eyes; his whole body was trembling nervously with happy excitement. I have tried to describe the uniquely expressive quality of his gestures to you several times already, but I cannot depict this one, for it conveyed ecstatic, supernal delight such as a human countenance seldom turns on us, comparable only to that white shade in which, waking from a dream, we think we see the countenance of an angel vanishing.

Why conceal it? I could not withstand that glance. Gratitude is delightful because it is so seldom found, tender feeling does one good, and such exuberance was delightfully new and heartwarming to me, sober, cool woman that I was. And with that crushed, distressed young man, the landscape itself had revived as if by magic after last night's rain. The sea, calm as a millpond, lay shining blue beneath the sky as we came out of the restaurant, and the only white to be seen was the white of seagulls swooping in that other, celestial blue. You know the Riviera landscape. It is always beautiful, but offers its rich colours to the eye in leisurely fashion, flat as a picture postcard, a lethargic sleeping beauty who admits all glances, imperturbable and almost oriental in her ever-opulent willingness. But sometimes, very occasionally, there are days when this beauty rises up, breaks out, cries out loud, you might say, with gaudy, fanatically sparkling colours, triumphantly flinging her flower-like brightness in your face, glowing, burning with sensuality. And the stormy chaos of the night before had turned to such a lively day, the road was washed white, the sky was turquoise, and everywhere bushes ignited like colourful torches among the lush, drenched green foliage. The mountains seemed suddenly lighter and closer in the cooler, sunny air, as if they were crowding towards the gleaming, polished little town out of curiosity. Stepping outside, you sensed at every glance the challenging, cheering aspect of Nature spontaneously drawing your heart to her. 'Let's hire a carriage and drive along the Corniche,' I said.

The young man nodded enthusiastically: he seemed to be really seeing and noticing the landscape for the first time since his arrival. All he had seen so far was the dank casino hall with its sultry, sweaty smell, its crowds of ugly visitors with their twisted features, and a rough, grey, clamorous sea outside. But now the sunny beach lay spread out before us like a huge fan, and the eye leapt with pleasure from one distant point to another. We drove along the beautiful road in a slow carriage (this was before the days of the motor car), past many villas and many fine views; a hundred times, seeing every house, every villa in the green shade of the pine trees, one felt a secret wish to live there, quiet and content, away from the world!

Was I ever happier in my life than in that hour? I don't know. Beside me in the carriage sat the young man who had been a prey to death and disaster yesterday and now, in amazement, stood in the spray of the sparkling white dome of the sun above; years seemed to have dropped away from him. He had become all boy, a handsome, sportive child with a playful yet respectful look in his eyes, and nothing about him delighted me more than his considerate attentiveness. If the carriage was going up a steep climb which the horses found arduous, he jumped nimbly down to push from behind. If I named a flower or pointed to one by the roadside, he hurried to pluck it. He picked up a little toad that was hopping with difficulty along the road, lured out by

235

last night's rain, and carried it carefully over to the green grass, where it would not be crushed as the carriage went by; and from time to time, in great high spirits, he would say the most delightful and amusing things; I believe he found laughter of that kind a safety valve, and without it he would have had to sing or dance or fool around in some way, so happily inebriated was the expression of his sudden exuberance.

As we were driving slowly through a tiny village high up on the road, he suddenly raised his hat politely. I was surprised and asked who he was greeting, since he was a stranger among strangers here. He flushed slightly at my question and explained, almost apologetically, that we had just passed a church, and at home in Poland, as in all strict Catholic countries, it was usual from childhood on to raise your hat outside any church or other place of worship. I was deeply moved by this exquisite respect for religion, and remembering the cross he had mentioned, I asked if he was a devout believer. When he modestly confessed, with a touch of embarrassment, that he hoped to be granted God's grace, an idea suddenly came to me. 'Stop!' I told the driver, and quickly climbed out of the carriage. He followed me in surprise, asking, 'Where are we going?' I said only, 'Come with me.'

In his company I went back to the church, a small country church built of brick. The interior looked chalky, grey and empty; the door stood open, so that a yellow beam of light cut sharply through the dark, where blue shadows surrounded a small altar. Two candles, like veiled eyes, looked out of the warm, incense-scented twilight. We entered, he took off his hat, dipped his hand in the basin of holy water, crossed himself and genuflected. When he was standing again I took his arm. 'Go and find an altar or some image here that is holy to you,' I urged him, 'and swear the oath I will recite to you.' He looked at me in surprise, almost in alarm. But quickly understanding, he went over to a niche, made the sign of the cross and obediently knelt down.

'Say after me,' I said, trembling with excitement myself, 'say after me: I swear … '—'I swear,' he repeated, and I continued, 'that I will never play for money again, whatever the game may be, I swear that I will never again expose my life and my honour to the dangers of that passion.'

He repeated the words, trembling: they lingered loud and clear in the empty interior. Then it was quiet for a moment, so quiet that you could hear the faint rustling of the trees outside as the wind blew through their leaves. Suddenly he threw himself down like a penitent and, in tones of ecstasy such as I had never heard before, poured out a flood of rapid, confused words in Polish. I did not understand what he was saying, but it was obviously an ecstatic prayer, a prayer of gratitude and remorse, for in his stormy confession he kept bowing his head humbly down on the prayer desk, repeating the strange sounds ever more passionately, and uttering the same word more and more violently and with extraordinary ardour. I have never heard prayer like that before or since, in any church in the world. As he prayed his hands clung convulsively to the wooden prayer desk, his whole body shaken by an internal storm that sometimes caught him up and sometimes cast him down again. He saw and felt nothing else: his whole being seemed to exist in another world, in a purgatorial fire of transmutation, or rising to a holier sphere. At last he slowly stood up, made the sign of the cross, and turned with an effort. His knees were trembling, his countenance was pale as the face of a man exhausted. But when he saw me his eyes beamed, a pure, a truly devout smile lit up his ecstatic face; he came closer, bowed low in the Russian manner, took both my hands and touched them reverently with his lips. 'God has sent you to me. I was thanking him.' I did not know what to say, but I could have wished the organ to crash out suddenly above the low pews, for I felt that I had succeeded: I had saved this man for ever.

We emerged from the church into the radiant, flooding light of that May-like day; the world had never before seemed to me more beautiful. Then we drove slowly on in the carriage for another two hours, taking the panoramic road over the hills which offers a new view at every turn. But we spoke no more. After so much emotion, any other words would have seemed an anti-climax. And when by chance my eyes met his, I had to turn them away as if ashamed, so shaken was I by the sight of my own miracle.

We returned to Monte Carlo at about five in the afternoon. I had an appointment with relatives which I could not cancel at this late date. And in fact I secretly wished for a pause in which to recover from feelings that had been too violently aroused. For this was too much happiness. I felt that I must rest from my overheated, ecstatic condition. I had never known anything like it in my life before. So I asked my protégé to come into my hotel with me for a moment, and there in my room I gave him the money for his journey and to redeem the jewellery. We agreed that while I kept my appointment he would go and buy his ticket, and then we would meet at seven in the entrance hall of the station, half-an-hour before the departure of the train taking him home by way of Genoa. When I was about to give him the five banknotes his lips turned curiously pale. 'No ... no money ... I beg you, not money!' he uttered through his teeth, while his agitated fingers quivered nervously. 'No money ... not money ... I can't stand the sight of it!' he repeated, as if physically overcome by nausea or fear. But I soothed him, saying it was only a loan, and if he felt troubled by it then he could give me a receipt. 'Yes, yes ... a receipt,' he murmured, looking away, cramming the crumpled notes into his pocket without looking at them, like something sticky that soiled his fingers, and he scribbled a couple of words on a piece of paper in swift, flying characters. When he looked up damp sweat was standing out on his brow; something within seemed to be choking him, and no sooner had he given me the note than an impulse seemed to pass through him and suddenly—I was so startled that I instinctively flinched back—suddenly he fell on his knees and kissed the hem of my dress. It was an indescribable gesture; its overwhelming violence made me tremble all over. A strange shuddering came over me; I was confused, and could only stammer, 'Thank you for showing your gratitude—but do please go now! We'll say goodbye at seven in the station hall.'

He looked at me with a gleam of emotion moistening his eye; for a moment I thought he was going to say something, for a moment it seemed as if he were coming towards me. But then he suddenly bowed deeply again, very deeply, and left the room."

Once again Mrs C interrupted her story. She had risen and gone to the window to look out, and she stood there motionless for a long time. Watching the silhouette of her back, I saw it shiver slightly, and she swayed. All at once she turned back to me with determination, and her hands, until now calm and at rest, suddenly made a violent, tearing movement as if to rip something apart. Then she looked at me with a hard, almost defiant glance, and abruptly began again.

"I promised to be completely honest with you, and now I see how necessary that promise was. For only now that, for the first time, I make myself describe the whole course of those hours exactly as they happened, seeking words for what was a very complicated, confused feeling, only now do I clearly understand much that I did not know at the time, or perhaps would not acknowledge. So I will be firm and will not spare myself, and I will tell you the truth too: then, at the moment when the young man left the room and I remained there alone, I felt—it was a dazed sensation, like swooning—I felt a hard blow strike my heart. Something had hurt me mortally, but I did not know, or refused to know, what, after all, it was in my protégé's touchingly respectful conduct that wounded me so painfully.

But now that I force myself to bring up all the past unsparingly, in proper order, as if it were strange to me, and your presence as a witness allows no pretence, no craven concealment of a feeling which shames me, I clearly see that what hurt so much at the time was disappointment ... my disappointment that ... that the young man had gone away so obediently ... that he did not try to detain me, to stay with me. It was because he humbly and respectfully fell in with my first attempt to persuade him to leave, instead ... instead of trying to take me in his arms. It was because he merely revered me as a saint who had appeared to him along his way and did not ... did not feel for me as a woman.

That was the disappointment I felt, a disappointment I did not admit to myself either then or later, but a woman's feelings know everything without words, without conscious awareness. For—and now I will deceive myself no longer—for if he had embraced me then, if he had asked me then, I would have gone to the ends of the earth with him, I would have dishonoured my name and the name of my children—I would have eloped with him, caring nothing for what people would say or the dictates of my own reason, just as Madame Henriette ran off with the young Frenchman whom she hadn't even met the day before. I wouldn't have asked where we were going, or how long it would last, I wouldn't have turned to look back at my previous life—I would have sacrificed my money, my name, my fortune and my honour to him, I would have begged in the street for him, there is probably no base conduct in the world to which he could not have brought me. I would have thrown away all that we call modesty and reason if he had only spoken one word, taken one step towards me, if he had tried to touch me—so lost in him was I at that moment. But ... as I told you ... the young man, in his strangely dazed condition, did not spare another glance for me and the woman in me ... and I knew how much, how fervently I longed for him only when I was alone again, when the passion that had just been lighting up his radiant, his positively seraphic face was cast darkly back on me and now lingered in the void of an abandoned breast. With difficulty, I pulled myself together. My appointment was a doubly unwelcome burden. I felt as if a heavy iron helmet were weighing down on my brow and I was swaying under its weight; my thoughts were as disjointed as my footsteps as I at last went over to the other hotel to see my relatives. I sat there in a daze, amidst lively chatter, and was startled whenever I happened to look up and see their unmoved faces, which seemed to me frozen like masks by comparison with that face of his, enlivened as if by the play of light and shade as clouds cross the sky. I found the cheerful company as dreadfully inert as if I were among the dead, and while I put sugar in my cup and joined absently in the conversation, that one face kept coming before my mind's eye, as if summoned up by the surging of the blood. It had become a fervent joy to me to watch that face, and—terrible thought!—in an hour or so I would have seen it for the last time. I must involuntarily have sighed or groaned gently, for my husband's cousin leant over to me: what was the matter, she asked, didn't I feel well? I looked so pale and sad. This unexpected question gave me a quick, easy excuse; I said I did indeed have a migraine, and perhaps she would allow me to slip away.

Thus restored to my own company, I hurried straight to my hotel. No sooner was I alone there than the sense of emptiness and abandonment came over me again, feverishly combined with a longing for the young man I was to leave today for ever. I paced up and down the room, opened shutters for no good reason, changed my dress and my ribbon, suddenly found myself in front of the looking glass again, wondering whether, thus adorned, I might not be able to attract him after all. And I abruptly understood myself: I would do anything not to lose him! Within the space of a violent moment, my wish turned to determination. I ran down to the porter and told him I was leaving today by the night train. Now I had to hurry: I rang for the maid to help me pack—time was pressing—and as we stowed dresses and small items into my suitcases I dreamt of the coming surprise: I would accompany him to the train, and then, at the very last moment, when he was giving me his hand in farewell, I would suddenly get into the carriage with my astonished companion, I would spend that night with him, and the next night—as long as he wanted me. A kind of enchanted, wild frenzy whirled through my blood, sometimes, to the maid's surprise, I unexpectedly laughed aloud as I flung clothes into the suitcases. My senses, I felt from time to time, were all in disorder. And when the man came to take the cases down I stared at him strangely at first: it was too difficult to think of ordinary matters while I was in the grip of such inner excitement.

Time was short; it must be nearly seven, leaving me at most twenty minutes before the train left—but of course, I consoled myself, my arrival would not be a farewell now, since I had decided to accompany him on his journey as long and as far as he would have me. The hotel manservant carried the cases on ahead while I made haste to the reception desk to settle my bill. The manager was already giving me change, I was about to go on my way, when a hand gently touched my shoulder. I gave a start. It was my cousin; concerned by my apparent illness, she had come to see how I was. Everything went dark before my eyes. I did not want her here; every second I was detained meant disastrous delay, yet courtesy obliged me at least to fall into conversation with her briefly. 'You must go to bed,' she was urging me. 'I'm sure you have a temperature.' And she could well have been right, for the blood was pounding at my temples, and sometimes I felt the blue haze of approaching faintness come over my eyes. But I fended off her suggestions and took pains to seem grateful, while every word burned me, and I would have liked to thrust her ill-timed concern roughly away. However, she stayed and stayed and stayed with her unwanted solicitude, offered me eau de Cologne, would not be dissuaded from dabbing the cool perfume on my temples herself. Meanwhile I was counting the minutes, thinking both of him and of how to find an excuse to escape the torment of her sympathy. And the more restless I became, the more alarming did my condition seem to her; finally she was trying, almost by force, to make me go to my room and lie down. Then—in the middle of her urging—I suddenly saw the clock in the hotel lobby: it was two minutes before seven-thirty, and the train left at seven thirty-five. Brusquely, abruptly, with the brutal indifference of a desperate woman I simply stuck my hand out to my cousin—'Goodbye, I must go!'—and without a moment's thought for her frozen glance, without looking round, I rushed past the surprised hotel staff and out of the door, into the street and down it to the station. From the agitated gesticulating of the hotel manservant standing waiting there with my luggage I saw, well before I got there, that time must be very short. Frantically I ran to the barrier, but there the conductor turned me back—I had forgotten to buy a ticket. And as I almost forcibly tried to persuade him to let me on the platform all the same, the train began to move. I stared at it, trembling all over, hoping at least to catch a glimpse of him at the window of one of the carriages, a wave, a greeting. But in the middle of the hurrying throng I could not see his face. The carriages rolled past faster and faster, and after a minute nothing was left before my darkened eyes but black clouds of steam.

I must have stood there as if turned to stone, for God knows how long; the hotel servant had probably spoken to me in vain several times before he ventured to touch my arm. Only then did I start and come to myself. Should he take my luggage back to the hotel, he asked. It took me a few minutes to think; no, that was impossible, after this ridiculous, frantic departure I couldn't go back there, and I never wanted to again; so I told him, impatient to be alone, to take my cases to the left luggage office. Only then, in the middle of the constantly renewed crush of people flowing clamorously into the hall and then ebbing away again, did I try

to think, to think clearly, to save myself from my desperate, painful, choking sense of fury, remorse and despair, for—why not
admit it?—the idea that I had missed our last meeting through
my own fault was like a knife turning pitilessly within me, burning and sharp. I could have screamed aloud: that red-hot blade,
penetrating ever more mercilessly, hurt so much. Perhaps only
those who are strangers to passion know such sudden outbursts
of emotion in their few passionate moments, moments of emotion like an avalanche or a hurricane; whole years fall from one's
own breast with the fury of powers left unused. Never before or
after have I felt anything like the astonishment and raging impotence of that moment when, prepared to take the boldest of
steps—prepared to throw away my whole carefully conserved,
collected, controlled life all at once—I suddenly found myself
facing a wall of senselessness against which my passion could
only beat its head helplessly.

As for what I did then, how could it be anything but equally
senseless? It was foolish, even stupid, and I am almost ashamed
to tell you—but I have promised myself and you to keep nothing back. I … well, I went in search of him again. That is to
say, I went in search of every moment I had spent with him. I
felt irresistibly drawn to everywhere we had been together the
day before, the bench in the casino grounds from which I had
made him rise, the gaming hall where I had first seen him—yes,
even that den of vice, just to relive the past once more, only
once more. And tomorrow I would go along the Corniche in
a carriage, retracing our path, so that every word and gesture
would revive in my mind again—so senseless and childish was
my state of confusion. But you must take into account the lightning speed with which these events overwhelmed me—I had
felt little more than a single numbing blow, but now, woken too
abruptly from that tumult of feeling, I wanted to go back over
what I had so fleetingly experienced step by step, relishing it
in retrospect by virtue of that magical self-deception we call

memory. Well, some things we either do or do not understand. Perhaps you need a burning heart to comprehend them fully.

So I went first to the gaming hall to seek out the table where he had been sitting, and think of his hands among all the others there. I went in: I remembered that I had first seen him at the left-hand table in the second room. Every one of his movements was still clear before my mind's eye: I could have found his place sleepwalking, with my eyes closed and my hands outstretched. So I went in and crossed the hall. And then ... as I looked at the crowd from the doorway ... then something strange happened. There, in the very place where I dreamt of him, there sat—ah, the hallucinations of fever!—there sat the man himself. He looked exactly as I had seen him in my daydream just now—exactly as he had been yesterday, his eyes fixed on the ball, pale as a ghost—but he it unmistakably was.

I was so shocked that I felt as if I must cry out. But I controlled my alarm at this ridiculous vision and closed my eyes. 'You're mad—dreaming—feverish,' I told myself. 'It's impossible. You're hallucinating. He left half-an-hour ago.' Only then did I open my eyes again. But terrible to relate, he was still sitting there exactly as he had been sitting just now, in the flesh and unmistakable. I would have known those hands among millions ... no, I wasn't dreaming, he was real. He had not left as he had promised he would, the madman was sitting there, he had taken the money I gave him for his journey and brought it here, to the green table, gambling it on his passion, oblivious of all else, while I was desperately eating my heart out for him.

I abruptly moved forwards: fury blurred my vision, a frenzied, red-eyed, raging desire to take the perjurer who had so shamefully abused my confidence, my feelings, my devotion by the throat. But I controlled myself. With a deliberately slow step (and how much strength that cost me!) I went up to the table to sit directly opposite him. A gentleman courteously made way for me. Two metres of green cloth stood between us, and as if looking down from a balcony at a play on stage I could watch his face, the same face that I had seen two hours ago radiant with gratitude, illuminated by the aura of divine grace, and now entirely absorbed in the infernal fires of his passion again. The hands, those same hands that I had seen clinging to the wood of the prayer desk as he swore a most sacred oath, were now clutching at the money again like the claws of lustful vampires. For he had been winning, he must have won a very great deal: in front of him shone a jumbled pile of jettons and louis d'ors and banknotes, a disordered medley in which his quivering, nervous fingers were stretching and bathing with delight. I saw them pick up separate notes, stroke and fold them, I saw them turn and caress coins, then suddenly and abruptly catch up a fistful and put them down on one of the spaces. And immediately that spasmodic tic around his nostrils began again, the call of the croupier tore his greedily blazing eyes away from the money to the spinning ball, he seemed to be flowing out of himself, as it were, while his elbows might have been nailed to the green table. His total addiction was revealed as even more dreadful, more terrible than the evening before, for every move he made murdered that other image within me, the image shining as if on a golden ground that I had credulously swallowed.

So we sat there two metres away from each other; I was staring at him, but he was unaware of me. He was not looking at me or anyone else, his glance merely moved to the money, flickering unsteadily with the ball as it rolled back to rest: all his senses were contained, chasing back and forth, in that one racing green circle. To this obsessive gambler the whole world, the whole human race had shrunk to a rectangular patch of cloth. And I knew that I could stand here for hours and hours, and he would not have the faintest idea of my presence.

But I could stand it no longer. Coming to a sudden decision, I walked round the table, stepped behind him and firmly grasped his shoulder with my hand. His gaze swung upwards, for a second he stared strangely at me, glassy-eyed, like a drunk being laboriously shaken awake, eyes still vague and drowsy, clouded by inner fumes. Then he seemed to recognise me, his mouth opened, quivering, he looked happily up at me and stammered quietly, in a confused tone of mysterious confidentiality, 'It's going well … I knew it would as soon as I came in and saw that he was here … ' I did not understand what he meant. All I saw was that this madman was intoxicated by the game and had forgotten everything else, his promise, his appointment at the station, me and the whole world besides. But even when he was in this obsessive mood I found his ecstasy so captivating that instinctively I went along with him and asked, taken aback, who was here?

'Over there, the one-armed old Russian general,' he whispered, pressing close to me so that no one else would overhear the magic secret. 'Over there, with the white sideboards and the servant behind him. He always wins, I was watching him yesterday, he must have a system, and I always pick the same number … He was winning yesterday too, but I made the mistake of playing on when he had left … that was my error … he must have won twenty thousand francs yesterday, he's winning every time now too, and I just keep following his lead. Now—'

He broke off in mid-sentence, for the hoarse-voiced croupier was calling his '*Faites votre jeu!*' and his glance was already moving away, looking greedily at the place where the white-whiskered Russian sat, nonchalant and grave, thoughtfully putting first one gold coin and then, hesitantly, another on the fourth space. Immediately the fevered hands before me dug into the pile of money and put down a handful of coins on the same place. And when, after a minute, the croupier cried '*Zéro!*' and his rake swept the whole table bare with a single movement, he stared at the money streaming away as if at some marvel. But do you think he turned to me? No he had forgotten all about me; I had dropped out of his life, I was lost and gone from it, his whole being was intent only on the Russian general who, with complete indifference, was hefting two more gold coins in his hand, not yet sure what number to put them on.

I cannot describe my bitterness and despair. But think of my feelings: to be no more than a fly brushed carelessly aside by a man to whom one has offered one's whole life. Once again that surge of fury came over me. I seized his arm with all my strength. He started.

'You will get up at once!' I whispered to him in a soft but commanding tone. 'Remember what you swore in church today, you miserable perjurer.'

He stared at me, perplexed and pale. His eyes suddenly took on the expression of a beaten dog, his lips quivered. All at once he seemed to be remembering the past, and a horror of himself appeared to come over him.

'Yes, yes … ' he stammered. 'Oh, my God, my God … yes, I'm coming, oh, forgive me … '

And his hand was already sweeping the money together, fast at first, gathering it all up with a vehement gesture, but then gradually slowing down, as if coming up against some opposing force. His eyes had fallen once more on the Russian general, who had just made his bet.

'Just a moment,' he said, quickly throwing five gold coins on the same square. 'Just this one more time … I promise you I'll come then—just this one more game … just … '

And again his voice fell silent. The ball had begun to roll and was carrying him away with it. Once again the addict had slipped away from me, from himself, flung round with the tiny ball circling in the smooth hollow of the wheel where it leapt and sprang. Once again the croupier called out the number, once again the rake carried his five coins away from him; he had lost. But he did not turn round. He had forgotten me, just like his oath in the church and the promise he had given me a minute ago. His greedy hand was moving spasmodically towards the dwindling pile of money again, and his intoxicated gaze moved only to the magnet of his will, the man opposite who brought good luck.

My patience was at an end. I shook him again, hard this time. 'Get up at once! Immediately! You said one more game … '

But then something unexpected happened. He suddenly swung round, but the face looking at me was no longer that of a humbled and confused man, it was the face of a man in a frenzy, all anger, with burning eyes and furiously trembling lips. 'Leave me alone!' he spat. 'Go away! You bring me bad luck. Whenever you're here I lose. You brought bad luck yesterday and you're bringing bad luck now. Go away!'

I momentarily froze, but now my own anger was whipped up beyond restraint by his folly.

'I am bringing you bad luck?' I snapped at him. 'You liar, you thief—you promised me … ' But I got no further, for the maniac leapt up from his seat and, indifferent to the turmoil around him, thrust me away. 'Leave me alone,' he cried, losing all control. 'I'm not under your control … here, take your money.' And he threw me a few hundred-franc notes. 'Now leave me alone!'

He had been shouting out loud like a madman, ignoring the hundred or so people around us. They were all staring, whispering, pointing, laughing—other curious onlookers even crowded in from the hall next door. I felt as if my clothes were being torn from my body, leaving me naked before all these prying eyes. '*Silence, madame, s'il vous plaît*,' said the croupier in commanding tones, tapping his rake on the table. He meant me, the wretched creature meant me. Humiliated, overcome by shame, I stood there before the hissing, whispering curious folk like a prostitute whose customer has just thrown money at her. Two hundred, three hundred shameless eyes were turned on my face, and then—then, as I turned my gaze evasively aside, overwhelmed by this filthy deluge of humiliation and shame, my own eyes met two others, piercing and astonished—it was my cousin looking at me appalled, her mouth open, one hand raised as if in horror.

That struck home; before she could stir or recover from her surprise I stormed out of the hall. I got as far as the bench outside, the same bench on which the gambling addict had collapsed yesterday. I dropped to the hard, pitiless wood, as powerless, exhausted and shattered as he had been.

All that is twenty-four years ago, yet when I remember the moment when I stood there before a thousand strangers, lashed by their scorn, the blood freezes in my veins. And once again I feel, in horror, how weak, poor and flabby a substance whatever we call by the names of soul, spirit or feeling must be after all, not to mention what we describe as pain, since all this, even to the utmost degree, is insufficient to destroy the suffering flesh of the tormented body entirely—for we do survive such hours and our blood continues to pulse, instead of dying and falling like a tree struck by lightning. Only for a sudden moment, for an instant, did this pain tear through my joints so hard that I dropped on the bench breathless and dazed, with a positively voluptuous premonition that I must die. But as I was saying, pain is cowardly, it gives way before the overpowering will to live which seems to cling more strongly to our flesh than all the mortal suffering of the spirit. Even to myself, I cannot explain my feelings after such a shattering blow, but I did rise to my feet, although I did not know what to do. Suddenly it occurred to me that my suitcases were already at the station, and I thought suddenly that I must get away, away from here, away from this accursed, this infernal building. Taking no notice of anyone, I made haste to the station and asked when the next train for Paris left. At ten o'clock, the porter told me, and I immediately retrieved my luggage. Ten o'clock—so exactly twenty-four hours had passed since that terrible meeting, twenty-four hours so full of changeable, contradictory feelings that my inner world was shattered for ever. At first, however, I felt nothing but that one word in the constantly hammering, pounding rhythm: away, away, away! The pulses behind my brow kept driving it into my temples like a wedge: away, away, away! Away from this town, away from myself, home to my own people, to my own old life! I travelled through the night to Paris, changed from one station to another and travelled direct to Boulogne, from Boulogne to Dover, from Dover to London, from London to my son's house—all in one headlong flight, without stopping to think or consider, forty-eight hours without sleep, without speaking to anyone, without eating, forty-eight hours during which the wheels of all the trains rattled out that one word: away, away, away! When at last I arrived unexpectedly at my son's country house, everyone was alarmed; there must have been something in my bearing and my eyes that gave me away. My son came to embrace and kiss me, but I shrank away: I could not bear the thought of his touching lips that I felt were disgraced. I avoided all questions, asked only for a bath, because I needed to wash not only the dirt of the journey from my body but all of the passion of that obsessed, unworthy man that seemed to cling to it. Then I dragged myself up to my room and slept a benumbed and stony sleep for twelve or fourteen hours, a sleep such as I have never slept before or since, and after it I know what it must be like to lie dead in a coffin. My family cared for me as for a sick woman, but their affection only hurt me, I was ashamed of their respect, and had to keep preventing myself from suddenly screaming out loud how I had betrayed, forgotten and abandoned them all for the sake of a foolish, crazy passion.

Then, aimless again, I went back to France and a little town where I knew no one, for I was pursued by the delusion that at the very first glance everyone could see my shame and my changed nature from the outside, I felt so betrayed, so soiled to the depths of my soul. Sometimes, when I woke in my bed in the morning, I felt a dreadful fear of opening my eyes. Once again I would be overcome by the memory of that night when I suddenly woke beside a half-naked stranger, and then, as I had before, all I wanted was to die immediately.

But after all, time is strong, and age has the curious power of devaluing all our feelings. You feel death coming closer, its shadow falls black across your path, and things seem less brightly coloured, they do not go to the heart so much, they lose much of their dangerous violence. Gradually I recovered from the shock, and when, many years later, I met a young Pole who was an attaché of the Austrian Embassy at a party, and in answer to my enquiry about that family he told me that one of his cousin's sons had shot himself ten years before in Monte Carlo, I did not even tremble. It hardly hurt any more; perhaps—why deny one's egotism?—I was even glad of it, for now my last fear of ever meeting him again was gone. I had no witness against me left but my own memory. Since then I have become calmer. Growing old, after all, means that one no longer fears the past.

And now you will understand why I suddenly brought myself to tell you about my own experience. When you defended Madame Henriette and said, so passionately, that twenty-four hours could determine a woman's whole life, I felt that you meant me; I was grateful to you, since for the first time I felt myself, as it were, confirmed in my existence. And then I thought it would be good to unburden myself of it all for once, and perhaps then the spell on me would be broken, the eternal looking back; perhaps I can go to Monte Carlo tomorrow and enter the same hall where I met my fate without feeling hatred for him or myself. Then the stone will roll off my soul, laying its full weight over the past and preventing it from ever rising again. It has done me good to tell you all this. I feel easier in my mind now and almost light at heart … thank you for that."

With these words she had suddenly risen, and I felt that she had reached the end. Rather awkwardly, I sought for something to say. But she must have felt my emotion, and quickly waved it away.

"No, please, don't speak ... I'd rather you didn't reply or say anything to me. Accept my thanks for listening, and I wish you a good journey."

She stood opposite me, holding out her hand in farewell. Instinctively I looked at her face, and the countenance of this old woman who stood before me with a kindly yet slightly ashamed expression seemed to me wonderfully touching. Whether it was the reflection of past passion or mere confusion that suddenly dyed her cheeks with red, the colour rising to her white hair, she stood there just like a girl, in a bridal confusion of memories and ashamed of her own confession. Involuntarily moved, I very much wanted to say something to express my respect for her, but my throat was too constricted. So I leant down and respectfully kissed the faded hand that trembled slightly like an autumn leaf.